D1371516

Postcards From The Edge

1

ST. JOHN THE BAPTIST PARISH LIBRARY
2920 NEW HIGHWAY 51
LAPLACE, LOUISIANA 70068

"Love's gonna get you killed, but pride's gonna be the death of you and me." – Kendrick Lamar, "Pride"

"Why am I waking up out of my sleep thinkin' of you, babe? You had a hold on me." – 6lack, "Free"

1

Shyhiem

Messiah's lips enveloped Shyhiem's, as he caressed the side of her face. He'd yearned for the feel of her mouth on his for weeks. The tangy taste of her wicked tongue reminded him of the salty taste of blood that poured from his lips after she shot him point blank in the heart. Only she could stop the bleeding. She was the cause of the unbearable pain he experienced day in and day out. Messiah was a murderer. She'd left him for dead and never looked back.

And yet, he still yearned for her touch with each breath he drew and released. She was his and would always be. When he was with her, nothing else in the world mattered. Time was a distant memory known to man, a figment of his imagination suspended in time. The only thing that existed was him and her. He'd hoped their love would stand the test of time. For a minute, he'd begun to believe that they weren't meant to be; but there she was, lying on top of him, kissing him ever so softly, causing him to tremble from her touch.

The hold she had on him was beautiful, Creole magic. From the moment he'd laid eyes on her, Shyhiem knew she'd be the death of him. A woman like Messiah couldn't be contained. She couldn't be tied down or controlled. She was a monster - just like he was. She'd held him captive from the second their eyes connected. He was her prey from the start. He'd stalked her but she captured him. She'd gnawed at his heart until it was raw and unrecognizable. Messiah was determined to find shelter inside the cold confines of his heart.

4

Once she'd found comfort in knowing she'd etched herself inside his bloodstream, she disappeared, but Shyhiem couldn't shake her. She lived inside of him. She'd unknowingly changed his life. There was no living if she wasn't around. The moans that escaped her full lips paralyzed his soul. She straddled his lap and stared down at his face. The whites of her eyes were gone. He gazed up into a black abyss. This wasn't the Messiah he knew and loved. This was a demon terrorizing his dreams - but he wasn't afraid.

It was time for takeoff. His hips rocked, as she bounced up and down on his hard, rigid shaft. Shyhiem was determined to enjoy every second he had with her. Messiah rode his cock with reckless abandon, bucking wildly. He wanted to caress her face but his arms and legs were paralyzed. The demonic version of Messiah had complete control.

Shyhiem was a prisoner and there was nothing he could do to escape. Messiah had him right where she wanted him. He didn't want to succumb to the wicked rotation of her hips, but each thrust of her ass into his shaft made his dick harder. She wasn't going to stop until she fucked the life out of him. Shyhiem didn't want her to. As soon as he came, she'd vanish; just like every other night when she entered his dreams. Each night, he tried his best to prolong her visits; but no matter what, the dream would end the same.

There was no keeping her there with him. The reality was, she wasn't real - but damn did she smell good. This notion became clearer as his body quaked in his sleep. Shyhiem released a soft moan from his lips. Messiah had clenched her pussy walls around his cock. She bounced harder and faster. He tried to slow her down; but like a wild stallion, she couldn't be reeled in. Once she got what

5

she wanted, she'd leave him stranded with only memories of her to haunt him. Moaning her name, Shyhiem planted his seeds deeply inside her womb, while enjoying the last few seconds of being inside her.

Her pussy was home. It was his safe haven. Messiah stared at him once more with her blacked-out eyes. Her wild, curly, dark hair fell over her forehead. Able to move his arms, Shyhiem instinctively raised his hand to push her hair off her face but his hand didn't make it in time. Messiah whispered, "I love you," and then evaporated into thin air.

"Messiah!" Shyhiem called out, as he jumped out of his sleep.

When he didn't get a response, it was then that he realized that it was all a dream - again. The only remnant of her was the sticky cum inside his boxer briefs. Shyhiem ran a clammy hand down his face and sat up straight. It was the middle of the night. His body was full of sweat. The only company he had was the moon shining into his bedroom, but he had to find Messiah.

He refused to believe that his mind was playing tricks on him again. She had to be there. He could smell her scent all around him. The sweet trace of lavender honey floated through the air. Shyhiem searched every room of the loft, hoping to see her smiling face, but she was nowhere to be found.

"Daddy? You woke me up." His daughter, Shania, stepped out of her room and rubbed her eyes.

Realizing he was trippin', Shyhiem scooped her up in his strong arms.

"I'm sorry, baby. Daddy had a bad dream." He placed her back in bed. "Everything's ok. Go back to sleep." He pulled the covers up and tucked her in nice and tight.

Thankfully, her twin brother, Sonny, was sound asleep in his bed next to her. Sonny could sleep through anything. Distraught that he'd let his dreams take ahold of him once again, Shyhiem made his way to his bedroom and lay on his back.

"You gotta pull it together, nigga." He told himself.

A month had passed since he last laid eyes on Messiah. Each night, he dreamt of her. The dreams were getting more vivid by the day. They seemed so real that he couldn't decipher what was his imagination and what was reality. Shyhiem had done everything to get over her but nothing seemed to work. He'd buried himself in his job and drank himself to oblivion, but Messiah kept permanent residency in his heart.

He'd been staying at his brother's loft since the fateful night he choked Keesha out and beat a dude's ass at Blank Space. A month had gone by since everything went down. He wished he could go back and change the events of that night; but with life, there was no rewind button. He'd fucked up royally and now had to pay the consequences for his actions. He regretted everything, except putting his hands on Keesha. He hated her with a fucking passion. Shyhiem felt she deserved everything bad that came her way.

He was determined to get his kids away from her. They didn't deserve to be subjected to her ignorance and cruel behavior. Shania and Shyhiem, his six-year-old twins, deserved nothing but greatness. He planned to give them

7

nothing but the best of him. With Messiah out the picture, there was nothing holding him back from diving head first into the dope game again. Shyhiem was determined to stack as much paper as he could, gather his kids and get the fuck out of St. Louis. There was nothing there for him.

The city, and the people in it, made him sick. He had no mother and his father, who he wanted nothing to do with, was on his death-bed. Mayhem, his half-brother, was the only family he had that he cared about; but Shyhiem couldn't stick around for him. He had to do what was best for him and his children. It was only a matter of time before they were on a plane to L.A. Shyhiem would be able to start all over and build a new life. He'd go to film school and live out his dreams in peace. The only wrinkle in his plan was the absence of Messiah.

She was supposed to be right there by his side but she wanted nothing to do with him. He'd practically gotten down on his knees and begged her to choose him and she couldn't. She didn't love him enough to put her past behind her and move forward. The man who'd ripped her heart to shreds was back and staking claim on her heart. Shyhiem just knew she'd see right through her ex-fiancé's bullshit, but Messiah fell hook, line and sinker. She clung to her ex's words, as if they were gold. The love she had for him outweighed everything she and Shyhiem built.

He thought he'd shown her just how special she was to him. When he stared into her eyes, he saw stars and planets that had yet to be discovered. Nothing came before her. She'd stolen his heart. Messiah was all he'd ever wanted. The month and a half they spent together was the best time of his life. Shyhiem never imagined he'd fall head-over-heels in love with the raven-haired, dimpled-chin beauty. But there was no controlling his feelings when it came to Messiah. She was the love of his life.

He looked past her insecurities and the sadness that rested in her brown irises. She was fragile and on the edge of insanity, but he was determined to love the lonely out of her. He tried his best to numb the pain she was going through. Shyhiem thought he'd gotten through to her after she opened up about her past. She'd begun to smile more and laugh lines were starting to form around her pretty, plump lips. A flicker of fire burned in her eyes. Then, he ruined it by acting like a jealous asshole.

He should've just taken her home and fucked her until the moon disappeared behind the sun. Instead, he let his anger get the best of him and allowed his brother to amp him up to beat a man senseless, outside of a nightclub. Messiah hated violence. She'd warned him several times that she wouldn't tolerate it but he didn't listen. Now, here he was, alone with a semi-hard dick and cum-soaked boxer briefs, wishing upon a star that she'd come back home. Shyhiem would hand over all his worldly possessions to have her back, but Messiah didn't want him. She'd chosen another; and no matter how hard that pill was to swallow, he had to accept that.

"I know you probably hate me for always fuckin' wit' your head." – Lyrica Anderson, "Don't Take It Personal"

2
Shyhiem

"Daddy, do we gotta go home? I wanna stay wit' you." Sonny poked out his bottom lip and dragged his book bag behind him.

"Yeah, Daddy, I wanna stay wit' you too." Shania agreed, as they approached the door to their mother's apartment.

"I wish y'all could stay with me too, but it's your mommy's turn to spend time with you guys. Plus, you gotta go to school tomor'. Y'all can come back to my house next weekend, ok?" Shyhiem replied.

"*Okay*." Sonny rolled his eyes, not pleased with his father's answer.

Noticing the look of disappointment on his son's face, Shyhiem bent down so he could be at eye level with the twins. His heart ached for his kids. They were his lifeline. Shania's milk chocolate skin shined underneath the dim light of the afternoon sun. She had long, thick, natural, black hair that her mother kept in ponytails or braids. Her little, chubby stomach always poked out of the bottom of her shirt, but Shyhiem knew it was only baby fat. His daughter was beautiful - even though she looked just like her evil-ass mama, who he couldn't stand.

Sonny, however, was the spitting image of his father, except he had dimples and eyes as big as the moon. Shyhiem loved his mini-me. He was perfect in his eyes. The only problem was, Sonny wasn't as rough and tough as Shyhiem would've liked. He was the complete opposite of how his father was as a child. Sonny didn't like sports, roughhousing or getting dirty. He loved musicals, playing with dolls and wearing his sister's clothes. He made it known that he thought other little boys were cute and even asked Shyhiem if he could kiss a boy.

The fact that his six-year-old son was gay was something Shyhiem didn't even want to consider, until he was forced to face reality. The night Keesha beat Sonny for wearing his sister's nightgown to bed was too much. The incident ended worse than Shyhiem ever imagined, with him putting his hands on her and Keesha threatening to call the police. At first, Shyhiem hated the notion that his son could be gay. It wasn't until Messiah schooled him on the subject that his son's sexuality was a little easier to tolerate. He hadn't fully accepted that Sonny was gay, but with time and understanding, he was willing to come to terms with it.

"You know I love you both to the moon and back, right?" He looked them both in the eye.

"Yes." The twins nodded.

"If you need anything or if something bad happens, call me. It don't matter what time, a'ight?" Shyhiem stared at Sonny.

The request was more for him than Shania. Keesha had an infinite urge to be extra mean to him whenever Shyhiem wasn't around to defend him. Shania and Sonny nodded their little heads sadly. Neither wanted to leave. It was much calmer and cleaner at their dad's place. When they were at home with Keesha, things were always chaotic and the house stayed dirty. Keesha barely spent any time with them. She was always on the phone with her friends or getting ready to go out.

Shyhiem hated when he had to drop them off. A portion of his heart cracked each time. The pain only motivated him to work harder at getting custody of them. It was only a matter of time before the kids were with him on a full-time basis. Standing up straight, he used his knuckles and knocked on the door.

On the inside of the apartment, Keesha sat on the couch smoking a Whitney Houston special: a blunt laced with cocaine. She heard Shyhiem knock but took her sweet time answering. Whenever she had the opportunity to get under his skin, she took it. She got off on pissing him off.

He'd thrown her and their relationship away, so she was determined to make his life a living hell. If he didn't want her, then in her mind, Shyhiem had to suffer. There was no way he was going to go on with life without her and it be all good. He was her safety net. He took care of her. Keesha never had to lift a finger to do a thing. Now that he'd moved out, she was forced to fend for herself. Well, that was all about to change. She refused to work a 9 to 5 job. Pretty bitches like Keesha were accustomed to the finer things in life.

She used her looks and feminine wiles to get what she wanted. Keesha was bad. Her honey-colored skin, 42DD breasts, slanted eyes, slim nose, cinched waist, round hips and Jennifer Lopez booty kept niggas in her face. She stayed in the streets and was always dressed in the hottest and latest fashions. There wasn't a week that went by where she didn't get her hair and nails done.

Keesha had a reputation to protect. She didn't give a damn that she stayed looking good but her house and kids stayed dirty. She cleaned up when company came over and made sure the kids looked nice when they were around people she knew. Other than that, household chores and the twins' hygiene wasn't on her list of priorities. After several knocks, she rolled her eyes hard and slowly rose from the couch. As if she'd been inconvenienced by having to answer the door for her children, she swung it open and let out a heavy sigh.

"Hi, Mommy!" Shania wrapped her arms around her mother's shapely legs.

"Hi, mama's baby." She rubbed Shania's little back. "I missed you."

"I missed you too, Mommy."

"Hi, Mama." Sonny spoke timidly.

"Get yo' butt on in here." She waved him inside, instead of speaking back.

"See ya, Pop." Sonny hugged his father, one last time, and then placed his head down and walked into the apartment.

It took every bit of willpower Shyhiem had not to pull his son back into his arms and take him back home with him. The only reason he didn't was because Keesha would call the police and claim he'd kidnapped him. He didn't need the cops involved in his life. He had too much shit going on to have any unwanted eyes on him. Instead of spazzing out, Shyhiem counted to 10 in his head to calm himself down. He wasn't going to allow Satan's spawn to ruin his day.

"I washed their clothes and they ate dinner. I'll be back to get them Friday, after I get off work." He finally acknowledged Keesha's presence.

"I'ma need some more money." She held out her hand.

"For what? I just gave you $400 for the month. You'll get another $400 next month."

"I need more than that. It cost a lot to take care of these kids by myself," she spat.

"Bullshit. They got everything they need. I just bought them winter clothes and shoes. Four hundred dollars is enough to make sure that they got money for food and anything they need for school. Anything other than that is on you."

"Umm... excuse you, but your kids consume more than just food. They use the lights and heat up in this bitch. I need help with that too." Keesha pursed her lips.

"That's your responsibility not mine. I got my own bills to take care of, so I suggest you get off yo' fat ass and get a job."

"DON'T CALL ME FAT!" Keesha shouted, stomping her foot. "I'm thick."

Shyhiem chuckled. He knew whenever he called Keesha fat she'd lose her shit.

"If that make you feel better," he smirked.

"So you really not gon' give me no more money?"

"What part of no don't you understand?"

"Don't act like you ain't got it. I know what you and Mayhem been up to." Keesha whispered, squinting her eyes.

Shyhiem curled his upper lip and wondered why his brother would tell Keesha, of all people, about their business dealings. He knew Shyhiem didn't like her knowing about the moves he made out in the street. What made matters even worse, was that this wasn't the first time he'd told her his personal business. Shyhiem made a mental note to confront his brother about his shady behavior.

"I don't give a fuck about what you know." Shyhiem got in her face and mean-mugged her. "Know I'm not giving yo' ass no more money. How 'bout that?"

Pissed that he'd talked about her weight and refused to meet her demands, Keesha decided to hit him where it hurt.

"Here; you gon' have to do something about this." She handed him a stack of mail. "I'm sick of collecting your mail for you. You need to get a change of address before I tell yo' P.O. you don't stay here no more."

"Why would you do that?" Shyhiem furrowed his brows.

"'Cause, nigga, you don't stay here. What I'ma lie for? You ain't my man. You ain't helping me with shit around here."

"So that's what this is about? You mad 'cause I moved out." He looked at her with disbelief. "After all the shit I done did for yo' raggedy-ass, you won't even let me use this address so I won't get in trouble with my parole officer?"

"Use the address you're living at." Keesha rolled her neck.

"You know damn well I can't use Mayhem's address. He's a convicted felon too. I can't be associated with him."

"Sound like a personal problem to me." Keesha clicked her tongue against the roof of her mouth. "Use your li'l girlfriend address."

The mere mention of Messiah made Shyhiem's blood boil.

"We ain't together no more."

Keesha doubled over in laughter. Shyhiem stood pissed that she found his misery so funny.

"I told you that bitch was gon' leave you. That's what yo' ass get. You thought you was gon' leave me and ride off into the sunset with Pollyanna. Her bougie-ass saw you for the ain't shit, crazy-ass nigga you are and bounced. Hump, God don't like ugly, my nigga."

"You got a lot to say for a bitch that can't even keep a man. You done fucked half of St. Louis, including me, and ain't none of these niggas claiming you. You and yo' infested pussy washed up."

Keesha sucked her teeth and breathed heavily. She wanted to spit in his face for disrespecting her - once again - but decided not to let him see her sweat.

"Either move back here and help me with the bills and rent, or figure it out on your own. I'm done protecting you," she sneered.

"Protecting me? Bitch, you ain't never did shit for me except get on my fuckin' nerves."

"Yeah-yeah-yeah. Wah-wah-wah. Whatever." Keesha mocked him. "Let you tell it, yo' middle name Captain Save-A-Ho. Nigga, please."

"You know what? I'm not about to argue wit' you. You ain't gotta worry about my mail coming here no more.

I'll handle it." Shyhiem stormed off, before she could get another word in edge wise.

Pleased that she'd pissed him off and rattled his cage, Keesha closed the door with a huge smile on her face. Shyhiem had no idea of all the wonderfully cruel things she had in store for him. Making him find another address was just the beginning of the hell she was about to rain down on him. Making her way back over to the couch, she pulled her panties out of her butt and raised her fingers to her nose to smell it. Normally, she didn't let Shyhiem's comments get to her, but she had to know if her box had a foul stench to it. Taking a deep breath in, Keesha inhaled and winced. In between her legs smelled like day old fish that had been sitting out in the sun. The odor made her gag; but instead of doing anything about it, she plopped down on the couch and resumed smoking.

"You actin' like we were more than a summer fling."– SZA, "Love Galore"

3

Shyhiem

After having a wonderful weekend with the twins, the last thing Shyhiem wanted was to let Keesha ruin his good mood. His life had been so much better, now that she was no longer in it. The only fucked up part about not living at home, was the fact that he didn't see his kids on a daily basis anymore, like he was used to. Sonny and Shania were his motivation to keep on living. Without having them around consistently made Shyhiem's life bleak and dreary.

Since he'd left, it felt like he was coasting through life. The only thing he did was work, help his brother, drink and smoke all day. Shyhiem didn't like that he was back on the same shit that got him locked up before. But the urgent need for a better life drove him to push the limits of his freedom. He'd gladly risk it all to accomplish his goal. Without his anchor, Messiah, around to keep him grounded, he sailed hopelessly in the wind.

Being in the same building in which she lived was pure torture. Every time he came to pick the twins up, he wanted to board the elevator and go up to her apartment, but his ego kept him at bay. Shyhiem let her hurt him once. There was no way his pride could take her rejecting him twice. The first time damn near wiped him out. Low-key, it was a good thing she wasn't in his life anymore. The shit he was up to now, she would never put up with.

Dying to get out of the apartment building from hell, Shyhiem jogged down the steps to his brand new car. He'd purchased a cocaine white 2017 Range Rover Sport. Shyhiem loved his new baby. He still had his Cadillac CTS-V sedan though. With the extra money he was bringing in from moving weight, he decided to treat himself. He deserved the expensive present. After all the bullshit he'd been through in the last few months, he deserved the car and much more.

In desperate need of a stiff drink, Shyhiem opened his glove compartment and took out five, mini Jack Daniel bottles and downed them. The potent liquor burned his chest but it made him feel good. Buzzed, he threw the bottles out the window and started up the truck. The liquor had rushed to his head but he didn't care. Being in a drunken state helped him cope with his fucked up life. As he pulled out the parking space, instead of focusing on the road, he focused on changing the CD in the disc changer.

Without looking, Shyhiem wheeled the car into the street, just before a loud thump on the hood caught his attention. Immediately, he slammed on the brakes and looked out the windshield. His heart raced a mile a minute. He knew for sure he'd hit someone. The last thing he needed was to go jail.

"What the fuck is wrong wit' you? Watch where you going!" Messiah yelled, holding her chest, flustered.

The truck was inches away from hitting her, as she crossed the street. Seeing that it was her, Shyhiem placed his car in park and quickly hopped out. Messiah's doe-shaped eyes widened at the sight of him. Shyhiem was the last person she expected to find behind the wheel of the car. Her heart was beating so fast it constricted the air in her lungs. Messiah swallowed hard and stepped back, as he came close. Being near Shyhiem was the last thing she needed at that moment.

His six foot tall, athletic frame towered over her. Messiah gazed up into his soothing, diamond-shaped eyes and became lost in the essence of him. He was hypnotically gorgeous. Shyhiem had the smoothest Godiva chocolate skin, full beard and kissable, brown lips. His spinning waves and 180-pound physique, made from pure muscle, was begging to be licked.

Jesus be a fence, she prayed silently to herself. Messiah had just gotten off work from her job at the cable company, Charter Communications. All she wanted was something to eat and a quick nap before she had to head to her second job at Joe's Diner. She didn't have time to have her heart beat through her pussy. Being around Shyhiem always put her in a state of confusion. She couldn't function when he was near.

"My bad. You a'ight? Did I hurt you?" He searched her body for injuries.

As he looked her over, Shyhiem couldn't help but drink her in. She was just as beautiful in person as she was in his dreams. Messiah's golden skin glowed, despite the obvious anger in her eyes. He couldn't front like he didn't notice that she acted like she didn't want to be around him. Nervous, Shyhiem placed his hands inside his pockets, just so he wouldn't reach out and take her into his arms. At that moment, it became crystal clear that he needed this woman more than he needed air to breathe.

Her wild, black, curly hair framed her perfectly-crafted face. Shyhiem adored her thick, arched brows, warm, brown eyes, long lashes, pronounced nose, razor sharp cheekbones, luscious, full, pink lips and dimpled-chin. Again, he thought that she and the actress Yara Shahidi could've been twins. She was only 5'5 in height. Messiah had a small physique but her 34C breasts and small, round booty gave her the womanly curves that turned Shyhiem on to the fullest. She was the epitome of beauty, class and grace. It was damp and cold outside, so she wore a fake, black, leather jacket, burgundy V-neck, bell sleeve, rayon dress and black, suede, thigh-high boots that laced up the back. Shyhiem wanted nothing more than to sit her on top of the hood of his truck and fuck the shit out of her in those boots.

"I'm fine." Messiah finally remembered how to speak.

Shyhiem had rendered her speechless. It wasn't a good idea for her to be anywhere near him. Just being in the same vicinity was too much. The last time she'd seen him, she'd ripped his heart to shreds. If she stayed a second longer, she'd only end up doing it again. A lot had changed since she last saw him. She didn't want to subject him to anymore unnecessary pain. Shyhiem didn't deserve that.

"Just watch where you going next time." She started to walk away.

"Hold up." Shyhiem couldn't stop himself from pulling her back.

"Shyhiem... let me go." She pleaded, sadly.

The touch of his strong hand on her small arm felt so right, but deep down, she knew it was wrong. She'd made her decision and she was sticking to it.

"I just... wanted to make sure you was alright. You've been on my mind a lot lately." He gazed into her eyes, looking for any sign that she still loved him.

Shyhiem didn't see anything. Messiah was great at concealing her feelings, when she wanted to. Only apprehension and regret was written on her pretty face.

"I'm fine." She slowly pulled her arm away. "You?" She asked, even though she knew she shouldn't. "I can smell the liquor on your breath."

"Drinking's the only thing that makes me feel better." He responded honestly.

"Obviously, that's not helping any." Messiah looked at him with pity in her eyes.

Shyhiem was a shell of the man he once was and it was all because of her. She'd warned him that she'd ruin him but he wouldn't listen.

"I haven't seen you around. Where you been staying?"

"The loft."

"Oh... I see you got a new car." She pointed.

"Fuck the car." He stepped into her personal space and caressed her cheek. "Can't you see? I'm fuckin' miserable without you. I miss you." He cupped her face in his hands and kissed her lips passionately.

Messiah relished the domineering kiss and then pulled her head away. The enthralling scent of his cologne was stirring emotions inside of her she'd tried to bury, so she closed her eyes. Shyhiem closed his eyes too and rested his forehead on top of hers. This wasn't a dream. She was right there with him. For Shyhiem, life didn't get any better than this. He loved Messiah with every fiber of his being. She had quickly become his best friend, trusted confidant and the love of his life. It fucked him up that she acted like their relationship never even mattered.

"Baby, please, come home." His deep voice cracked with desperation. "I can't live without you another day." He cried.

A single tear slipped from his eye and landed on Messiah's cheek. A part of her died right there in the middle of the street. She couldn't give Shyhiem what he wanted. Her mind was made up. She'd walked away from him once, and hated to do it again, but it had to be done. She was no good for him. What they had was just a fun, summer fling. It was never meant to move past that. She'd put what they had behind her and moved on. The decision she made was best for her to move forward. She hoped and prayed he would find the strength to let her go.

"I can't, Shyhiem." She opened her eyes and watched as his heart cracked in two.

"Why? I know you still love me." His chest rose and fell with every word.

Messiah bit down into her bottom lip. Her entire body was trembling. He was making this harder than it had to be. She'd avoided him on purpose, so she wouldn't have to deal with this conversation.

"I don't." She uttered, feeling faint.

"What?" Shyhiem stepped back.

Suddenly, her skin felt like hot coals on the palm of his hands.

"Why you doing this?" He asked, as he died several, slow, excruciating deaths.

Shyhiem knew she was pushing him away on purpose. He needed to know why.

"I'm sorry." Messiah shook her head.

Before she allowed him to see a tear fall from her eye, she made a mad dash into the building. Shyhiem watched as she ran away. He wanted to run after her but his legs stayed planted on the concrete. Once again, he'd put himself out there and she'd shot him down. His heart couldn't take the constant pounding from her dismissal of his love. No matter how much he longed for Messiah to be in his bed at night, she made it abundantly clear that she didn't want him anymore.

Burying his feelings inside his steel heart, he climbed back inside his Range and sped off. Somehow, someway, he'd get over the raven-haired beauty that had stolen his heart. He didn't know how he was going to do it, but for his sanity, it was a must.

"If you're an African American man, you have to have ego." –Van Jones, "Footnotes for 'Kill Jay z'"

4
Shyhiem

"You're late!" Shyhiem's boss said, as he clocked in.

Shyhiem looked at his supervisor, Tom, and scowled. Today was not the day for him to be fucking with him. He was not in the mood. He was still hungover from the night before. It had been a little over a week since his run-in with Messiah. He'd drunk himself into a stupor every night since. His head was banging, and the loud-ass barking Tom was doing was making it worse. He hated that fat muthafucka anyway. Tom was an overweight, racist, asshole with a comb over that rivaled Donald Trump's. He had white, splotchy skin and was always sweaty and out of breath.

He got off on fucking with Shyhiem and all the other employees who were black and on parole. Since the day he started, Shyhiem let off an energy that being an UPS driver was beneath him. He was grateful for the position because it provided him a legit means to take care of his kids, but it would never be the career choice of his dreams. It was strictly a means to an end. He had bigger dreams than delivering packages. He wanted to create films and documentaries. The one he'd been working on, featuring Messiah, was his first masterpiece. He'd planned on showing it to her once it was finished, but after the way things ended, that wouldn't be happening anytime soon. He loved the girl; but since the night they met at Blank Space, she'd been fuckin' with his brain.

Shyhiem blamed himself for the breakdown of their relationship. He was controlling, angry and aggressive. There was no beginning, middle or end with him. He went from 0 to 100, real quick. Living life on a short fuse was a hindrance for him. He'd tried to change his dramatic ways but it was all he knew. Growing up in the streets, he was conditioned to be hard. Having vibrato and a big ego got you far in the hood. The cockier you were, the more people respected you.

Being a black man in America was hard. Add being poor and dark-skinned on top of that - you were destined to fail. Shyhiem had skin the color of coal, so it was extra tough for him. Since he was a teenager, it didn't go unnoticed that white women clutched their purses when he walked by. White men feared him 'cause he had eyes that didn't show fear and a back that wouldn't bend. Because he was a black man in America, he had to work extra hard to survive - financially and physically.

Every time he walked out of the house, there was a target on his back from his own people, who wanted to take him out because he'd made thousands selling cocaine and got all the pretty girls. White police officers targeted him because, in their eyes, he was a wild gorilla without a leash. It didn't matter how much he achieved; to both sides, he'd always and forever be a nigga. Despite the obstacles he faced, Shyhiem refused to die broke and destitute. In life, you had to take chances to get ahead. He wasn't going to let his environment, his criminal record, skin color or his racist-ass boss get in his way. He knew there was power in his African blood. He didn't fear any man on earth. The only man he feared was God Himself.

Shyhiem gave zero fucks. He especially didn't give a fuck about his punk-ass job at UPS. With each day that passed, he hated it more. The pay was cool, but he was a man used to making racks on top of racks. The little pay, grueling schedule and shitty boss wasn't worth the headache. They all made scraps while the white owners made millions off their hard work. It was legal slavery. He would never take driving a delivery truck seriously. He wanted to be in the owner's shoes. He wasn't built to be a worker. He was made to be a boss. With everything going on his life, Shyhiem's last concern was making sure he got to work on time. He didn't give a fuck about the job or Tom. Both could kiss his natural, black ass.

"I know you hear me, boy." Tom furrowed his brows and placed his hands on his wide hips.

Shyhiem looked over his shoulder and glared at him.

"Watch yourself, Tom." He warned, on edge.

He knew Tom wanted him to snap and do something stupid. He was waiting for Shyhiem to fuck up so he could fire him. He loved getting under his skin. Shyhiem's life was basically in his hands. Tom knew he needed the job. Having a steady job was a part of his parole stipulation; as well as, having an approved residence and passing all mandatory drug tests. Shyhiem was on strike number two at his job. One more violation and he was gone. He couldn't let that happen. His parole was up that coming January. He'd come too far to fuck up now.

"Listen up, everyone!" Tom got the rest of the guys' attention. "If you are continuously late, like Shyhiem here." He gripped him by the back of his neck, aggressively.

Shyhiem's nostrils flared. Tom was pushing it. Shyhiem could take him embarrassing him in front of everyone, but putting his hands on him was a no-no.

"I will dock your pay and add extra deliveries to your shift. Let Shyhiem be an example of what not to do. I know some of you are on parole, like he is, and value your freedom. Don't take this job or me for granted. Just as quick as I hired you, I will fire you. You got that?" Tom looked around the room.

All the men nodded their heads and went back to work. With no one looking, he whispered into Shyhiem's ear, "One more fuck up and your black ass is out of here. You hear me, boy? One more time." He flashed him a devilish grin.

Shyhiem balled his fist; his natural reaction was to grab Tom by the neck and slam his head into the wall. He'd watch with glee, as his face caved in with each blow. But Shyhiem wasn't going to let Tom get the best of him. In a few months, he'd be out of there anyway. After the last of the coke shipment was gone, he'd have enough money stashed away to start a new life in California. Until then, his hands were tied. He'd have to bite his tongue and be the good, li'l house nigga Tom wanted him to be.

"You left and I ain't seen you for all these years. you ain't shit and I don't fuck wit' you."– Jay Z, "Footnotes of 'Adnis'"

<u>5</u>

Shyhiem

Later that day, Shyhiem drove the UPS truck he was assigned into a circular driveway and placed the car in park. The trek out to the gated community had been a long one. He'd thought about turning back several times but his foot stayed on the gas. Veering off course while on the clock could get him fired, but he had far more pressing matters going on in his life than delivering packages. Now that he was at his destination, he wanted to throw up.

Never in a million years did he think he'd ever be back in the neighborhood, let alone, parked in front of the mansion his father stayed in. He'd despised the man practically his entire life. Shyhiem had made it his business to act like Ricky Simmons didn't exist. It was payback for the disappearing act he played on him as a young boy. In Shyhiem's eyes, his father was nothing but a living, breathing, piece of shit.

He couldn't respect a man that raised one child while forsaking the other. His father's absence in his life molded Shyhiem into the man he was. He'd lived a hard life growing up. Plenty of nights went by where he went to bed hungry. The lights and gas were always being cut off. His mother couldn't afford brand new, brand name clothes, so all his clothes came from the thrift store. Shyhiem hated being poor. Kids constantly teased him because of how little he had.

He didn't understand why his father was in and out of his life and didn't help his mother take care of him. Shyhiem resented the fact that his brother got the love and affection from their father that he always craved. He would've traded anything he had to be in his position but he wasn't. Their father wanted nothing to do with him. Shyhiem was nothing but a nut that shouldn't have been bust that was forced to raise himself. Growing up in St. Louis fatherless was a struggle. Shyhiem spent most of his time fighting to prove his worth. If he wasn't defending his own battles, he was protecting Mayhem.

By the time he was 20, he was done with scrimping and saving just to afford food each week. Money was coming in hand over fist. Being a drug dealer was intoxicating. He was on top of the world. He became high off the life, even though he knew the career path would end with him being dead or in jail. Secretly, he hoped that when word got back to his pop that he was running the streets, he'd either rescue him from the life or earn his respect.

Ricky was an ex dope dealer turned real estate mogul. Shyhiem never heard anything from his father. He wasn't there for him as a child or when he got locked up for three years for a gun charge. Shyhiem didn't understand how someone could be so cruel and heartless. He swore, from that moment on, to hate his father till the day he took his last breath.

Now, here he was at the mercy of the man he loathed. Shyhiem's back was up against the wall and he had nowhere else to turn. His father was the only person who could come to his aid. Sullen, Shyhiem hopped out the truck and reluctantly walked up the steps to ring the bell. The $17 million, 15,000-square foot, limestone-clad mansion his father lived in was exquisite. Shyhiem couldn't even believe that someone he knew, let alone his father, resided in a place so grand. A few seconds later, the huge, wooden door opened.

"May I help you?" The housekeeper asked.

She was a middle-aged, pudgy, black woman with gray hair that was pulled back into a bun.

"Yeah, I'm here to see Ricky." Shyhiem replied, nervously.

"Are you here to drop off a package?" She eyed him quizzically.

Shyhiem looked down at his uniform.

"No," he chuckled. "I'm here on a personal visit."

"And you are?"

"Shyhiem."

"Is Mr. Simmons expecting you?" She questioned, holding the door.

"No, but I'm his—"

"I'm sorry," The housekeeper cut him off. "But Mrs. Simmons didn't say anything about Mr. Simmons having any visitors today. She's not here, so I'm afraid I can't let you in." She stepped back to close the door.

"But—" Shyhiem pushed the door back open.

"Excuse you! You betta back up for I mace yo' ass!" She demanded, holding the tiny can up, ready to strike.

"Gloria, who is that at the door?" Ricky yelled from the top of the stairs.

"Mr. Simmons, get back in bed. I got this!"

"Obviously, you don't. I hear you all the way up here. Now, who's there?" His voice strained.

"Someone name Shyhiem!" Gloria glared at him with disdain.

Shyhiem shook his head. *I knew I shouldn't have come here,* he thought. His father's own staff didn't even have a clue who he was. It was just another sign of how little he meant to him.

"Let him in! That's my son." Ricky held onto the rail, weakly.

Shyhiem hated him even more now. Heated, he stepped inside the lavish abode. He made sure that he mean-mugged the fuck outta Gloria, as he bypassed her. Everything in him was saying, *leave, you don't need this nigga, Shyhiem,* but his legs kept moving in the direction of the man who never attempted to raise him. A little joy filled his heart to see his sperm donor die a slow, painful death. Ricky was on his last leg. He had stage 4 lung cancer. Shyhiem had convinced himself that he could care less. To him, his father was finally reaping all the evil he'd sewn into the earth.

A man was nothing if he didn't take care of his family. After years of living the high life, he was suffering from his transgressions. Shyhiem wanted to laugh in his face and be like, *ah ha, nigga, that's what you get.* Karma was a bitch. The same disease that claimed his dear mother's life was now claiming his. Wanting to get this dreadful reunion over with as quick as possible, he followed his father upstairs to his master bedroom.

He'd only been inside the room once, two months prior. The massive size of his dad's bedroom was astounding. The apartment he once shared with Keesha could've fit inside the one room alone. The master bedroom was immaculately decorated. Hues of sky blue, cream, gold and tan filled the room. Crown molding with gold designs gave the white walls a royal effect. A sky blue canopy draped over the back of the king-sized, cushioned headboard. A crystal chandelier hung from the ceiling over the bed. His and her nightstands, a Victorian bench and the softest carpet he'd ever been blessed to walk on decorated the lavish boudoir.

Attached to the room was an en-suite made for lounging and watching television. Sky blue, Tiffany vases, a vintage chaise lounge and an antique rug filled the area. The room was fit for a king. Shyhiem stood by the door, feeling out of place. He didn't belong. He wasn't connected to the man making his way across the room. His kids were his only family. Shyhiem placed his hands inside his pants pocket and watched as his father feebly sat on the side of the bed.

Ricky caught his breath and took a long, hard look at Shyhiem. He hadn't seen much of his second born son over the years but he could tell something was wrong. The solemn look on his face was hard not to notice. Shyhiem looked like he had the weight of the world on his shoulders. Ricky knew that look all too well. He'd worn the same expression many times himself. Shyhiem was suffering from a broken heart.

"After our last meeting, I didn't think I would see you again." Ricky situated himself.

His health was deteriorating fast. Shyhiem could see the life in his eyes gradually fading away. Bottles of water, tons of medication and a portable potty for adults was by the bed.

"I prayed to God that I would, but I didn't believe it," Ricky continued.

"What's the point of praying if you don't believe?" Shyhiem challenged. "I mean, ain't a prayer just a plea? A hope, a desire to believe there's something better on the other side of it?"

"Good point," Ricky chuckled. "I'm happy to see you, so—" He stopped himself from calling Shyhiem son.

He hadn't earned the right, plus Shyhiem loathed when he did.

"I mean... Shyhiem." He corrected himself. "What brings you by?"

"Umm," Shyhiem hesitated.

The words he was about to say hurt him to the core.

"I need your help."

Ricky's eyes widened. His youngest son made it a priority in life to never ask him for shit. He admired and hated that about him. Shyhiem stood on his own, two feet, which was good. He didn't take handouts, but his pride often got in the way of him making level-headed decisions. His prideful ego was a gift and a curse. He didn't know it, and would probably hate it, if he knew he'd gotten the trait from him. Shyhiem was the total opposite of his brother. Mayhem had it easy in life and often took his good fortune for granted.

"You know I'd do anything for you," Ricky responded, after the initial shock of Shyhiem's request wore off.

"Do I?" Shyhiem raised his brow. "You and I both know that ain't true. I only know what you won't do for me, which is be my father."

"Shyhiem, I know you think I'm some kind of monster, but I swear you have it all wrong, so— I mean, Shyhiem."

"Look, I ain't come here for all that." Shyhiem waved him off. "I need to use your address as my place of residence for my P.O. Can you help me or not?" He scowled.

Ricky wanted to press the subject of their relationship. There were things that needed to be clarified and explained, but getting through to Shyhiem was futile. He was as pigheaded as he was, but Ricky would take him however he could get him. The fact that Shyhiem was turning to him for assistance with a problem meant a lot. It warmed Ricky's heart to know that his son needed him. It meant that they were a step closer at building some kind of relationship with one another.

"Of course." He said eagerly.

"Appreciate it," Shyhiem replied, dryly.

On the outside, his face was stone, but on the inside, he was jumping for joy. Having a legit address for his parole officer was one less thing he had to worry about. It was also one less thing Keesha could hold over his head. Coming in, he didn't know what kind of response he would get from Ricky. They were practically strangers, instead of father and son. It wasn't like Shyhiem could depend on him. He'd never been there; but that day, he was. Shyhiem still didn't fuck with his father but appreciated his support. Deciding not to be a complete asshole, he stared at him out of the corner of his eye and asked, "How you been?"

"I have my good days; but lately, it's been more bad than good."

Shyhiem licked his bottom lip and sighed. Everything in him wanted to remain numb to the fact that his father was dying, but his heart wasn't made of stone. He wasn't a heartless man, no matter how hard he tried to be. The notion fucked him up far more than he'd like to admit. If he allowed the concept to sink in that he would be parentless, Shyhiem would drown. Since his mother's passing, he'd pretended like he was in this world alone; but in the back of his mind, it was always comforting knowing his dad was still within arm's reach.

"I'm sorry to hear that. How much more time are they giving you?"

"Less than six months."

A cold chill ran down Shyhiem's spine.

"Damn, that's fucked up." He massaged his jaw.

"Tell me about it," Ricky said somberly. "I've made my peace with it."

But I haven't, Shyhiem thought. It hurt him beyond belief to hear the life-altering news. The twins hadn't even gotten a chance to meet him yet. Now, it seemed they never would and he would never have the relationship with Ricky he'd secretly pined for.

"So, who is she?" Ricky interrupted his thoughts.

"Huh?"

"Who is she?" Ricky repeated.

"Who is who?" Shyhiem asked, confused.

"The girl that got you walkin' around draggin' yo' feet."

Damn, is it that obvious, Shyhiem wondered.

"I ain't come here to talk about all that." He flicked his wrist dismissively.

"C'mon, you can talk to me. I'm here. I ain't going nowhere. I got all the time in the world. At least for right now," Ricky joked.

Shyhiem winced at the badly timed joke.

"Her name is Messiah." He found himself admitting.

He didn't come there to discuss his love life, but if Shyhiem didn't talk about his troubles with someone soon, he was sure to combust.

"She must be pretty special to have you in yo' feelings."

"She's the best thing that's ever happened to me but she can't see it. She has a lot of issues and an ex that won't fuckin' disappear," Shyhiem balled his fist. "The more I try to love her, the more she pushes me away."

"Some women take a little longer to fall in love than others. She seems like she's a tough one. Women like her don't just go off words. You gotta take action. Make her see that your feelings match your words. Do something grand. Sweep her off her feet."

"I tried, but I let my temper get the best of me and pushed her away for good." Shyhiem said hopelessly. "She barely even wants to talk to me."

"You ain't hit her, did you?" Ricky asked, concerned.

"Fuck nah." Shyhiem lied, not wanting his father to know he was right. "Why would you ask me something like that?"

"'Cause I ain't raise you boys to put yo' hands on no women."

"You ain't raise me at all. You don't know shit about me," Shyhiem fumed. "Unlike you, I'm not a shitty boyfriend. I know how to treat a woman. I don't just leave when things don't go my way."

"I'm sorry. I ain't mean no harm. I was just making sure."

"Whatever. Thanks for letting me use your address." Shyhiem turned to leave, in a hurry.

"Shyhiem, wait!" Ricky called out.

"Nah, I'm gone!" Shyhiem yelled over his shoulder, as he jogged down the steps.

He had to get out of there before he snapped and started tossing shit. The fact that Ricky called him out on his bullshit infuriated him. *That nigga don't know me. What the fuck was I thinkin' coming here?* Shyhiem knew he had no business opening up to his father. He didn't deserve to get to know him on a personal level. His feelings and thoughts were his and his only, especially the ones he had for Messiah. She was off limits to everyone. His feelings for her were sacred. He didn't need anyone's advice on how to fix their situation. He knew exactly what he had to do to get her back.

"I never thought the circumstances would've changed you."– PartyNextDoor feat. Drake, "Come and See Me"

6

Shyhiem

It was now or never. Praying her away hadn't worked. Smoking and drinking only dulled the pain for a moment and clouded his brain. Working countless hours didn't help either. No matter what, Messiah was always there with him. Shyhiem hoped his longing for her would eventually go away but the feeling only intensified. He couldn't go another day without his dream girl by his side. Her place in this cold, cruel world was with him. He didn't see it any other way. They were meant to be. It was written in the stars. She was his rib. It was time to get his lady back.

Shyhiem was fully prepared to lay it all on the line. He'd beg; hell, even plead for her to give him a second chance. He'd control his temper and love her for the strong, sensitive woman she was. She completed him and he completed her too. Deep down, Messiah knew this to be true.

Nervous as fuck, he stood at her apartment door, holding a bouquet of pink roses. They were her favorite. The television was playing on the other side of the door, so he knew she was home. Before knocking, he wiped the sweat off his clammy hands onto the side of his jeans. No other woman had this kind of effect on him. Only Messiah could make him feel like - at any moment - he would throw up or pass out. Around her, he always felt weak. She was the only woman to bring him down to his knees. She had complete control over his emotions and mood.

Clearing his throat, Shyhiem raised his hand and knocked. When he heard the lock turn, he stepped back and prepared himself to see her gorgeous, angelic face. Shyhiem watched intently as the door creaked open. His entire body was racked with nerves. It was as if time was moving at a snail's pace. His limbs felt like wood, as he anticipated seeing her petite silhouette come into frame. Only… it wasn't Messiah that answered the door. Shocked at who he saw standing before him, he blinked profusely. Shyhiem looked from side to side to ensure he had the right apartment. He did. Messiah hadn't moved. Once that was cleared up, he died to know why in the fuck her lame-ass ex was answering her fuckin' door – shirtless, no less.

"Can I help you?" Bryson, Messiah's ex-fiancé asked, groggily, while wiping cold from his eyes.

Shyhiem dropped the flowers down to his side and examined the nigga standing before him. He was sure that steam was blowing from his ears, he was so furious. Bryson looked as if he'd just rolled out of her bed, even though it was mid-afternoon. Sizing him up, Shyhiem peeped that he was 6'3 with skin the color of caramel, had a bald head and a beard. He was muscular and wore nothing but a pair of plaid pajama bottoms that hung low off his waist. He was a good-lookin' dude, but he ain't have shit on Shyhiem. Bryson was a square. He was wacker than wack. A nigga like him didn't deserve to breathe the same air as Messiah, let alone, be laid up inside her crib.

"Yo, my man. Are you deaf? What you want?" Bryson asked aggressively.

He knew exactly who Shyhiem was. He was the nigga that had been fuckin' Messiah while they were separated. She'd made it clear that she didn't want to fuck with him, so why in the hell was he there?

"Is Messiah here?" Shyhiem looked Bryson square in the eyes.

Bryson hung his head low and chuckled.

"What you doing, man?"

"What the fuck you mean what am I doing?" Shyhiem's upper lip curled.

He hated to be questioned, especially from niggas that he felt wasn't on the same level as him.

"Why are you here?" Bryson stressed. "You look mad crazy. Listen, I know you and Messiah had a li'l thing there for a minute. You love her. I get it. Messiah's the type of girl you'd go to the end of the earth for; but this sad, desperate attempt to win her back, is making you look hella gay. She already told you it was over. Stop embarrassing yourself. She don't want you. She chose me. I'm the man she wants to be with. I'm the man she's gonna marry. Daddy's home where he belongs. So, I suggest," Bryson stepped closer to make himself abundantly clear. "You take your grocery store flowers and step."

Shyhiem clenched his jaw tightly. If he pressed down any harder, he'd crack a tooth. His fist was balled and ready to strike, but flipping out and being violent was part of the reason Messiah had left him in the first place. Besides, fuckin' up this fake-ass Carlton Banks wasn't even worth it. Bryson was the type of cornball that would call the police if you laid a hand on him and then turn around and sue. Shyhiem wanted nothing more than to beat him to a bloody pulp, but that wouldn't change the fact that Messiah had chosen him over Shyhiem. The temporary joy of wiping the smug look off Bryson's face wouldn't stop the outpour of blood spilling from his heart.

All his hopes and dreams had been dashed in a matter of minutes. It was really over between him and Messiah. The love she claimed she had for him was only momentary. Maybe she never really loved him at all. How could she? She'd chosen a nigga that made her cry, broken her heart, lied, cheated, had a baby on her and treated her like she was beneath him, over a man that treated her as an equal and loved her - scars and all.

Boiling with anger, Shyhiem gave Bryson a death stare and then turned his back to leave. It didn't matter how badly he wanted to stomp a hole in his face. There was no reason to argue with Bryson. He'd won the grand prize. Shyhiem boarded the elevator and leaned against the wall. A billion emotions ran through him. The biggest one being: relief. Shyhiem closed his eyes and said a silent prayer to God, thanking him for preventing him from making the biggest mistake of his life. Tears stung his eyes but he was determined not to let them fall.

It was abundantly clear that Messiah wasn't the woman he thought she was. Maybe he'd built her up in his mind to be more than she was. She'd played with his heart and his time. He'd lost himself loving her. He'd given her his all only to be cast aside. The pain in his chest was nauseating. For weeks, he'd worn himself ragged trying to prove his love to her. Shyhiem felt like a fuckin' fool, as he reached inside his pocket and pulled out a small, velvet box. The soft fabric stung the palm of his hand. Inside, was the ring he was gonna propose to her with but she'd never get to see the 3.78CT, pear-shaped diamond, trimmed in rose gold.

Messiah had literally sucker-punched him in the face with her idiotic decision to get back with the nigga that constantly shitted on her. Sure, Shyhiem was new to this love shit. It was a foreign feeling that he really didn't know

47

how to convey. The only emotions he was familiar with were anger, hurt, selfishness and control. Other than that, he was emotionally unavailable.

He didn't believe in miracles. Loving someone, outside of his kids, wasn't on his list of priorities. Maneuvering his way through the gritty streets of St. Louis was the only way he knew to survive. Love didn't rule his world until Messiah entered it. She affected him in a way he never knew was possible. Before her, he let his ego and pride rule his actions. He never wanted to be responsible for holding himself accountable for breaking a woman's heart. Now, there he stood, with his head pressed against the elevator wall in shambles. He'd mourn this death forever. Their love was one for the ages.

Thankfully, Shyhiem had dodged a bullet. Messiah would never see or hear from him again, after this day. Being a begging, pleading, please, baby, please-ass-nigga wasn't even him. Before her, Shyhiem had never given his heart to a woman. After this bullshit, he never would again. Love was for suckers. It used you up and tossed you aside like a used piece of gum, when it was done with you. He'd opened his heart and allowed himself to feel something soul-stirring. The feeling didn't last as long as he'd hoped but that was life. Nothing good ever lasted forever. Messiah wasn't an angel sent down from heaven. She was nothing but one of hell's executive managers. She was on the fuckin' board.

He was done with her. She could choose to live out her days being another man's second choice if she wanted. Shyhiem had tried to show her that real love was tangible and pure. She claimed she wanted more for her life but she would always be stuck in the mud. There was no way she could prosper wit' a man that didn't even measure up in her life. That wasn't Shyhiem's problem though. From that day, moving forward, the raven-haired goddess with the dimpled-chin didn't exist. Like Keesha, she was nothing but an ain't-shit-lyin'-ass bitch he despised.

"I realize I'm just too much for you."–
Beyoncé, "Don't Hurt Yourself"

7
Messiah

Every muscle on Messiah's body ached. With every step she took, it felt as if needles were being pricked into the soles of her feet. A hot bubble bath was calling her name, as she exited the elevator and made her way to her apartment door. The only problem was: she didn't have any bubbles. She'd have to use dish washing liquid, again. Afterward, she might be a little itchy, but she didn't care. As long as she got to soak her throbbing body, she'd be alright.

Working two jobs and taking ballet lessons was effecting her body in ways she never imagined. She was constantly sore from being on her feet at the diner. Adding the rigorous routine of attending ballet class, had her body feeling like it was going to break in half. Everything on her hurt, including her hair follicles, but she wouldn't trade the strain she was putting herself through for all the gold in the world. Working two jobs was a must because she was heavily in debt with creditors and loan companies. It would be years before she would be able to pay everything off.

The stress of her financial issues drove Messiah insane; but when she was on the dance floor, all her worries floated away. She'd avoided dancing for six years, until Shyhiem forced her to dance for him. For years, Messiah felt like she was alone. After the tragic accident that took the lives of her parents and unborn son, she wished that she'd died along with everyone else. She hated being the lone survivor. She wanted desperately to reunite with her parents and son. The only thing that kept her alive was her love for Bryson. Messiah and her older sister, Lake, weren't particularly close. She had no one except Bryson and her best friend, Bird.

Messiah poured her all into her relationship with Bryson, praying he'd do the same. After six years of loving and holding him down, he repaid her loyalty and devotion by cheating and impregnating a girl he went to school with. To say Messiah was heartbroken was an understatement. She died a thousand deaths. Her whole, entire world had been turned upside down. She believed in Bryson and their love, so she never gave up hope that he would come to his senses and return to her. She knew that their love could survive his betrayal.

They weren't even broken up two months before he came crawling back on his hands and knees. The girl he got pregnant lost the baby halfway through the pregnancy. With nothing holding them together, Bryson realized what a huge mistake he'd made and begged for Messiah's forgiveness. There was no denying that she still loved him. He would forever be etched inside her heart. He was the first, and only man, she'd ever slept with, until Shyhiem. He was the first man to tell her 'I love you'. He was the first man to ask for her hand in marriage. Despite how angry and hurt she was by his actions, she couldn't pretend like none of that had transpired.

Messiah loved Bryson and always would, but as she walked inside of her apartment and flicked on the light, her anger boiled to new heights. Her crib was her place of peace. It was a direct reflection of who she was. Normally, her house was spotless; but that day, her house was a mess. Bryson lay on the couch scratching his balls, while asleep on his back. She loved him dearly, but at that moment, it was abundantly clear that she wasn't in love with him anymore.

"Uh ah! Get yo' ass up!" She threw her purse and keys down on the kitchen counter.

Messiah was livid. Here she was tired as fuck from working all day and this nigga was laid up on his ass. Dishes from the night before were piled up in the sink. The trash hadn't been taken out. Red Kool-Aid stains stuck to the bottom of her shoes. Leftover, Chinese, takeout boxes were on the coffee table. Bryson's clothes and shoes were sprawled all over the floor and the living room smelled like feet. Instead of getting up like she asked, he rolled over onto his stomach and groaned.

"I know you hear me! Don't roll over and play dead! Get yo' ass up!" She smacked him hard on the ass. "It's 8 o'clock. Why are you still sleep? What have you been doing all day?"

Bryson rubbed his face and opened his eyes. He hadn't done shit but eat, sleep and fart. Oh, and lie and tell her ex that they were back together. He wasn't going to tell her that though. Messiah would throw him out on his ass. She could never know what he'd done. He'd never win her back if she did. She'd hate him even more than she did now. Instead, he replied, "Messiah, I'm in mourning or have you forgotten?"

Messiah rolled her eyes and inhaled deeply. She was over his whining.

"I understand that you're sad. I get it. Remember, we lost a child too, but you can't sleep your misery away. Well, you can if you want to, but you can't do it here. Life goes on. I was being nice by letting you stay here for a while but it's been a month. You gotta go, my nigga." She pointed to the door.

"You really gon' kick me out? Messiah, I need you." He sat up and planted his long feet on the floor.

"You need me? Are you fuckin' kidding me?" Messiah stopped dead in her tracks. "I needed you but you wasn't there for me! No, I need you to clean up this fuckin' mess and take yo' ass back to Philly! Talkin' 'bout you need me..." She looked him up and down with disgust.

"You should've thought about that before you left me for that bitch! You got yo' nerve. I need my fuckin' money back! How 'bout that? I need all the times I cried over yo' ass back! I need the time I invested into this punk-ass relationship back. Hell, I need my baby back, but guess what? I ain't gon' get it!" Messiah tossed her head from side to side.

"Talkin' about you need some fuckin' body. Nigga, please. You need a goddamn clue. That's what you need. Shit. I don't live like this! You got my house lookin' like a fuckin' pigsty. And let me tell you one thing." She pointed her finger in his face, like he was a child. "If I see a roach crawl around this bitch, I'ma stick my foot so far up yo' ass, you'll be shittin' leather for weeks," she hissed.

"Ok, ok; I'ma clean up." Bryson sighed, picking up the takeout boxes.

"No, when are you leaving? Don't you gotta go back to school?"

"I do but I need more time. This has been really hard on me. I lost two fuckin' babies and... you. I ain't got shit right now."

"And whose fault is that? You had the world but you left it for a bitch you knew for five minutes. Now, you gotta suffer. Now, you gotta live the rest of your life knowing you will *neeeeeever* get me back. Us not being together is the best thing that has *EVER* happened to me. 'Cause guess what? I ain't no dummy. You never loved me for real. You used me as a fuckin' ATM machine."

"That's not true." He said, visibly hurt. "You know damn well I love you. I would do anything for you."

"Ok, then give me back my money." She held out her hand, palm up.

"I told you, I'ma pay you back. I just need you to reconsider giving me another chance. Messiah, I love you."

Messiah held her head back and let out a loud groan. She couldn't believe that at one point in time she was madly, head-over-heels in love with this clown. Bryson was like a pesky little brother she couldn't get rid of now. There was no attraction to him at all. Her heart belonged to one person and one person only.

"Bryson, you don't love me. The only person you love is yourself. You cheated on me and had a baby on me, but here you are, trying to lay a guilt trip on me! Narcissistic much? You are a fuckin' asshole!"

"C'mon, Messiah, don't be like that. We can work this out." He tried to reach for her hand.

"Noooo! Uh ah... don't touch me." She yanked her hand away. "Go work shit out with the bitch you was just wit'. Don't you think she needs you? I forgot. It's all about your pain. Fuck everybody else feelings. Well guess what, nigga? *I'm tired*! Look at me!" She stomped her foot and looked over her uniform.

"I'm covered in grease, my hair is dirty, my feet hurt, I haven't slept in days, I'm in debt up to my ass because of you, and yet you're the victim? Do you see how fucked up that is? I am *tired*!" Messiah stressed at the top of her lungs. "All I want is peace! I want my life back! I wanna be happy!"

"I'm sorry. I didn't mean to make you upset." Bryson apologized, feeling like shit.

He hated to see Messiah in such distress, especially, because of him. Despite all he'd put her through, she'd found it in her heart to be a shoulder for him to lean on. Most women wouldn't have given a damn about his feelings. She was honestly and truly an angel on earth. He didn't deserve to have her in his life. He wasn't worthy of her friendship - let alone her love. The selfish part of him still wasn't going to stop until he made her his girl again.

"You got one more week, then you gotta get the fuck outta here." Messiah shot past him and headed to her bedroom. "And clean up my fuckin' house!" She slammed the door closed behind her.

Alone, she sank down onto the concrete floor and leaned her head up against the door. Tears formed in her eyes. *This can't be my life,* she thought, pulling her knees up to her chest. Moments like this reminded her of why she hated living sometimes. She needed a break. She was tired of people taking her kindness for weakness. Everyone around her seemed to take her kind, good nature for granted, including Shyhiem.

After the incident at Blank Space, where he beat a guy that was trying to hit on her and accidentally backhanded her in the process, Messiah had no choice but to detach herself from him. She loved Shyhiem with all her heart. He was her soulmate, but his violent tendencies scared the shit out of her. She couldn't have that kind of negative energy in her life. The way he loved her so intensely, so quickly, scared her even more. She wasn't used to someone making her a priority in their life.

Plus, his issues with his ignorant-ass baby mama didn't help either. It was all too much too soon. She missed him with every breath she took, but things between them were moving too fast for comfort. She didn't want to go from one fucked up relationship to another. Shyhiem didn't deserve to have just half of her. He deserved to have all of her or nothing at all.

Messiah was still trying to figure her shit out. She didn't know who she was as a woman. To give herself to Shyhiem or any other man, she had to be a whole, complete person. Until then, she was trapped inside her own house, her own head and in her own, personal misery.

"His family history pimpin' and bangin'. He was meant to be dangerous."– Kendrick Lamar, "Duckworth"

8

Shyhiem

The damp smell of rain water and mildew filled the empty warehouse where Mayhem and Shyhiem were at. Several mice scurried around the space, looking for food and shelter. Broken glass crackled under their feet, whenever they walked. Mayhem sat in a metal folding chair, puffin' on a blunt. It was cold and his back hurt from sitting in the hard chair for so long. Being at the warehouse was the last place he wanted to be, but one of his premiers needed to re-up. Shyhiem sat beside his brother. He was Mayhem's distro, so it was his responsibility to make sure everyone stayed in line and all the money was collected.

They were under a lot of pressure to move the 132 kilos of product within 60 days. They couldn't afford any fuck ups. Victor Gonzalez, the plug and head nigga in charge, would have their heads on a platter if they did. Shyhiem wasn't willing to die. He'd survived this long without getting a bullet in his brain. He was determined to get the job done without being touched. Getting back into the game was his only way to get to Cali faster. The longer he stayed in St. Louis, the more stir-crazy he became. Shyhiem had become a hardened man. He now gave negative zero fucks. His kids were the only thing keeping him alive. Other than that, he didn't have anything to live for.

The li'l bit of heart he had left shriveled up and died once he learned Messiah was back with her ex. Nothing good in the world existed, in his eyes. The world had become an even darker, grittier place. The monster inside of him had taken over. When he looked in the mirror, he didn't recognize the man staring back at him. Messiah had ruined him forever.

"Yo, where is this nigga at?" Shyhiem said, becoming weary.

He hated waiting on people. Being late was his #1 pet peeve.

"He said he was on his way," Mayhem answered, becoming agitated as well.

"I need to ask you something anyway." Shyhiem lowered his voice so their workers wouldn't hear.

"What?"

"Why you tell Keesha I was back in business?"

Mayhem thought of a quick lie. He couldn't tell his brother that he'd slipped up and started pillow-talking with her one night.

"My bad, bro. I ain't know it was supposed to be a secret."

Shyhiem eyed him suspiciously. Mayhem knew damn well he hated Keesha. Anything regarding his personal life was off limits to her.

"What was you doing talkin' to her anyway?" He continued to probe.

"Look who decided to show up." Mayhem changed the subject, as Esco approached the door.

Esco showing up when he did was a blessing in disguise. He wasn't prepared to answer Shyhiem's questions. Mayhem's men patted Esco down before he entered. Once he was cleared of having any weapons, Esco strolled in casually, which pissed Shyhiem off even more. He hated when muthafuckas wasted his time. Plus, he couldn't stand Esco. He was a loudmouth Puerto Rican that talked way too much and always had some slick shit to say.

"I may be late but I'm always on time." Esco showed Mayhem love by giving him dap.

"Goodnight! What it do, playboy?" He held out his hand for a five.

Shyhiem ice-grilled him, refusing to raise his hand.

"Damn, it's like that? Who pissed in your cereal?"

Shyhiem continued to stare him down.

"A'ight, be like that then." Esco sat a duffle bag full of money down on the table.

Shyhiem unzipped the bag and rummaged through it. The bag was light.

"Where the fuck is the rest of it?" He asked, not in the mood to play.

"Look at this guy," Esco laughed. "Is he always so serious? You know, stress can kill you."

"And so can a gunshot to the head," Shyhiem responded coldly.

"Answer the fuckin' question, Esco," Mayhem ordered.

"We had a bad week. Didn't sell as much."

Shyhiem called bullshit. Esco couldn't even look him or Mayhem in the eye when he lied. Esco was not only loud and annoying, but the dude was usually plain as shit. He was never flashy with his style. However, that day, he wore designer everything. Shyhiem also noticed the brand new 18k gold Audemars Piguet watch on his wrist.

"I swear, I'll have the rest for you next week," Esco said to Mayhem, sincerely.

"You had a short week, huh?" Mayhem repeated.

"Yeah." Esco said confidently.

Mayhem looked over at his brother and laughed.

"Can you believe this nigga?" He said to Shyhiem, standing up. "You had a bad week? Shit, I can't tell. You designer down. Ferragamo belt." He tugged at his pants. "Gucci shoes, Robin jeans; you lookin' good than a muthafucka, if you ask me."

"What the fuck I got on got to do wit' anything? I ain't never played y'all and I haven't been short yet. Like I said, I'm working on gettin' y'all the money now." Esco shot back.

"First off, recognize where the fuck you at and who the fuck you talkin' to wit' all this 'like I said shit'." Mayhem pointed his finger in his face. "So, tell me. What is it? What's the change? You got a new bitch? You snortin' it? 'Cause you ain't never come around this muthafucka designer down."

"Ain't shit changed. Like I said, we had a bad week. Things ain't move how they should've moved."

"So, you short and the first thing you decide to do is swag out?" Shyhiem quizzed, becoming more and more irritated by the second.

"Man." Esco waved him off. "Are we done here?"

"Are we done? You hear this nigga?" Mayhem looked back at Shyhiem and then turned around and backslapped Esco in the mouth and then choked him. "Nigga, we done, when I say we done." He squeezed his neck causing his veins to pop out.

Esco clawed at his hands to remove them from around his neck but Mayhem's grip was too tight.

"Don't ever disrespect me, nigga!" He squeezed harder.

Mayhem got off on the sight of Esco's face turning blue. Everyone, except Shyhiem, watched in horror, as he damn near cut off Esco's air supply. Shyhiem was used to his brother's violent outbursts. The lids of Esco's eyes fluttered, as he gasped for air. At any moment, he was sure to die, but today was his lucky day.

"As a matter-of-fact, come up out that shit, nigga!" Mayhem threw him down onto the ground. "That's my shit now!"

Esco scooted back in fear.

"C'mon, man, you trippin'." He said, trying to catch his breath.

"What size shoes are those anyway? Them look like my size, nigga." Mayhem hovered over him, as Esco began to strip down.

Once he was down to nothing except his socks and underwear, Mayhem slapped him again. "Everything, Ese."

Esco tearfully pulled down his underwear and revealed his pink, little dick. Some of the goons in the room laughed, while others shook their heads and looked away.

"No wonder you always talkin' shit. Muthafuckas like you always overcompensating for something," Mayhem teased.

"Mayhem, please. I'm sorry. I'll get the rest of your money today!" Esco pleaded.

"You damn right, you gon' run me my money. The next time you steal from me will be the last day you walk this earth. But today, I'ma let you live, li'l nigga. See you next week." Mayhem patted his tear-stained cheek, mockingly, and then stood up straight.

POW! The sound of a gun shot rang through the air and caused Mayhem to flinch. For a second, he thought he'd been hit, until Esco's lifeless body fell back onto the ground. Mayhem looked to his right and saw Shyhiem aiming the gun at what was once Esco's head. His brains had been blown out and his blood was now splattered all over their clothes.

"Yo, what the fuck?" He laughed, in a state of disbelief.

Shyhiem wasn't a shooter. He'd never taken a life before. He was known for throwing down with his fists. Mayhem looked at his little brother with brain fragments all over his face. The fact that he'd killed someone not only stunned Mayhem but surprised the hell out of him. He was the devil himself, compared to Shyhiem, but he hadn't even batted an eyelash. Mayhem didn't know what had gotten into him but he welcomed the drastic change.

"It needed to be done. The nigga disrespected you. If we let him slide, what would the others think?" Shyhiem wiped his fingerprints off the gun, before handing it back to him.

Shyhiem didn't know what had gotten into himself. He was losing his mind. There was so much pent up anger inside of him, he couldn't contain it.

"You know this ain't gon' be the end of this, right?" Mayhem smiled.

Shyhiem shot him a stone-cold look.

"A'ight. Just so you know. One of y'all niggas clean this shit up." Mayhem ordered. "Fuck." He looked down at his shirt. "Now I gotta put this nigga shirt on for real. You got blood on mine."

"You got a bangin' booty and a tight waist."– New Edition, "Hot 2Nite"

9
Shyhiem

Shyhiem looked down at his phone. His thumb hovered over the keyboard. Everything in him wanted to text Messiah and tell her how fuckin' stupid she was for breaking his heart. He wanted to tell her that his days were dim because she wasn't in it but the inner nigga wouldn't allow it. He'd die before he exposed his heart to her again.

Shyhiem was on the edge of insanity. Every which way he turned, he thought he saw her face. He was living recklessly but there was no slowing him down. Memories of Messiah filled his brain, clouding his judgement, causing him to make brash decisions. The memory of what they used to be haunted his psyche.

No matter what he did, Shyhiem couldn't escape her. Getting faded off liquor and weed didn't stop him from thinking about her. He'd randomly smell her scent in the air or hear her voice. Shyhiem ran his hands down his face. He couldn't continue to live in misery. It was fucked up because he had the world at his fingertips. He had access to the finest jewels, cars and homes; but none of it meant a thing, since she wasn't around to bask in the riches. From sun up to sun down, he wondered if she was thinking about him the way he was thinking about her. Shyhiem would give it all up to have her back in his world.

Shaking his head, he glared at the bottles of Cîroc on the table before him. *Take another sip. You know you want to,* Shyhiem's inner demon whispered. Alcohol numbed the hollowness in his chest. It helped soothe the nightmare he'd been having. If he wasn't dreaming of Messiah, Esco's lifeless body taunted him. Taking a life was harder to live with than he thought. He didn't know how Mayhem went through life so casually. Shyhiem didn't think his life could get any worse - until he received papers from the state saying Keesha had filed child support on him.

Every month they were going to take $900 out his check. Shyhiem would never be able to get a crib of his own now. The only way he could afford it is if he used his dirty money. He couldn't do that 'cause that would raise a red flag with his P.O. Once again, Keesha had found a way to screw him over. Usually, he'd have Messiah to talk to about stuff like this. Now, he had to carry the burdens of the world on his own. He wanted to get over her so badly but it wasn't that easy.

She was the woman he was convinced would someday be his wife and the mother to his kids. They were supposed to be a family. None of that would come to be. They'd never move to the West Coast together and live out their days underneath the California sun.

She didn't want him. Dealing with the realization was harder than surviving three years in prison. The first, and only, time he'd opened his heart to a woman led to internal bloodshed. Shyhiem wasn't used to feeling anything besides anger, distrust and lust. This love shit was too fuckin' stressful. He hated it; and what felt even worse, was loving someone that didn't love him in return. Outside of Mayhem and the twins, he had no one. He thought Messiah would be the one to save him from his misery, but she didn't. She betrayed him in the worst way. And yeah, he'd fucked up majorly by accidentally putting his hands on her, but that didn't warrant this kind of punishment. He'd never hurt Messiah on purpose. It was his job to protect her.

Drowning his sorrows with vodka at a nightclub he didn't want to be at was the only thing that made him feel somewhat alive. He didn't want to be posted up in a private booth around a bunch of goons and hoes that only wanted him for his looks and money. He'd much rather be laid up in bed between Messiah's warm, caramel legs. Yet, there he was, chugging down a bottle of Cîroc with his brother and his mans.

The Olive Bar was packed from wall-to-wall. The hip-hop-inspired club had a rooftop patio, eight, private booths, bottle service, 16 video screens, large, outdoor patio and a full-service restaurant. The DJ was playing a mix of Too Short's *Blow the Whistle*. Everyone was lit and having a good time. Shyhiem stood next to Mayhem, holding court. He hadn't smiled once but Shyhiem wasn't the type to smile much anyway. For the past month, they'd been hitting the club nonstop. Every weekend, they were in the spot.

He should've been riding high on his good fortune. He and Mayhem had been flooding the streets with cocaine. Shyhiem hadn't seen this kind of money in years. It felt good not to have any financial worries. He could have whatever, whenever he wanted it but he didn't make any foolish purchases. He wasn't stupid. He knew from experience to lay low. The only worry he had was Esco's crew retaliating for his death. If, and when, the day came, he'd be ready.

Mayhem, on the other hand, was wilding out. He'd bought three cars, several diamond chains, two Cartier watches and a new home. Shyhiem told him to stop spending so recklessly but Mayhem was hardheaded and wouldn't listen. If he kept on flossing, Shyhiem was out. He'd be damned if he went back to jail because of his brother's stupidity. Jumping back into the coke game was only for the betterment of his kids. He had no plans on it being a lifelong career. Shyhiem wanted to be a filmmaker. While dating Messiah, he'd filmed tons of videos of her that he planned on turning into a mini documentary based on the way he saw her through his eyes. Messiah had no idea how special and unique she was. She often went through life hiding herself from the world.

Now that they'd broken up, he couldn't bear to look at the footage. It hurt too much to see her innocent face. Just thinking of the way she used to smile at him caused Shyhiem's heart to constrict. *She chose him over you,* his inner voice taunted him. *Are you surprised? Why would she want a nigga like you? Look at you. You're a drunk and a murderer. How can you call yourself a man when you're killin' your own people for personal gain?* Shyhiem closed his eyes and rolled his neck around in a circle, to work out the kinks. He had to get these fucked up thoughts out of his head.

They were eating him alive. Getting blasted every night was only making it worse. The bass from the music wasn't helping either. The voices in his head were louder than ever. He had to figure out a way to kill all the noise. Instead of trippin' off his old love, it was time to get under something new. Shyhiem searched the club for someone to take home. It didn't take too much time to find someone. Chicks had been eye-fuckin' him since he walked through the door. None of them caught his attention, except one.

She was the opposite of Messiah. This girl was the type he'd normally go for. She had the whole Instagram baddie look that made his dick super hard. Shyhiem locked eyes with the cutie and signaled for her to come over. The girl tucked her hair behind her ear and sauntered over to him. The gesture reminded him of Messiah, which pissed Shyhiem off. The reason he wanted to stick his dick in another woman was to get over her, not think about her even more.

Face-to-face, he looked the chick over. She had silky smooth, mocha-colored skin, just like him. Her 30-inch weave was parted down the middle and flat ironed bone straight. Her makeup was tastefully done, but the dress she wore was downright sinful. She rocked a skin-tight, red, bodycon dress that dipped down to her navel, exposing her firm, succulent, DD breasts. This girl's body was insane. She was thick in all the right places. Her figure reminded him of the cartoon character Jessica Rabbit. Her hips and ass were round and curvy - just how he liked it. Shyhiem didn't even need to know her name. She would do just fine.

"Hi. What's your name?" The woman smiled, flashing her come-fuck-me eyes.

"Goodnight." He introduced himself, extending his hand.

"Lincoln." She placed her hand in his, mesmerized by his good looks.

"You lookin' at me like you can handle everything you askin' for," Shyhiem flirted.

"Boy, you ain't talkin' about nothing," she blushed.

"Why we still here then?"

"I'm ready to go whenever you are."

"Smuggle bricks for China."– Yo Gotti
feat. Nicki Minaj, "Rake It Up"

10

Keesha

"Loan me 50 dollars." Keesha's mother, Debra, held out her hand.

"I ain't got it," Keesha lied, sitting at the kitchen table.

The twins were in the living room watching TV, while they had grown people talk.

"Yes, you do. You betta be happy I ain't asking you for more than that. C'mon now. I'm tryin' to go on the boat tonight."

"Huuuuuh," Keesha groaned, digging inside her Michael Kors purse. "Here, girl, don't ask me for nothin' else." She slammed a one-hundred-dollar bill down onto the table.

"I knew yo' ass was lyin'." Debra stuffed the bill inside her bra and then resumed rolling up a blunt. "You talk to Mayhem?"

"Everyday." Keesha replied, munching on a bag of Rap Snacks.

"What about Shyhiem?"

"Nope. He call his self being mad 'cause I filed child support on him," Keesha laughed.

"That's what his ass get. He should've never left home to be with that high yella bitch. I bet his ass regret now," Debra chuckled.

"I ain't thinkin' about Shyhiem. He'll be a'ight. As long as he don't skip no payment, we straight."

"And what you gon' do about Mayhem? Is that nigga ever gon' step up to the plate and take care of his kids?" Debra said loudly.

"Shhhhhhhh! What you talkin' so damn loud for?" Keesha looked towards the living room to see if the kids heard anything.

The twins were all into the TV and hadn't heard a thing.

"Girl, don't you shush me! You in my damn house, remember? I can talk as loud as I want to. I pay the bills up in this muthafucka. You just mad 'cause you know I'm right." Debra lit the blunt and took a puff.

"Mayhem helps me in other ways."

"What, by supplying you wit' coke and dick? How dumb can you be?"

"Ain't you the pot callin' the kettle black," Keesha scoffed. "You askin' me for money but you got a whole nigga in the other room that's damn near my age."

"'Least I ain't stashing shit for his ass. I know that's what you over there doing."

Keesha sat quietly and continued to eat her chips.

"Mmm hmm. That's what I thought." Debra pursed her lips. "You over there taking care of his kids and stashing coke. Meanwhile, he engaged to a whole bitch and get to roam the streets free. I wouldn't be surprised if his sorry-ass was on the down low too." Debra rolled her eyes and passed Keesha the blunt. "You can't trust none of these niggas nowadays. All of 'em like they booty tampered with. Don't be no fool like I was and get tricked by a gay man like ya daddy. Nasty fucka."

"Mayhem ain't shit like that sick fuck," Keesha snarled.

"You don't know what that man is, li'l girl. You ain't around him 24 hours a day. Hell, him and Shyhiem probably gay. Frankly, both of 'em some old, dick-in-the-booty-ass niggas to me. You need to take both of 'em for all they got. I still can't believe yo' daddy left me for that ole Lionel-Richie-lookin' muthafucka."

Keesha clenched her jaw and kept quiet. Whenever her mother went on a tangent about her homosexual father, it was best not to argue with her. Keesha didn't have much to argue anyway. She hated the muthafucka. Since as far back as she could remember, her mother had instilled in her that being gay was wrong. Her mother hated homosexuals, whether gay or lesbian. She thought being gay was an abomination and a slap in the face to God.

Anyone with common sense knew the real reason Debra hated the gay community was because Keesha's father left her for another man. She was blindsided by the betrayal. To make him suffer, she filled Keesha's head with beliefs that gay men were of the devil and liked to rape and beat little boys and girls. When Keesha's father tried to see her, she'd be too afraid to be alone with him. Growing up in the hood with a gay father was humiliating. Everyone knew and would roast her for it, which made her want to distance herself even more. She didn't want a faggot as a father.

As an adult, Keesha put all of that behind her, but the past had a funny way of sneaking up on her. Seeing her only son showcase feminine behavior sickened her to the core. It made her feel like her bloodline was tainted. Her father not only abandoned her mother for another man, but now his homosexual gene had passed on to her child. Maybe it was payback for not telling Shyhiem the truth about the paternity of the kids. The secret ate at her flesh every day, but Keesha was too far in it to tell the truth now. She couldn't risk not having Shyhiem around to help her financially and physically with the twins. Mayhem was unreliable. He wasn't father material. He didn't know the first thing about raising a child. Hell, she was barely getting by.

Keesha knew filing child support would put a greater wedge between her and Shyhiem, but a point had to be made. He could not hurt her feelings and get away with it. It wasn't ok that he was messing around with a girl that lived in their building. It was fuckin' humiliating. Everyone in the building knew. Keesha couldn't go to the mailbox without someone staring at her like she was a wounded bird. Shyhiem had to pay for what he'd done. The way to do it, was by making him see that no matter what, she'd always have control over him. She was Debra's child. Just like she'd made her father suffer, Keesha would do the same.

"For all we know, we may never meet again."– Donny Hathaway, "For all we know"

11

Messiah

Messiah's morning had just begun but she wished it was over already. The day was November 2, 2016. It was the most dreadful day of the year for her. It was the day that haunted her dreams and gave her nightmares. If she could've, she would've stayed hidden underneath the covers until the day passed. Unfortunately for Messiah, her life didn't work that way. She didn't have the luxury to take a day off. She had to work, if she wanted to eat and pay bills. She didn't have anyone that she could turn to in her time of need - which was often.

Normally, she didn't have enough money to pay rent and buy groceries, despite working two jobs. Her raggedy, ole car had been in the shop for months because she couldn't afford to get it out. Bryson should've been the person she turned to but he was of no help. Since he'd been crashing on her couch, he'd thrown her a couple of dollars and bought some toiletries for the house but that was about it. Other than that, she was still on her own.

Messiah felt like an idiot for giving him a place to stay when she was barely getting anything in return - except a headache. It was her fault that she was in such financial debt. She'd helped put Bryson through school by taking out several loans and maxing out credit cards. She did it with the notion he'd pay her back. She thought she was helping her man shape the future they'd have as husband and wife. Little did she know, but marriage for she and Bryson was nowhere in her future.

Her inability to tell him no and put her needs first fucked up her life in more ways than one. The guilt she carried from her parents' death caused her to put other people's needs ahead of her own. She never wanted anyone to be upset with her. Her circle was small and she didn't want to lose anyone else because of her selfishness. It would kill her. Telling Bryson off the way she had was huge for her. Messiah hated confrontation and she hated conflict even more. She was a peaceful person who craved balance. Yet, her life was the most off-kilter it had ever been. She was always in a piss-poor mood. Lately, the only time she felt any kind of happiness was when she was dancing. On the dance floor, she soared. She felt as free as a bird. All her worries, fears and inner demons vanished.

That day, she knew she'd feel no joy. Nothing good would come out of visiting this place. The heel of her boots sunk into the moist grass, as she walked to her parents' and son's grave. The rainy weather expressed her somber mood to a T. This was the last place she wanted to be before heading to work. Being at their gravesite would only make an already shitty day, shittier. But it would be a slap in the face to her parents' memory if she didn't come and show her respect on the anniversary of their death.

As she neared their headstone, she saw a woman dressed from head to toe in designer duds. The woman wore a $4,546, black and white, Balmain, double-breasted, houndstooth midi coat. The chick looked and smelled like money. It didn't take long for Messiah to figure out who the woman was. *Really, Jesus? Really? You gon' do me like this today,* she thought, rolling her eyes extra hard. Messiah knew exactly who the woman was. She'd done a great job of avoiding her sister until now. She'd only spoken to Lake once since their showdown at the bridal salon. It was when Messiah put her pride to the side and asked her for help when her lights got cut off and Lake refused to offer assistance. After that, Messiah vowed to never speak to her again. She couldn't stand Lake. She was nothing but a condescending, egotistical, spoiled, prima donna.

Messiah trudged her way through the muddy grass, as Bird waited for her in the car. Messiah didn't plan on being there long. She was going to leave flowers on each of their graves, say a quick prayer and leave. Lake heard sloshy footsteps behind her and turned around in a panic. It was already bad enough she was in a cemetery at the wee hours of the morning. She didn't need some psycho, serial killer running up on her. She expected to be alone. Lake held her chest and caught her breath, once she realized it was nobody but her pesky, little sister.

"Holy shit. You scared the hell out of me." She turned back around and faced the headstones.

"If I would've know you were gonna be here, I would've came later or not at all." Messiah bent down and placed the flowers on her parents' grave.

"Rude." Lake flipped her hair over her shoulder. "But whatever, I'm low-key happy you're here. I hate coming here by myself year after year."

Messiah tuned her sister out and focused on the fact that her parents' dead bodies were underneath her feet. The realization made her sick to her stomach, because the feeling that it was her fault still hadn't gone completely away.

"Please don't tell me you're still mad 'cause I wouldn't pay your li'l punk-ass light bill. If so, you really need to take a Xanax and chill." Lake waved her off.

Messiah looked over her shoulder at her sister. If they weren't at her parents' grave, she would've slapped the taste out of her mouth. She loathed her sister's smug attitude, as much as she hated her beautiful guts. Lake was a bitch but she was a gorgeous bitch. Her naturally curly, auburn hair framed her picture-perfect face. Lake's sun-kissed skin, arched brows, round, brown eyes and beauty mark above her plump lips made her every man's wet dream. She had a long neck, was 5'7 and wore a size 4. Lake was a fucking bombshell and she used her magnificent good looks to get through life. She used men for money and fame and it had paid off well. On New Year's Eve, she was set to marry St. Louis Cardinals pitcher, Austin Rhodes. He had a 200-million-dollar contract, milky, white skin and a killer smile.

Ever since their parents' death, Messiah had suffered one loss after another. She just couldn't get her shit together. Meanwhile, Lake soared through life, forsaking anyone that got in her way. She loved to belittle Messiah about the way she dressed, the company she kept, the men she dated and the decisions she made regarding her life. Instead of arguing with Lake on such a sacred day, Messiah focused her attention on her son's headstone. Dried up leaves covered his name. Messiah brushed the leaves away and willed herself not to fall apart. She had to keep it together. Even though her baby was dead, he didn't deserve her tears. She'd cried enough to last them both a lifetime. To honor his short life, she would remain stoic.

"Mama loves you," she whispered, before rising to her feet.

Every time she visited the gravesite, a piece of her died inside. It didn't help that each year she visited alone. Bryson refused to come. He said he wasn't strong enough to relive the pain.

"So, you gon' act like you don't hear me? Oh my God, you are such a child." Lake shook her head.

"Shut up talkin' to me. I ain't got shit to say to you." Messiah dusted off her pants.

"You can be mad at me all you want but you're still in my wedding."

"Heffa, please. No, I'm not. Ask one of them bougie bitches you pledged with to be your maid of honor."

"If I hadn't promised Mama that whenever I got married you'd stand up for me, I would've, but you're my sister. You gotta be there for me."

"You know what?" Messiah snapped. "I am so sick of people tellin' me what I gotta do. I don't owe none of you niggas shit! You ain't never been there for me. Ever since Mama and Daddy died, I've been on my own."

"Stop it with the Orphan Annie sob story, Messiah. Just because I made something of myself doesn't mean I had it any easier than you." Lake wrinkled her brow.

"Bullshit! You have had everything handed to you on a silver platter. Mama and Daddy worshiped you. They acted like you were the second coming of Jesus. You were Malibu Barbie and I was Skipper up in this bitch. I had to struggle for everything I got, including Mama and Daddy's affection."

"Oh, stop it! Mama and Daddy loved your dirty drawz. Maybe if you're attitude wasn't so shitty, you would get further in life, Scrooge McDuck. You don't have to struggle. You struggle 'cause you choose to."

"That's the dumbest thing I've ever heard. Who chooses to struggle?" Messiah retorted, indignantly.

"You! Nobody told yo' dumbass to put a nigga that ain't even yo' husband through school. I told you not to do it but you did it anyway. *'Cause you was in love.* Now look at you." Lake gave her the once-over. "Walkin' around in your hand-me-down fashions, lookin' like you're beggin' for change. I have told you time and time again to set that monkey out to a real nigga. Somebody that's gon' take care of you. But you just dead set on being somebody's *ride or die. Somebody's wifey.*" Lake made air quotes with her hands.

"Ugh, it's fuckin' pathetic. Haven't you learned anything? Love is for the weak."

"I swear to God you're a White Walker. No way do we have the same parents. You have no soul. Sometimes, I hate to even call you my sister." Messiah said in disbelief.

"You know, I realize we haven't been close, but I guess I never realized just how much you hate me." Lake wrinkled her brow.

"I hate you?" Messiah scoffed. "Oh, it's the other way around, sweetheart. You're the one who constantly attacks me."

"I don't hate you." Lake stood tall. "It's just that I love you more when I'm not with you. It's like we're allergic to each other."

"You got that right." Messiah agreed with a laugh.

"I really do want you in my wedding, but you gotta shave your armpits though."

"Bitch, I do shave under my arms!" Messiah pushed her playfully.

"Oh, you do? You know you incense burnin' bitches like to be natural." Lake scrunched her nose.

"Whatever. You want a fuckin' slave. You want me to do your grunt work 'cause them goofy-lookin' bitches won't do it. They're on the same level as you. You look at me like I'm nothing."

"Is that really what you think of me?" Lake asked, appalled.

"Didn't Daddy tell you not to ask questions you already know the answer to?" Messiah raised her brow.

Lake cleared her throat. She hated being nice, but Messiah was forcing her to let down her guard.

"Well, despite what you think, I do care about you, Messiah. I might not always show it; but deep down inside this cold, black heart lies feelings for you. You're my little sister. I give you shit all the time because I want the best for you."

"Mmm hmm." Messiah pursed her lips, unimpressed by her speech.

"I pour my heart out to you and that's how you respond?" Lake mean-mugged her. "I'm serious, Messiah. You have to be in my wedding. It wouldn't be the same without you. Plus, Mama and Daddy would turn over in their graves if you weren't. And ain't nobody got time for their ghosts to be haunting me. She is too cute for that."

"I'm not gonna be in your wedding." Messiah said flatly.

"But whhhhy," Lake whined, stomping her feet. "I already bought your dress."

"Nobody told you to do that." Messiah shrugged.

"I knew you couldn't afford it. That's why I did it, asshole. I was tryin' to be nice. Don't make me regret it."

"What you want me to say, thank you, 'cause I'm not."

"Ooooooooooh… you are such a spiteful li'l bitch! I love it. Keep it up," Lake smiled devilishly. "Now, seriously; c'mon, Messiah, be my damn maid of honor. Please don't make me beg. I'm wearing Balmain. You can not beg in Balmain! It's disrespectful."
"I said… no."

"Here." Lake reached inside her Birkin bag and pulled out six, crisp, one-hundred-dollar bills. "I'm sorry, ok? I should've helped you with your light bill. I must have been PMS'ing that day. You obviously needed it or you wouldn't have asked."

Messiah looked down at the money.

"Take it. I know you need it."

"Fuck you 'cause I do." Messiah snatched the money and placed it inside her bra. "I'm still not gon' be in yo' tacky, overpriced, snooty-ass wedding." She stormed off.

"I love you too! It was nice catching up! I'll see you at the rehearsal diner! It's the night before the wedding; and please, wear something that doesn't smell like mothballs!" Lake yelled after her.

Messiah shot her the middle finger, as she got inside Bird's warm car.

"What she do now to piss you off?" She asked, starting the engine.

"I'm back in the wedding." Messiah placed on her seatbelt.

"You are such a glutton for punishment." Bird shook her head.

"She's my sister. She's the only family I have left. I can't just say no. Plus, she gave me $600," Messiah grinned, showing off the money.

"I guess, but when things go left, and we both know it will, remember this day."

"Oh, trust me. I know Lake is gon' piss me off. I just need a drink. I need to blow off some steam before I lose it."

"You need several drinks and some dick." Bird pulled off. "Ooooh… I got an idea. Let's go out."

"Oh hell to the nah. The last time I went out with you, I got slapped. The time before that, I almost got shot. Nah, bruh. I'm good."

"Let's just forget that happened. We need to kick it, friend. I promise we'll have a good time. Won't nothin' bad happen."

"Why can't we just go out to eat? It ain't like I ain't got money."

"Nope… we're going to the club. We gon' find you some dick."

"Huuuuuh… it bet not be Blank Space."

"Fine; we won't go to Blank Space. We can go to this new club I've been hearing about called The Olive Bar.

"Asking god to… please, forgive me. for messing up the blessing he gave to me. I see everything clearly now." – Jagged Edge, "Walked Outta Heaven"

12

Messiah

Nothing can stop me, I'm all the way up! The crowd sang, going wild. Fat Joe and Remy Ma's hit song, *All The Way Up,* had been the hit song of the year. Even though it was winter, the summertime anthem still banged. While Bird, and everyone else inside the club, jammed to the music, Messiah yawned and stretched her back. Nightclubs just weren't her thing. She hated crowds. People were always bumping into her, and for some reason, the craziest of men were always attracted to her. Bird tried to get her to loosen up and have a good time but Messiah just wasn't feeling it. She wanted to go home.

The club and Messiah didn't mix. She never danced. It was weird because she could dance on stage in front of hundreds of people, but for some reason, whenever she was in a club she froze up. Messiah always felt uncomfortable and out of place. Leaning against the wall, she positioned her weight from one foot to another. The balls of her feet were on fire. She hated wearing heels. The muthafuckas hurt like hell.

Buying an outfit, shoes, getting her hair and nails done to pay to get into a club and order drinks she couldn't afford was asinine. Yet, she'd done it anyway. After some persuading from Bird, the two girls hit up the mall. Messiah couldn't even enjoy the shopping excursion. She always felt guilty when it came to spending money on herself. Her whole, adult life had been spent paying bills and rent, as well as taking care of others. She never had any extra money to do anything nice for herself.

Stores like H&M, Aldo and Macy's were a splurge for her. When Messiah did go clothes shopping, it was mainly at thrift stores or garage sales. With Bird's persistence, they hit up a store Messiah never even dreamt of going in. Anthropologie was the hippie-chic girl's Mecca. It was a store meant for bitches that didn't have credit problems. A store Messiah should never step foot in. They're clothes, however, were fabulous and matched her boho-chic style perfectly. Messiah didn't even have to try anything on. She simply bought the outfit the mannequin was wearing in the front of the store. It was vintage-inspired, sexy and unique.

Messiah looked like a million bucks. For the first time in years, she flat ironed her curly hair straight. On her lips, she wore a brown matte lipstick with a gray undertone. Around her neck, was a rhinestone choker, rosary beads and two, gold, cross necklaces. The blue, velvet, spaghetti strap, jumpsuit with dusty rose pink flowers embroidered onto it hugged the curves of her hips flawlessly. The strategically-placed cut-outs on each side of her torso exposed her flat, toned stomach. She finished the 70's look off by rockin' a blue, faux fur, cropped jacket off her shoulders.

All night long, Messiah had garnered attention from the opposite sex. Several men had offered to buy her drinks and asked for her number but she declined all the advances. She couldn't fix herself to talk to another man. Even though she and Shyhiem weren't together anymore, it felt like cheating. Thoughts of him ruled her world. Being without him had been harder than she ever expected. She craved his touch and soft, chocolate kisses. When she lay down at night to sleep, he invaded her dreams.

Many nights went by where she lay awake touching herself. She knew they should be together. The only person she was hurting was herself by keeping them apart. Messiah kept telling herself that some distance would do them both some good. But as she looked around at everyone, including her best friend, boo'd up, loneliness seeped in. She could've got on one of the men that tried to holla but none of them were her type. After dealing with a nigga like Shyhiem, she couldn't possibly go back to dating a lame.

She didn't want any man she met in the club. The only man she wanted was him. Nightlife was built on frontin'. The whole thing was a façade. Everyone was trying to be something more than what they actually were. No one was themselves. It was a disheartening sight to see. Messiah didn't even go out much. It sickened her that every time she did hit up the club, she saw the same muthafuckas each time. She swore some people took up residence inside the club.

Messiah would've had more fun laying up in bed watching Project Runway or reading a good book. But her home wasn't her home anymore. Bryson had taken over her sanctuary. Her home was once a place of peace. Now, it was a place she avoided at all cost. If Bryson wasn't funking up the place, he was getting on her goddamn nerves. From the moment she woke up, to the time she went to sleep, he was in her face, begging her to take him back. Messiah couldn't take it anymore. His ass had to go. She'd gone back on her word and let him stay after his week deadline was up. He looked so pitiful that she couldn't throw him out on his ass. But it was time now. She had to have her house back.

Messiah glanced down at her watch. It was 2:15am. The club let out at 2:30. If it wouldn't have been weird, she would've jumped for joy. *Thank God, I'm finally getting my ass out of here,* she thought. Once again, she'd wasted a totally chic outfit on a bunch of rowdy-ass niggas and bitches that wore spandex dresses and Malaysian weave. Messiah couldn't wait to get out of there. Her stomach was growling like crazy. She was hungry as fuck. A double cheeseburger with cheese on the fries from White Castle was calling her name. She'd be farting for the next two days, but the salty, mini burgers were worth it. Maybe the cabbage-smelling farts would prompt Bryson to leave earlier than requested. Messiah could only hope.

As the clock neared 2:30, Messiah became even antsier. She couldn't last another second in the five-inch, platform heels. What made matters worse, was that a guy named Romon wouldn't get the fuck out of her face. The nigga looked like Travis Scott on steroids. He was friends with the guy that was tryin' to get on Bird. Bird happened to like the dude she was with, which was cute for her, but Messiah just wanted his homeboy to leave her the fuck alone. Despite how many times she turned him down, he wouldn't take the hint. Messiah was in pure hell. Every time he leaned over to talk in her ear, she gagged. His breath smelled like sour milk from all the liquor he'd consumed that night.

"You sure you don't want a drink?" He asked extra loud.

"Nah, I'm good. I don't drink." Messiah leaned her head to the right, so she wouldn't have to smell his hot breath.

"You don't drink? That's like not being on Facebook." He eyed her quizzically.

"I'm not on Facebook either." Messiah held her breath as long as she could.

"Damn..." Romon bit his bottom lip. "You classy as fuck." He grabbed his dick, turned-on. "I bet if I got you drunk that liquor would go straight to that pussy!"

Messiah's mouth dropped open, as she eyed him with disdain.

"You are disgusting and it's obvious you don't know how to take a hint. So, let me put this in terms you 'll understand. Get the fuck out my face," she said sternly.

"I like that feisty shit. Mmm." He looked Messiah up and down, hungrily. "You keep it up and you gon' be my sixth baby mama."

"Please, go play in traffic."

"You can't fool me, baby girl. I know under all that animal magnetism, you're hiding something." Romon licked his bottom lip, intrigued by her resistance.

"Yeah, a knife to stab you with. You got the wrong one, homeboy. Look, you seem like a nice guy, but I like titties and ass. Me no likey no dick. You ain't got shit I want." She pretended to be a lesbian.

"Shiiiit... I always wanted my girlfriend to have a girlfriend. A nigga like me don't mind a li'l bit of competition."

"Oh my God," Messiah groaned. "Somebody shoot me now." She ran her hand through her hair, exasperated.

"C'mon, I know you wanna go on an ate."

"A what?" Messiah screwed up her face.

"An ate. If you're good, I'll give you the D later." Romon winked his eye.

"Oh my God. I'ma throw up." Messiah held her stomach.

"What you doing for Thanksgiving?"

"Forgetting you exist."

"I'm diggin' you so much, I want you to meet my mama. You wanna come over for Thanksgiving?"

"NO!"

"Why not? Let me stuff yo' turkey." He tried to wrap his arm around her.

"Ah uh, I'm done!" Messiah pushed him away.

"C'mon now. Don't be like that. Let me click yo' mouse. Can I refresh yo' page? Let me download yo' document."

"Bird! Are you ready to go?" She looked past him and over at her friend.

"Give me a second." Bird said, smiling all up in the French Montana look-alike's face.

"I'ma be outside. My feet are fuckin' killin' me." Messiah prepared to leave.

"Where you going?" Bird's boo asked. "My homeboy tryin' to get at you."

"I'm good. He's not my type."

"Word?" Romon smirked. "It's like that? I was gon' take you out for breakfast. Hell, I was even gon' pay for you; but now, fuck it. It's 2016; I ain't finna be runnin' up in behind no bougie bitch just 'cause she light skin."

"Who the fuck you talkin' to?" Bird spat, before Messiah could respond. "You betta get yo' li'l dusty-ass friend before I slap him. As a matter-of-fact, he can't come with us out to eat. Messiah, girl, you alright?"

"It's all good, friend. I'ma be outside," Messiah assured.

The cold, November, night air was sharp and brisk, as Messiah stepped onto the sidewalk. The wind blew harshly causing her hair to fly in her face. Messiah tucked her long hair behind her ear and wrapped her arms around her body tightly. Bird had parked the car all the way down the block. *Fuck, I should'a got the keys,* she thought. Shaking her legs back and forth, Messiah did her best to keep warm. It was hard to, being that it was 42 degrees outside.

Despite the blistering cold weather, the energy outdoors was invigorating. If Messiah wasn't so exhausted and sore, she would've enjoyed it. There were tons of cars driving up and down the street blasting music. There were a few street vendors on the block selling hot dogs and pretzels, which made her hungrier. People were filing out the club left and right, but none of them were Bird. Messiah started to become aggravated. She didn't want to come to the club in the first place. Now, it was up to Bird when she got to go home. *I gotta get my fuckin' car out the shop.*

Freezing from her barely there outfit, she continued to bounce her body up and down, as a group of girls walked past her. Messiah couldn't help but overhear one of the girls say, "Look at my baby Goodnight." Time immediately stood still. Messiah's heart started to beat at a snail's pace.

94

Miraculously, she didn't feel cold anymore. The faux fur she wore felt like a sauna, as she searched the crowd of people for the man she knew as Shyhiem. It didn't take long for her to find him. Messiah watched as the girl left her friends and switched over to him.

Her heart dropped down to her freshly-pedicured toes. She and Shyhiem weren't in a relationship anymore, but she never thought he'd move on to someone new so quickly. Just a few weeks prior, he'd professed his love for her in the middle of the street. Messiah's chest heaved up and down. She didn't want to care but she did. The sight before her was worse than any nightmare she'd ever had. Shyhiem stood posted up against the wall with one leg propped up. His arm was draped around the thick, chocolate woman's waist, while his hand rested on her behind.

He was dressed in all black. The monochromatic look added to his bad boy sex appeal. He donned a leather-sleeved varsity jacket, hoodie, ripped jeans and classic Van sneakers. The only jewelry he wore was a simple, gold watch. Messiah's nipples hardened at the sight of him. How she'd ever denied his beauty was unfathomable. His twinkling eyes, pearly white teeth and full beard enhanced his mahogany skin. He hadn't had a haircut, which was unlike him, but he still was the finest man within miles.

For weeks, she'd tried to be tough and act like she didn't want him, but seeing him with another woman killed her softly. There was no hiding it any longer. She'd always want him. As she eyed him, it was crystal clear he was all she would ever need. Drought or famine couldn't keep her away from him. Life wasn't worth living if Shyhiem wasn't in it. She thought distancing herself from him was the best thing for both of them but it was the worst decision she'd ever made.

Messiah didn't even realize till she was halfway there that she'd begun to walk in his direction. Her body naturally gravitated towards him. At first, he didn't see her coming, but it didn't take long before he felt her presence. He and Messiah were like magnets. Messiah's legs felt like jelly, with each step she took. She wanted to run and jump in his strong arms but someone had already taken her place. On the outside, Shyhiem seemed as cool as a cucumber but Messiah knew him better than most. His eyes spoke what he was truly feeling. Resentment resonated in his dark irises.

There was a coldness there that wasn't there before. She didn't know what had changed, but she was sure as hell gonna fix it. Shyhiem was her baby, her future husband and the love of her life. Whatever was upsetting him, she'd kiss the problem away. All he had to do was focus on her and their love and everything else would be okay.

However, as she inched closer, the more hatred for her pumped through his veins. Messiah was the last person he wanted or expected to see. She hated the club, but there she was, looking like a fuckin' sex kitten. He'd completely forgotten about the chocolate beauty in his arms. She was just a seat filler for Messiah anyway. She was a cute girl and had a banging body, but she wasn't in Messiah's lane. No other girl on the planet could compete with her, in his eyes. The way she looked that night proved it. It was the first time he'd ever seen her with her hair straightened. Shyhiem liked it but preferred her hair in its natural state. *Fuck her, her hair and her pretty fuckin' smile,* he thought. It didn't matter how good she looked or how much his dick swelled inside his jeans. Messiah was public enemy #1.

"Hey." She spoke softly.

"What's up?" He placed his leg down and stood up straight.

The stern expression on his face caused her to quake in his presence. Messiah longed for the loving look he'd given her the last time they ran into each other. There was no emotion on his face, besides anger. It was as if he hated her. Messiah didn't know what had changed. It wasn't lost on her either that he hadn't moved his arm from the girl's waist. He had to have known it would hurt her to see him be so affectionate towards another woman. Messiah was a ball of nerves, as she and Shyhiem stared at each other in silence. Sensing the tension between the two of them, Lincoln decided to introduce herself.

"Hi, I'm Lincoln." She extended her hand for a shake.

Messiah blinked several times and focused on the girl. She was gorgeous, which was very intimidating. Messiah felt like a little girl playing dress up, compared to the buxom beauty. This girl was a full-blown woman. She had all the womanly curves Messiah wished she possessed. For the first time since she and Shyhiem met, her age became a factor. She was 22 and Shyhiem was 27. The five-year age difference seemed much bigger now that she'd seen him with her. Compared to Lincoln, she was a little-ass kid who was out of her league.

"Hi." Messiah shook her hand. "Nice to meet you. I'm Messiah."

"Nice to meet you too, Messiah. I love the name."

"Thank you."

"What does it mean?"

Shyhiem looked at Lincoln like she was dumb.

"It means the expected king and deliverer of the Jews," he answered, unimpressed by her lack of knowledge.

"Wow… that's deep. So, how do you two know each other?" She looked back and forth between him and Messiah.

"We used to be friends," he replied, staring deeply into Messiah's eyes.

His response was sure to kill her. He watched with pure joy as her soul left her body. Messiah drew in a sharp breath. She looked like she wanted to die. Shyhiem couldn't have been happier. She deserved every second of agony she felt.

"Used to be?" She finally uttered, feeling faint.

Shyhiem didn't respond. He wanted to see her in pain but the tears that were welling in her eyes was too much for even him to bear.

"Can I speak to you alone for a second?" Messiah asked, on the verge of crying her eyes out.

"We were just about to go," Lincoln responded.

"Give me a second." Shyhiem objected.

Uncomfortable with the situation, Lincoln wanted to push the subject about what was happening between him and Messiah, but she wasn't his girl. It wasn't her place to dig into his personal life - just yet.

"Ok." She said, feeling salty.

Lincoln stepped off to the side, giving them space to talk. She felt dumb as fuck but she really liked Goodnight. She didn't want to fuck things up before they even officially started. They'd only been talking a few weeks. If the stunning woman with the killer outfit was just an old acquaintance, then she had no choice but to believe him. Messiah reluctantly stepped closer to Shyhiem. His body stiffened as she neared.

"I didn't see you inside. Have you been here the whole time?" She asked, avoiding the elephant in the room.

"Nah, I came to pick her up." He replied, barely able to look at her.

"Oh." Messiah nodded. "She's pretty." She acknowledged, unsure of what to say.

"Yep."

"How long y'all been talkin'?"

"Why you wanna know?"

"I don't know. It was just a question." Messiah shrugged, tucking her hair behind her ear.

At any moment, she was going to breakdown and cry. Shyhiem was being extra cruel and she didn't understand why. Shyhiem pretended like he didn't see her nervous gesture. Messiah only tucked her hair behind her ear when she was anxious. Times like this was when she was most vulnerable. The part of him that still loved her wanted to reach out and hold her, but he couldn't allow himself to feel any emotion besides hate for her.

"You need a haircut." Messiah ran her hand over the top of his head, nervously.

"Stop." He grabbed her wrist.

His dick was so hard it felt like it was gonna break. Shocked, Messiah looked at his hand. His grip was so tight, her forearm started to turn red. Shyhiem could tell that he was hurting her but he wouldn't let go.

"You're hurting me." Messiah winced, trying to pull away.

"Now you see how it feels." Shyhiem flung her arm so harshly, she stumbled back.

"What the fuck is wrong with you?"

"You know exactly what's wrong with me."

"Clearly, I don't." Messiah spat.

"Baby, you ready?" Lincoln asked, tired of waiting.

"Yeah." He glared at Messiah, as he bypassed her and took Lincoln by the hand.

Heated, Shyhiem bumped shoulders with a guy, as he headed to his car.

"Aye, watch where you going, fam." He spun around ready for war.

"My bad, homey. It's all good." The Puerto Rican dude apologized with a sinister smirk.

Shyhiem eyed the dude for a second, wondering if he was a part of Esco's crew. His concerns were put to rest when the guy kept walking, but something about the encounter didn't feel right. It reminded him that he had to be on look out at all times.

Messiah massaged her wrist, as she watched Shyhiem get into his car. She didn't know what had just happened. Shyhiem treated her like she was a dog. She couldn't figure out, for the life of her, what she'd done to make him hate her so much.

"You okay?" Bird asked, concerned.

She'd seen everything that had gone down.

"You said nothing bad would happen." Messiah wiped away a tear from her eye.

"I know I did." Bird pulled her close. "I'm so sorry."

"Yeah… me too."

ST. JOHN THE BAPTIST PARISH LIBRARY
2920 NEW HIGHWAY 51
LAPLACE, LOUISIANA 70068

"We got options, but I wanna let you know that I decided. I finally realize that all I want is you." – H.E.R., "Changes"

13

Messiah/Shyhiem

What a mess I've made, Messiah thought, alone in the dark. Under the light of the moon, she sat in the center of her bed in a heap of tears. Tears the size of lemon drops strolled down her painted cheeks at a rapid speed. After the nauseating encounter with Shyhiem, she'd been stripped of everything she thought was true. The man she fell madly, deeply in love with was gone and replaced by a coldhearted monster.

This was the very reason she never wanted to love him. She'd shielded her heart for so long, only to be let down in the end. She tried to do right by Shyhiem and put his feelings first. She never wanted to disrespect what they shared. Their time together was far too precious to ever take lightly. He was everything that these plain niggas couldn't be. He had an unbreakable hold on her but none of that seemed to matter now.

Messiah tried to distract herself by falling asleep but all she could think about was him and Lincoln. They were probably at his place exploring each other's bodies with their tongues. The image wouldn't escape her brain. The more she visualized it, the harder she cried. This was all her fault. If she'd never played God with their relationship, she wouldn't have been in this position. She'd opened the door for another woman to walk in and take her place. A chick like Lincoln wouldn't let him go easily. Shyhiem was the type of man you fought for. Men like him didn't come a dime a dozen. Messiah knew this and still foolishly let him go. She should've never ended their relationship. They were on the cusp of greatness and she let her own insecurities and fear get in the way. Now, she sat suffering alone in the dark.

And no, she wasn't ready when he gave her his heart. For Messiah, things between them were moving at lightning speed. She needed a moment to catch her breath and analyze things. She didn't want to get swept up in lust and infatuation. She wanted to make sure that what they had was real. She'd spent six years of her life with a man that had promised to love her forever, then he turned around and betrayed her in the worst way possible. She couldn't risk her world being shattered once more. With Shyhiem, the pain would be 10 times worse.

She didn't want him to hurt her and vice versa. She needed time to heal the hole in her heart. Having one foot in and one foot out wasn't fair to either of them. He deserved to have all of her or nothing at all. Leaving him hadn't been an easy decision. She missed him every second of the day. Now, after some time apart, she could honestly say that she was ready to love him - always. He was the man she wanted to wake up to each morning. He was the man she wanted to grow old and gray with. With him, she'd give her all.

As soon as she got home, Messiah stripped down to her bra and panties. She never wanted to see or wear the outfit she had on again. It would always remind her of the night Shyhiem ripped her heart in two. He hated her now, and even though she didn't specifically know why, she couldn't blame him. She'd turned him down not once but twice. A man could only take but so much rejection before he'd say fuck it and throw in the towel. He'd obviously had his full of her bullshit. Messiah didn't know what she was gonna do. Losing Shyhiem wasn't an option. She always thought they'd make their way back to each other. They were meant to be. No other woman could love him like she could.

This Lincoln chick was cute and had a nice shape, but they'd never have the connection she and Shyhiem shared. The love they had was a once in a lifetime kind of thing. Messiah would be damned if she sat back and let another chick take her man. She'd fight to the death for Shyhiem. They could make it through the storm. She'd make him see that he could trust her with his heart.

Messiah didn't know what tomorrow might bring, but if Shyhiem wasn't in her future, she didn't wanna live. There still had to be some room for her inside his heart. She'd fucked up royally but she'd gladly spend a lifetime making up for it. Messiah was willing to put her pride and ego to the side. She didn't care if she had to cry, beg and plead. All she wanted was her man back in her arms.

Messiah knew what she was about to do was crazy but she had to see him. She didn't want to be away from him another second. *Fuck it, I'm going,* she thought. The fact that Lincoln might be there caused a cold sweat to wash over her body. If she was, it would tell Messiah everything she needed to know. If Shyhiem could so easily replace her with another woman, then his feelings for her were never real. She'd never let another man touch her. And yes, men were different than women. They weren't emotional creatures but Messiah was. She didn't want a man that could give what she felt was hers away.

Messiah looked down at her watch. It was almost 4:00am. An hour and a half had passed since the club let out. Shyhiem should be home, unless he'd gone to Lincoln's house or got a hotel room. Messiah wiped her face and hopped out of the bed. Quickly, she threw on a slouchy tank top, cut-off jogging pants, a leather jacket and a pair of Family Dollar, Ugg-inspired boots. Quietly, she crept out of her room. Bryson was asleep, snoring loudly. Messiah tiptoed over to the coffee table and grabbed his car keys. Driving his car without permission wasn't the right thing to do, but she didn't care. The nigga had been mooching off her for over a month. He'd be alright. Messiah wasn't going to let anything or anyone get in her way. She was going to get her man back or die trying.

Shyhiem stood in front of the bathroom mirror with a towel wrapped around his waist. He'd just finished showering and brushing his teeth. Ro James' *A.D.I.D.A.S* was playing softly in the background, setting the mood for pleasure. Shyhiem looked at his reflection in the mirror. He never went to the gym but his body was ripped. His biceps were carved in the shape of mountain peaks. While his pecks were chiseled and firm, Shyhiem's six-pack rippled like waves. The towel around his waist highlighted the Ken doll slits leading down to his 10-inch, mouthwatering cock.

If he kept on drinking the way he'd been lately, he'd have a gut in no time. All the pretty, fly girls that stayed on his dick wouldn't want him anymore. Thank God he had a fast metabolism and a baddie like Lincoln already on his arm. In a short amount of time, he'd grown to really like her. She was a nice girl. Unlike with Messiah, he didn't take his time with her. The same night they met, she found herself in his bed with her legs draped over his shoulders. He'd knocked her down several times since. After the disastrous run-in with Messiah, he planned on fuckin' her again and again. That night wouldn't be any different.

After dropping her off at the crib, Shyhiem went to handle some business with Mayhem. He'd promised Lincoln that after he was done he'd swing by her crib.

Being the clean freak he was, he stopped by his house to take a shower before heading her way. He didn't want to go over there smelling like outside. *Ring... Ring... Ring!* Shyhiem frowned. Why his phone was ringing at 4:20am was beyond him. His phone didn't ring at that time of the morning, unless it was an emergency. He prayed to God nothing was wrong with the twins. Worried, he raced over to the phone.

"Hello?" He asked in a rush.

"Mr. Simmons, this is Paul at the front desk. I'm sorry to wake you but you have a guest."
"I ain't expecting anybody." He said, confused.

No one besides his brother and Keesha knew where he stayed.

"Who is it?"

"She—"

"She?" Shyhiem wrinkled his nose.

"Yes, sir. She said her name is Messiah."

Shyhiem closed his eyes and let out a heavy sigh. He hadn't even recovered from seeing Messiah at the club that night. He wasn't mentally or physically prepared to see her again so soon. Plus, he was confused as to why she was there. She had a whole man at home who was sure to be pissed if he knew she was there trying to see him.

"Is it ok if I send her up?"

"Yeah... send her up." Shyhiem ended the call and stood still for a second.

His heart was racing wildly. His anxiety was at an all-time high. He didn't know what game Messiah was playing but he had no plans on participating. There would be no more allowing her to stomp all over his heart. He was just beginning to accept that they were over. He couldn't allow her to suck him back into her trap. Shyhiem left the bathroom and walked across the heated floor. He was mad annoyed that she decided to pop-up on him unannounced. She had no right to. Pop-ups were girlfriend privileges.

"Messiah, what you doing here?" He held the knob with the chain on the door.

"Shyhiem, let me in," she said loudly.

"Why are you talkin' so loud? You gon' wake my neighbors."

"I don't give a fuck about your neighbors. Let me in!" Messiah pushed the door.

"No, I'm not lettin' you in here. You actin' retarded."

"Open the fuckin' door!" She kicked it with her foot.

"You trippin', dawg." He shook his head.

"I'm trippin'?" Messiah's eyes widened to the size of saucers, when she noticed he was dressed in nothing but a towel.

The nigga looked freshly fucked. Messiah placed her detective hat on and quickly put two and two together. *This nigga just got done fuckin' that bitch,* she thought, enraged.

"Why the fuck is yo' dick hard?" She tried to reach her hand inside to hit him.

Shyhiem smiled. His dick was hard because of her. Seeing that she wasn't going to calm down until she got her way, he pushed her hand back and unlocked the door.

"Move!" Messiah pushed him out the way and barged inside.

Her forceful shove caught Shyhiem off guard, causing him to bump into the wall.

"What the fuck are you doing?" He slammed the door shut and followed behind her.

"Is she here? Where she at?" Messiah looked around the living room area and then the kitchen.

"Is who here?" He asked.

"The bitch you just left the club with!" Messiah headed to his bedroom, after not finding anyone in the front of the loft.

"Now she a bitch 'cause you think she in my crib?" He shot sarcastically.

"Shyhiem, don't play with me." Messiah pushed open the bedroom door.

The master bedroom was all gray. The walls had a gray and white chevron pattern on it. A gray, king size bed with a suede, tufted headboard sat in the center of the room. The gray, Egyptian cotton sheets were in disarray. The master bedroom was the only room with gray carpet. The best part of the room was the wall length mirror off to the side of the bed. Messiah used to get off watching herself in that very mirror as she and Shyhiem made love.

"Don't make me ask you again. Is she here?" She pulled back the shower curtain.

"Why?" Shyhiem watched, amused as she acted erratic.

"'Cause I wanna know, that's why!" She opened the closet.

"If she was here, do you think I would've let yo' crazy-ass in?"

"I'm not crazy." She glared at him with a crazy look in her eye.

"Stop actin' like it then."

Messiah knew she was acting like a madwoman but she'd lost her sanity a long time ago. Her female intuition was telling her he had that bitch there. If it took all night long, Messiah was going to open every cabinet and drawer to find her.

"You got a lot of fuckin' nerve. You know that?" Shyhiem looked at her like she was insane.

"Is she here or not?" Messiah spun around and faced him with a wild look in her eye.

"Why the fuck does it matter to you? Remember, you broke up with me! We not together no more!"

"I can't fuckin' believe you." Messiah's bottom lip trembled. "I knew you were full of shit, but damn, Shyhiem. I ain't know you could be this heartless." She stormed past him.

"I'm full of shit?" He grabbed her arm and pulled her back, forcefully.

"You fuckin' right. All that *I love you, I can't live without you, you gon' be my wife* was some straight bullshit. We ain't even been broken up two months and you already got yo' dick in somebody else. If that's what you call lovin' me, then I don't want that bullshit."

Shyhiem stared at her, hurt.

"I should bash yo' head in." He pushed her away, furiously.

She was showing out to get his attention and it was working.

"Oh, so you gon' hit me again?" Messiah spat, sarcastically. "Put yo' hands on me if you want to," she warned, arching her brow. "You know, everybody was right about you. Keesha was right too. You ain't shit but a dark skin Chris Brown. Ole Ike Turner wanna-be-ass. I wish you would put yo' hands on me."

"I'm a woman beater now? I guess I purposely put my hands on you, right?" Shyhiem nodded his head, getting angrier by the second.

"Yep, like you purposely walked out the club with that bitch tonight."

"You know what, get the fuck outta here." Shyhiem said, fed up with her antics. "Coming over here like we still together. Like I got some bitch up in here that I'm fuckin'. Get yo' delusional-ass outta here before you make me put my hands on you purposely."

"I hate I ever met yo' stupid-ass!" Messiah mushed him in the forehead, just to hurt him.

In a blind rage, Shyhiem lifted her by the arms and slammed her small frame down onto the bed. Messiah's back hit the crumpled sheets with a thud. Shyhiem lay on top of her, staring deep into her frightened eyes. He was so mad, his breathing was irregular. Messiah glared back at

111

him. The ferocious look on Shyhiem's face scared her to pieces but she pretended like she wasn't fazed. With the little range of motion she had with her arms, she reached up and slapped her hand across his face. Shyhiem didn't even flinch.

"Get the fuck off of me!" She hissed.

Furious that she'd put her hands on him, Shyhiem looked at her with disgust and sat up on his knees. He didn't want to be anywhere near her. The Messiah he fell in love with would've never put her hands on him. She hated violence. This insecure maniac was a stranger. Realizing what she'd done, Messiah gasped. A deafening silence filled the room.

"Shyhiem, I'm sorry." She quickly apologized.

This wasn't who she was. She wasn't the kind of girl to pop-up on a man starting all kinds of ruckus. The type of behavior she displayed was the kind you'd see on Love and Hip Hop. Messiah was way classier than that. She prided herself on being graceful under pressure. Somehow, she'd slipped and lost her way; but behaving like a ghetto banshee wasn't the answer.

"I'm so sorry." She reached up to touch his hand.

"Nah, man." He drew his hand away, so she couldn't touch him.

Messiah didn't know what to do. She could tell by the look on his face that she was losing him - if she hadn't lost him already.

"I don't know what I'm doing right now." She broke down and cried. "I'm trippin'. I ain't mean to come over here actin' like a fool. I just… had to come see you."

112

"What you wanna see me for?"

"'Cause I miss you, Shyhiem. I tried it my way. I tried to leave you alone. I thought things were moving too fast between us but I can't be without you. It hurts too much. I don't wanna go another day without you."

"Yeah, well you too late. I've moved on," he replied dryly. "And from the looks of it, you have too."

"What are you talkin' about? Don't say that. Look, I know I was all over the place. I was doubting you. I was doubting us, but I realize you're the one for me now."

"Messiah, go home."

"No." She sat up on her knees too. "I know you still love me."

"I'ma always have feelings for you but we ain't no good together."

"I may not be good for you, but nobody has the right to say what's good for me. Not even you. You think that I don't know everything that went wrong is my fault?" Tears slid from the corners of her eyes. "I fucked up. I'm sorry for letting you go. I let fear and a bunch of outside shit get in the way of what we had. But seeing you with ole girl tonight put everything into perspective. I wanna be your girl. I wanna be the one you come home to. I don't wanna see you with someone else."

"So that's what this is all about? You jealous 'cause you saw me wit' ole girl tonight?" Shyhiem scoffed. "You are unbelievable."

"Maybe I am… but Shyhiem, I can't be without you right now. I can't," she whispered, kissing the bridge of his nose.

"Messiah, stop." He groaned, hating that his entire body lit on fire from one single touch.

"Please," Messiah begged, as her lips brushed against his. "Make love to me… please." She held onto the sides of his face.

"Messiah, just go home," Shyhiem pleaded.

"You still love me. I know you do. A love like ours will never go away. It lives forever." She kissed his soft lips, repeatedly, as he pushed her jacket off her arms.

"I know you wanna love but I just wanna fuck." – Jacquees, "B.E.D."

14

Messiah/Shyhiem

Before Messiah knew it, she was naked on her back. A familiar heat rushed between her legs, as Shyhiem lay on top of her. He'd dreamt about kissing her succulent lips for weeks. His wish was finally coming true. Shyhiem ripped the towel from his waist and entered her swiftly. Messiah didn't even have enough time to prepare herself for his length. It always caught her off guard how big he was. Shyhiem filled her up to capacity. She couldn't breathe. Her nails racked over his well-developed back, as he drove his dick in and out her pussy at a slow, rhythmic pace. Her juices sheathed his cock, she was so wet.

Shyhiem could barely hold on, as he buried his face in the crook of her neck. Moans escaped his lips that he didn't even know he could make. She felt so good underneath him. This was where she belonged. Messiah wrapped her legs around his back and locked her ankles. His cock was so deep, she swore he hit her cervix. The deeper he stroked her middle, the wetter she became.

Shyhiem cherished every second of being inside her, but making love wasn't what he wanted. He and Messiah weren't on that level right now. He wanted to fuck… hard. Sitting up on his knees, he flipped her over onto her stomach. Messiah's breasts pressed against the sheets, as she stared at him through the mirror. She was on all fours with her ass in the air - just how he liked it. Shyhiem rubbed his cock and plunged deeply inside her tight pussy.

"Ahhhhhhh!" Messiah wailed, closing her eyes.

Shyhiem gripped her neck, firm and tight. Erotic sounds of his desire filled the room, as his pelvis slapped against her ass. Lack of oxygen caused Messiah's pleasure to heighten. The fear of fading into darkness turned her on. Just as she was about to black out, Shyhiem let go. Messiah gasped for air and moaned.

"Oh baby!" She squealed, as he took both her arms and folded them behind her back.

Messiah tried to keep up with his pace but it was hard to. Shyhiem was fucking the dog shit out of her.

"Yes-yes-yes-yes-yes-yes! Ahhhhhhhhhhh! You love this tight li'l pussy, don't you?"

"Yeah," Shyhiem growled loudly. "This pussy too good. Oh my God, it's fuckin' good. It gets better and better. Tighter and tighter."

Messiah's screams of desire were driving him wild. The harder he fucked her, the wetter she became. Shyhiem's stroke game was precise, tantric rotations of chiseled, hard, fuck flesh. Messiah was a dripping mess, as he pulled her hair. Her head tilted back and faced the ceiling. Messiah contracted her pussy walls. The feeling of being filled up to the point of breakage was so satisfying.

"That's it, baby," he whispered in her ear. "You love this dick, don't you?"

"You know I do," she whimpered like a little girl.

"You miss daddy's dick?"

"Yes, baby, I miss it! It's so big!" Messiah wailed. "Ahhhhhhhh… you're so fuckin' hard!"

"Take that dick." Shyhiem smacked her hard on the ass, making her booty bounce.

The way Messiah contracted around his cock blew his mind. With every stroke, her back arched and her toes curled. Shyhiem brushed his hands over her breasts and pinched her erect nipples. She would never get enough of him. They both watched each other in the mirror. Their sex faces on fully display. The vision was so erotic. Messiah wanted to stay like this forever. Shyhiem kissed her shoulder from behind. Messiah noticed the look of passion in his eyes. He didn't have to say it. She knew he still loved her.

"Shyhiem, make me cum! Make me cum!" She begged, as he fucked her at a rapid pace, causing her to cum all over his dick.

"Holy shit!" He roared, cumming too.

"Awwww... baby! More! I want more!" Her body quacked.

Shyhiem pulled out and looked at her through the mirror.

"What do I get?" He asked, stroking his cock.

"Whatever you want." She smiled devilishly, anxiously awaiting his assault.

Nowhere near done with her, Shyhiem inserted himself back inside her slit and massaged her clit while he wound his hips slowly. Over and over he fucked her until her legs trembled and she came. Both came so many times neither could keep count. They'd missed each other terribly. Messiah and Shyhiem's love was like an asylum. Madness consumed them. They were each other's drug of choice. Without one another, they'd go crazy. Together, they did more damage than good but neither could let the other go. No one else could save them.

By the time Messiah and Shyhiem finished devouring each other's bodies, the darkness from outdoors faded and the sun began to rise. Messiah lay on her back spent, trying to catch her breath. The things Shyhiem did to her body should've been illegal but it was exactly what she needed. She didn't understand how she'd lasted this long without his sex. For the first time in weeks, she felt whole. She missed being with Shyhiem like this.

Shyhiem reached over and grabbed his phone off the nightstand. He had two missed text messages from Lincoln. Conflicting emotions ran through his body. He'd completely forgotten about her. She'd probably fallen asleep, by now, after wondering where he was. Thank God she wasn't his girl and he wouldn't have to explain his whereabouts. He still felt bad for playing her to the left. When Messiah was around, the world stopped. The only thing that was important was her. He hated the control she had over his every move. It truly disgusted him. Messiah checked her phone too. Bryson had called several times. She didn't care about him blowing up her phone. Her focus was on the man lying next to her.

"That was nice." She leaned over to place a kiss on his cheek.

"You gotta go." Shyhiem sat up swiftly, causing her to face plant onto the pillow.

"What?" Messiah pushed herself up on her elbows, confused.

"Get yo' shit and go."

Messiah sat all the way up and held the sheet up to her chest to cover her breasts. She felt like a fool. She'd never been so embarrassed in her life. She never thought Shyhiem would fuck her and then make her leave.

"After everything I said, this how you gon' do me for real?"

"What part of we're not together no more don't you understand?" Shyhiem threw her clothes at her, one by one.

"So, I was right? You are fuckin' her?" Messiah shot, heated.

"If I am, that's my fuckin' business! You ain't my gal! You made your choice! Stick with it! Don't try to backtrack now! Go be with that wack-ass nigga you over there layin' up wit!" He placed on a pair of hooping shorts.

Messiah drew her head back.

"What?"

"Now you wanna act stupid? A'ight, Messiah. Just get yo' shit and go. I don't even know why you here right now. I thought I left all that dumb shit alone when I stopped fuckin' wit' Keesha, but you on the same shit."

"I know you ain't comparing me to that crazy bitch!" Messiah said in disbelief.

"You the one fuckin' somebody else. Not me. Then you had the nerve to flaunt her in my face like it was nothing." Her voice cracked. "I never thought you would do some shit like that to me."

"Yo, you can stop with the crocodile tears." Shyhiem waved her off.

"Why are you treatin' me like this? What have I done to you?"

Shyhiem ice-grilled her. He couldn't believe that she was trying to act like she was the victim.

"You think Bryson gon' like the fact that you were over here suckin' my dick tonight?"

Appalled by his choice of words, Messiah sat speechless for a second.

"What did you just say to me?" She held her chest to ensure she was still alive.

"You heard me. You can stop actin' stupid. I know you back fuckin' wit' that nigga. He told me."

"Who told you what?" Messiah questioned, still puzzled.

"Really? You gon' sit up here and act like you don't know what the fuck I'm talkin' about?" Shyhiem folded his arms across his chest. "Bryson... he told me y'all was back together."

"When did he tell you that?" Messiah tried to piece the puzzle together.

"When I came by to see you a few weeks ago." Shyhiem relived the horrific day.

"You came by to see me?" Messiah said shocked.

"Yeah."

"What did you want?" Her heart raced.

"It don't matter now." Shyhiem thought about the engagement ring on the shelf inside his closet.

"It matters to me." Messiah spoke, barely above a whisper.

Shyhiem clenched his jaw. This wasn't the conversation he wanted to have. He didn't want to think about the way he'd embarrassed himself that day. He never let another man have one up on him, but Bryson had made him look like a complete fool.

"Tell me. I wanna know." Messiah scooted closer to where he was at.

"You have no idea how much I loved you. If you did, we wouldn't be in this position right now." He massaged his jaw.

"You said loved, as if you don't anymore." Messiah's eyes watered.

"I was gon' propose to you." Shyhiem looked down at his feet, regretfully.

Messiah inhaled a sharp breath. She had no idea.

"I was gon' propose and ask you to move away with me and the kids. I had it all planned out. We were gonna get married and move to Cali. I'd go to film school and you'd start back dancing again."

Messiah didn't know what to say. Things between them were so fucked up. He had no idea she was already taking classes again. That piece of the puzzle was minuscule, in the grander scheme of things. Shyhiem wanted her to be his wife and she'd missed the opportunity, all because of Bryson. Once again, he'd fucked up her life in the worst way. What fucked her up the most, was that there was no way Shyhiem was gonna attempt to propose again, despite how desperately she wanted him to. He was a man with pride. To be so vulnerable was foreign to him. It would take an eternity to get him to open up like that again.

"If it's any consolation, I would've said yes." She said, with hope in her eyes.

"It's not. I'm high-key happy things went down the way they did. It's apparent we ain't supposed to be together. If it was, you wouldn't have got back with ole boy."

"He really told you we were together?" She repeated, to make sure she'd heard right.

"Ain't that what I said?"

"Shyhiem, Bryson lied to you. We are not together. I wouldn't touch that nigga again with a 10-foot pole."

"If y'all ain't together, then why is he at your crib?" He challenged.

"I'm just letting him sleep on my couch. The girl he got pregnant lost the baby and he came to me 'cause he knew I would understand."

"So, let me get this straight." Shyhiem dropped his head and chuckled. "The chick he cheated on you with, got pregnant and proposed to with the ring he gave you, lost their baby and you're letting him sleep on your couch?"

"I know it sounds crazy but—"

"Nah, you couldn't possibly know how stupid you sound."

"Don't talk to me like that." She warned.

"Talk to you like what, Messiah? What, you don't want me to tell you the truth? You got this nigga that treated you like yesterday's trash stayin' at yo' crib, and I ain't supposed to feel some type of way? Get the fuck outta here." He waved her off, heated.

Messiah sat quietly, looking like a deer caught in headlights.

"You know what, fuck my feelings." Shyhiem continued. "What about yours? How many times you gon' let this muthafucka play you before you've had enough?"

"You don't understand. Bryson was there for me when I ain't have nobody. I get it, he did me dirty and I will never forgive him for what he did, but I think I know Bryson a li'l bit better than you. Deep down inside, he does have a good heart."

"You know him? You ain't even know he told me y'all was back together. This muthafucka stay lyin' to you but you just keep going back for more. You might not see it, but anybody with two eyes can see that you still love that nigga."

"No, I don't! I love you! I wanna be with you! Bryson is like a brother to me!"

"That nigga ain't yo' fuckin' brother! He ain't yo' blood. Y'all ain't got the same mama and daddy! At one point, he had his dick up in you. For all I know, you still fuckin' him." Shyhiem balled up his fist.

He couldn't believe she'd fixed her lips to let some stupid shit like that come out her mouth.

"So now I'm fuckin' somebody I look at as my brother?" Messiah shrugged her shoulders, indignantly. "C'mon, Shyhiem, you know me better than that."

"I don't know shit!" He shot with venom. "What I do know is that you full of shit."

"Whatever, Shyhiem," Messiah scooted out of the bed. "I'm not gon' sit here and let you talk to me any kind of way. You can be mad all you want, but you not gon' disrespect me."

Shyhiem knew he was taking it too far but he couldn't stop himself. Messiah would never understand how much she'd hurt him. The damage she'd done could never be repaired. The only way she'd understand what she'd done is if he hurt her just as much.

"You say you love me but you got yo' ex living wit' you? Do you not see how fucked up that is?"

"I know exactly how fucked up it is. How soon we forget, but when we first started messing around, you were living with your baby mama. Did I throw that shit up in your face? No. I let you make the decision to move out on your own time." Messiah placed on her clothes - one article at a time. "For all I know, you could've been fuckin' me and then going home and fuckin' her!"

"Man, you know I wasn't fuckin' that girl."

"I don't know shit." Messiah used his words against him.

"It's like that?" Shyhiem questioned her.

"Yeah."

"Well, I guess we're even then." He leaned against the wall.

"I guess we are." Messiah grabbed her coat and left, as quickly as she came.

"I've been blowin' up yo' phone."–
Mack Wilds, "Explore"

15

Messiah

Furious at Shyhiem, their nonexistent relationship, her life and the lies Bryson spewed, Messiah barged inside her apartment. Her whole, entire body was on fire. She was shaking uncontrollably. If one more bad thing happened to her, she was sure to go postal and kill everyone. *How much more do I have to take, God,* she said to herself, as Bryson turned and looked at her. He'd been pacing the room with his cellphone up to his ear. Bryson had been blowing her phone up the entire car ride home. She didn't bother to answer any of his calls. The shit she had to say needed to be said face to face. She was over him taking her kindness for weakness. She'd tried pretending like he wasn't, but Bryson was a user and a manipulator, at the end of day. It was apparent now more than ever. She was done with him using her for his own personal gain. She'd allowed him to wreak havoc on her life long enough. The devil would no longer be able to use her as a punching bag.

Bryson looked her up and down. She looked like a madwoman. Her straight hair was flying everywhere. It was freezing cold outside and she wore a tank top, cut-off jogging shorts and knockoff Ugg boots. If he didn't know any better, he'd think she was on drugs.

"Where have you been? I've been callin' you for hours?" He asked, ending the call.

His bare feet slapped against the concrete floor, as he came near her. Messiah took a step back. She didn't want to be anywhere near him. The heat from his body made her feel sick. She was so upset, she didn't even respond. Instead, she reared her hand back and threw his keys at this face. Bryson ducked and dodged the attempt to take his head off. The keys banged against the wall with a loud clank and fell to the floor. Messiah's chest rose and fell with each heated breath she took.

"What the fuck is wrong with you?" He slowly stood up, afraid she'd throw something else.

"I want you out of my house! Now!" Messiah pointed her finger towards the door.

"Why? What I do?" Bryson screwed up his face, confused.

"You know exactly what you did!" She fumed, pointing her finger at him.

Bryson stood silent. Based off the crazed look in her eye, it was obvious she'd went to see Shyhiem. Bryson quickly closed his eyes and shook his head. He hadn't prepared for this. He thought she and him were over. He never expected the truth to come out so soon.

"Messiah, listen, let me explain," he begged.

"Explain what?" She said with a sudden fierceness. "That you're a fuckin' liar! He came here to propose to me! Did you know that?"

"Of course not, but I'm glad he didn't get the chance."

"Wow…" Messiah spun around in a circle. "You have absolutely no shame."

"When it comes to you, no, I don't. You were supposed to be my wife, goddammit."

"Yeah, and you fucked it up when you got that bitch pregnant and proposed to her with my ring!"

"You're right, I did. That was a scumbag thing to do and I will live with that regret for the rest of my life."

"You have to have a heart to regret something," Messiah challenged. "I let you stay in my home, despite my better judgment and all the foul shit you've done to me. And what do you do? You turn around and stab me in the back – again!"

"I was tryin' to protect you."

"Protect me? Protect me from what?"

"From yourself. I knew if you saw ole boy again you'd get right back sucked in. The nigga is a thug. He's a hoodlum. He's no good for you. You deserve better. You deserve a man like me. Someone who's going somewhere in life. Not a UPS driver with two kids and a baby mama that wears blue weave," Bryson shot arrogantly.

"If there is anyone I need to be protecting myself from, it's you!" Messiah pressed her index finger into his firm chest. "Shyhiem is a lot of things, but guess what? He ain't never lied to me. He ain't never cheated on me. He always treated me with the upmost respect. With him, I never had to lift a fuckin' finger or worry about thing!"

"So you tryin' to say I ain't never did shit for you?"

"Barely! Nigga, I took care of you. I've done so much shit for you over the years, I can't even keep count. Hell, I should've filed you on my income taxes as a fuckin' dependent."

"That's not fair. You know I was trying to finish school so I could take care of us."

"No, nigga, you were tryin' to fuck Ivy League bitches and use me as your moneybag to pay your way through school. Ever since I was 16, I have done nothing but love you and hold you down. My dumbass even gave you the insurance money my parents left me. Yet every opportunity you get, you use it to shit on me." She shook her head.

"But I can't even blame you, 'cause I let you do it. Not anymore, though. I'm done letting you walk all over me."

"C'mon, Messiah, don't be like that. You're my best friend. All we got is each other."

"Bryson, please, you got a whole bitch back in Philly waiting on you. Go drive her insane. I am done with you. I never wanna see you again. You hear me? I don't give a fuck if yo' dick set on fire; if yo' ugly-ass mama dies, don't call me. From this moment on, act like I don't exist. 'Cause as of today, you are dead to me. Now, get yo' shit and get the fuck out!" She held the door wide open.

Bryson reluctantly began to gather his things. He didn't want to leave. He wanted to stay and beg her forgiveness. When he'd lied to Shyhiem, he'd only done it so he'd have more time to win her back. He was gonna eventually tell her the truth. He was just biding his time until he won her back. Now, things between them were more fucked up than ever. He knew Messiah was far too good of a woman to ever be with a man like him. He was a douchebag who only looked out for himself. He was so used to having Messiah there to pick him up when he fell - which was often.

She was his safety net. Bryson was used to fucking up and having Messiah there to clean up his mess. It was wrong, but he used their son's death and the fact that he'd been there when her parents died to keep her tied to him.

130

He knew Messiah felt indebted to him for that. He'd held it over her head for years and would continue to hold it against her to get what he needed out of her, which was financial and emotional support. She was mad now, but after a little time passed, he'd figure out a way to worm his way back into her good graces. Messiah could never stay mad at him too long. History had proven him right.

"Me and you were meant to last forever."–Anthony Hamilton, "I'm A Mess"

16

Shyhiem

The light from the morning sky lit the entire loft, casting a gray hue over the spacious white kitchen. Shyhiem blasted James Blake's *The Colour in Anything*. It was his favorite album at the moment. James' hauntingly melodic voice and lyrics resonated deeply in his soul. The album set the mood perfectly that somber Monday morning. The track, *Radio Silence,* had been on repeat since he woke up. His mind and body were still tired, but each night he was only able to get a few hours of rest. Dreams of one of Esco's pot'nahs avenging his death by stabbing him in the heart, several times with a butcher's knife, kept replaying in his head.

Shyhiem jumped out of his sleep more than once in a cold sweat, gasping for breath. Ever since he'd pulled the trigger, he'd regretted it. He'd acted off emotion, instead of thinking things through. Now, there was no telling when his day would be up. Esco's death wouldn't go unanswered. It was no secret he'd done it. Everyone in the streets knew. Killing Esco, at the time, seemed like the only option to assert their dominance. They had to make an example out of him so no one else would test them.

As Shyhiem poured his morning cup of orange juice, he realized Esco's son would grow up fatherless because of him. He knew how it felt not to have a dad there to teach him all the things only a father could. Shyhiem didn't know what he'd do if Sonny and Shania had to grow up without him. With all the moves he'd been making lately, they probably would.

Like James Blake, all he wanted was more time. He needed time to better his relationship with Keesha, figure out his feelings towards Messiah, stack enough money to live comfortably in Cali and release the demons that had taken over his soul. Shyhiem yearned to go back to the way he was when he'd gotten out of prison. He was optimistic and hopeful with a new lease on life. Now, he was as bitter and angry as ever. Nothing pleased him. He'd seen and done things over the past few months that he'd never imagined doing.

Messiah wanted him back, but little did she know, Shyhiem wasn't the man she used to know. He'd changed for the worse. There was no going back. Too much had happened. He didn't see her the same. She was no longer innocent in his eyes. She was just as flawed as anyone else. It was best he forget about her and move on. They'd only dated a month and a half. That wasn't long enough to build a future on. But damn had that month and a half been good.

Shyhiem's long legs strode over to the kitchen island. The doorman had just dropped off a manila folder someone had left for him at the front desk. There was no return address on the front, just his name written in big, bold letters. Shyhiem cautiously peeled open the folder. It could've very well been a death threat from one of the many enemies he'd made over the last few months. Slowly, he peeked inside. Inside, was a stack of postcards. Puzzled, he dumped them onto the island. His heart thumped loudly, like a bass drum.

He didn't fuck with anyone out of state. All the postcards were from different cities in California. Shyhiem checked the sender's name and saw that they were all from Messiah. Dumbfounded, he leaned back against the kitchen sink to keep his balance. Here she was, once again, practically knocking him off his feet. Shyhiem swallowed hard and read the first one.

I miss you the most at night. When everything is quiet, the silence reminds me that I'm not sleeping next to you.

The next one said:

I fell in love with you because of a tiny, million things you never knew you were doing.

Another one read:

Dear Shyhiem,

Maybe our past was meant to be so damn broken, so that when we met, we'd fit together so perfectly that nothing would ever be able to break us again.

The one that really fucked him up read:

The first time I met you, it wasn't love at first sight. My love for you formed gradually. Your personality, your voice, your hair, your eyes, your humor, the way you looked away and smiled; gradually, it all came clear to me you were exactly what I was looking for.

The postcards went on and on. There must've been at least 20 of them. The tough, hard as nails nigga inside of him wanted to act unfazed, but she'd caught him in her web again. Her sweet words touched the parts of his soul he thought couldn't be reached. Shyhiem couldn't front. He was lost without her. He was a complete and utter mess. Lincoln was a nice distraction but she didn't hold a candle to Messiah. They were meant to live and die together.

Shyhiem wanted to pick up the phone and call her but his pride kept him at bay. Too much damage had been done. She'd hurt him - twice. Who's to say she wouldn't do it again? Shyhiem wanted to take the risk but couldn't take the chance.

"Can you love me where we are or am I reaching for the stars?" –Alex Isley, "For The Stars"

17

Messiah

Now that she'd gotten her house back to herself, Messiah couldn't wait to go home when she got off work at night. It had taken several cans of Febreze and a few scented candles to get the Frito-Lay smell from Bryson's stanky feet out of her house, but it was gone. He'd texted her numerous times, apologizing for his behavior, but she wasn't ready to forgive him. There was no way she could. He'd interfered in her happiness - once again. It was like he got off on seeing her miserable. Besides, he could apologize until he was blue in the face, there was no excuse or reasoning for what he'd done.

She could've been engaged to the love of her life, if it weren't for him. Messiah would've been the happiest girl in the world if she'd known Shyhiem wanted to propose. Her life would've changed for the better. She'd finally have the life she'd always dreamt of as a little girl. From as far back as she could remember, she'd always wanted to be married. Being someone's wife and mother meant the world to her. Since she was told it was highly unlikely she'd ever be able to conceive again, having a child wasn't in the cards for her.

For years, the fact that she probably wasn't going to have another child tormented her. Meeting and falling in love with Shyhiem, a man who already had a son and daughter, was a gift from God. She'd already have the ready-made family she'd always wanted. Bryson destroyed all of that. There was no telling if she and Shyhiem would ever get back together, let alone, get married.

Anytime Messiah started to doubt their connection, she had to remind herself that they completed each other. Shyhiem was made for her. He made her want to be a better woman. Because of him, she'd begun to stick up for herself more. She was over being a wallflower. Being passive got you nowhere, when you're dealing with snakes. All her life, she'd let people like Bryson and Lake chew her up and spit her out. Well, no more. It was a new dawn and a new day. Messiah was taking charge of her life. It hurt like hell that Shyhiem wouldn't be around to see her growth. Since their blow up, she'd tried reaching out to him, but it wasn't via phone, email or text. Messiah decided to step outside the box and do something different. After hearing his revelation that he wanted to take her and the twins and move away, she decided to send him love notes via postcards.

It was the only way she could get through to him. She had to make him see that she was sure about them now. There were no more doubts in her head. Shyhiem wasn't too good to be true. He was a good man who'd given his love to her abundantly and freely. It was high time she give it back. It took some time, but Messiah finally realized that she deserved good things to happen in her life. Everyone wasn't out to destroy her or let her down. Shyhiem had only been a blessing. Because of him, she knew what real love looked and felt like. He'd changed her world for the better. She'd never find another man that would love her as much as he did.

Messiah didn't care what she had to do. She'd get down on her knees if that's what it took to get him back. She didn't want to live in doubt and misery anymore. She wanted to live life to the fullest. Decades and centuries could go by and she'd still love him. There was no one else for her. All the feelings she had bottled up, she was ready to reveal.

Messiah waited with baited breath for some type of response from him but didn't get any. Over a week had gone by. It hurt like hell that he could possibly not be in love with her anymore. And yes, she still felt some kind of way about the things he'd said and done. Nothing, however, would stop her from loving him. Messiah wouldn't dream of giving up on what they shared. The sound of his voice was the sweetest harmony she'd ever heard. He was the man God made especially for her. No matter how long it took, she was gonna make him her husband. Messiah was fully prepared to give her all to him. He just had to let down his guard long enough to allow her back in.

She refused to ever believe he didn't love her anymore. He was hers and she was his. They'd fallen apart but they'd make their way back to one another. Messiah had to stand firm in that belief; or her world would spin out of control. Positive thinking was key. Messiah wasn't a big believer in God but the universe had to have her back on this one. Their love could withstand the odds. It was concrete and unbreakable. She couldn't take anymore L's.

Zipping up her coat, Messiah stepped outside the diner door. After a six-hour shift, she was finally able to go home and get a few hours of rest, before getting up and doing it all over again. Her neck and shoulders were aching. She needed a massage, like yesterday, but the pain quickly became a distant memory when she spotted Shyhiem waiting for her outside. Her heart paused and the walls of her pussy contracted. When she was around him, all she wanted to do was strip naked. When their bodies

140

were pressed together in the dark was when she was at her best.

Nasty thoughts of her placing her mouth on his mic filled her head. Messiah loved his dick. It was long, wide and thick. Every time he entered her, the size of him filled her up. She wanted him desperately. The naughty shit he made her do, she never dreamt she'd do in a million years; but for Shyhiem, she'd do anything. He brought out her inner freak. She prayed that he was there to take her home so he could fuck her until the sun came up.

Then, she remembered that she looked a hot mess. She hated when he caught her off guard. Dealing with a nigga like Shyhiem, she had to stay on her P's and Q's. She never knew what he was going to do or what side of him she was going to get. He could be the sweet and attentive Shyhiem she adored or the cocky, dismissive bastard he'd been lately. On the low, she'd take either. Just to have him in her presence was a blessing. She'd take whatever side of him she could get.

It didn't hurt that he looked like a snack she wanted to devour. His car was parked down the street. His warm, brown skin faded into the dark night. He leaned up against the passenger side door of his Range. On his head was a black, leather, fitted cap with the word SKILLED written on it in white. He donned an army fatigue, longline, hooded jacket with the hood draped over the hat. The rest of the outfit consisted of an expensive, black sweatshirt, black jeans ripped at the knee and black, suede Tims. Shyhiem was doing the damn thing. All the new shit he'd copped hadn't gone unnoticed. Messiah wondered where he was getting the money to buy all the stuff.

Those questions would have to wait till later. Visions of them dancing the night away, as he kissed her lips, ran through her head. Their life could be so perfect, if he allowed it. She'd wake him with breakfast in bed and take the kids to school. He'd never have to worry about a thing. Till death do them part. He'd be her #1 priority. All he had to do was promise that he'd never let her go.

As Messiah neared, the glimmer from his brown eyes lit up the night sky. She missed having him there when she got off work. It was one of the little things she took for granted, when she had him. She wouldn't do it anymore. She'd cherish each moment they shared as if it were their last.

Messiah smoothed back her curly hair. It was all over the place. Normally, she wouldn't care, but for Shyhiem, she always wanted to look her best. She wanted to take a whiff under her arm but he'd see. There was a pretty good chance she smelled like ass, but there was nothing she could do about it. He would have to take her as she was or not at all.

Shyhiem pushed his weight off the passenger door and approached her slowly. There was no one on the block except him and her. The unfriendly, November weather kept everyone at home. A sheet of snow crunched underneath their feet, as they came face to face. Shyhiem gazed down at her face and studied her freckles like they were the constellation. There was hesitation in her eyes. She was afraid of what he might say. Good. She needed to be scared. He wasn't there for a bunch of pleasantries. She'd been sending him postcards in the mail for over a week. At first, he was able to keep his defenses up, but the more they came, the more her words of love penetrated his heart.

He swore to God he didn't want to love her anymore. They were no good together. One of them would end up hurting the other. They were both train wrecks on the edge of going off the tracks. Two broken people couldn't heal each other. All they'd do is more damage to one another. He understood all of this but still couldn't stay away. The only way he could save himself, was if he saved her too. God had brought them together for a reason. What that reason was, he hadn't figured out yet. The one thing he knew for sure, was that she was the holy water he needed to survive.

Shyhiem was a strong man but Messiah made him weak. She was his kryptonite, his Achilles heel. Without her, the weight of the world became heavier. No other woman made him feel like she did. For her, he would give his money, his life and soul. Since he laid eyes on her, everything in his life became centered around her. He'd told himself that he was through loving her; but there he was, crawling right back on his hands and knees. Shyhiem was starting to think he was addicted to the pain she inflicted on him. For her, he'd bleed himself dry. Whatever it was that pulled them together like magnets, hurt so good, he couldn't let go.

The way she smiled, her pretty eyes, the sway of her hips - hypnotized him. She wore no makeup, just how he liked. She didn't need it. Messiah was the most gorgeous woman on the planet. Black ringlets of hair fell onto her forehead and down to her shoulders. Bushy brows framed her wide eyes and long, natural lashes. Her sharp cheekbones, plump, pink lips and dimpled-chin is what drew him in the most. God was having a splendid day when he created her. He'd tried staying mad but he'd had enough. Shyhiem didn't want to live another second or minute without her.

"You put that nigga out?" He asked, instead of saying hi.

"You done fuckin' that bitch?" Messiah cocked her head to the side.

Shyhiem stared at her for a second before answering.

"We were never together." He skirted the question.

"I did." Messiah finally admitted.

"Good." Shyhiem placed his hands inside the pocket of his jeans.

"So, what now?" Messiah asked helplessly.

If he said he still didn't want to be with her, she wasn't sure what she was gonna do. It had been torture not having him around. She couldn't go another day without having his arms wrapped around her on a daily.

"I don't know." He shrugged.

I don't know was not what Messiah wanted to hear. She wanted him to say that he loved her to the moon and back. She wanted him to drop down on one knee and propose. She was sick of playing games. It was clear as day they were meant to be.

"What you mean you don't know? I love you and I wanna be wit' you. I know you feel the same way too."

"Do you really?" He quizzed.

"I wouldn't tell you I love you if I didn't mean it."

Shyhiem looked past her and at the diner.

"Do you know I used to come here every day, twice a day, sometimes… Just so I could see you. All I ever wanted to do was be around you." He resumed eye contact.

"I already feel bad enough. You don't have to keep rubbing it in."

"See, that's the problem. You think I'm tryin' to be funny but I'm not. You cut me deep. I'd never do that to you."

"Maybe 'cause you're a better person than I am. I don't know. All I know, is that I'm sorry and I love you. We can make this work, Shyhiem. I know we can." She placed her small hand on his firm chest.

"I love you too. I never stopped, but I honestly think we need to take it one day at a time and see what happen. I don't wanna just jump back into things and then they get right back fucked up."

"I get that, but what's the point of us just being friends? I've had your dick in my mouth, for God's sake," she joked.

Shyhiem laughed.

"I get what you're sayin' but just do this for me, please." He pulled her close.

"Is that really what you want?" She asked, disappointed.

Shyhiem wanted to tell her that she'd carved out chunks of his heart with a paring knife when she left, and that he'd cried more times than he'd care to admit, but his pride would never let him reveal any of that. He'd been vulnerable with her once and it had gotten him nowhere. Shyhiem had learned from his mistake. This time, when dealing with Messiah, they'd do things his way.

"I'm not over everything that's happened yet. I need more time."

"So, what are we looking at here: an open relationship, friends with benefits, the old dog and bone situation?" She held onto him for dear life.

"Let's just be us. We don't need to put a label on it." He said, as he kissed her lips tenderly.

As their lips pressed against one another under the November moon, a large, black crow sat on top of the street light, watching their every move.

"Bad times turn to good memories."–
Jay Z, "Smile"

18

Shyhiem

"I put my hands up. They're playin' my song, the butterflies fly away. I'm noddin' my head like, yeah. I'm movin' my hips like, yeah!" Sonny and Shania sang at the top of their lungs, as Miley Cyrus' song, *Party In The USA*, played.

Messiah sat on the couch, laughing hysterically. Watching the twins dance and sing was a delight. She loved to see them express themselves. They'd just finished decorating the Christmas tree. The finished product came out great. They'd even put some gifts under the tree. Messiah's gift to Shyhiem sat inside a gold box. She couldn't wait to see his face on Christmas morning. He'd be stunned to see what she'd gotten him.

They'd only been back together a few weeks. On the surface, everything seemed good. He'd officially introduced her to the kids, but only as a friend. The title bothered her but she kept her poker face on. Shyhiem needed time to trust her with his heart again. She was a woman of her word and planned on giving him the time he needed to adjust to their new normal. As long as she got to be with him - that was all that mattered.

That night, they were spending the night in with the kids. After a few weeks of not being able to see Shania and Sonny, Keesha finally eased up and let him have them for the weekend. He figured she must've needed a babysitter so she could go out or have some nigga over. Whatever the reason, he didn't care. He missed the twins like crazy.

They'd grown at least an inch since the last time he saw their angelic faces. Shyhiem never wanted to be apart from them a day, let alone, a few weeks. Keesha was playing a dirty game by holding the kids hostage. It wasn't fair. He was their father and he loved them dearly. Just because he didn't want to be with her didn't mean that he shouldn't be able to see his kids. Shyhiem thought when he moved out, he'd be free of Keesha and her shenanigans, but the situation only got worse.

She had him by the balls. Child support was taxing his check and she was playing a game of Red Light, Green Light when it came to visitation regarding the twins. Once he and Mayhem were done with the supply, Shyhiem was going to make it his business to take her ass to court for sole custody. He was tired of Keesha having all the say-so when it came to the twins. Especially, since she was the most unfit parent he'd ever met.

That night, none of that mattered. He had his best girl and his kids by his side. Pillows and blankets covered the floor for their slumber party. Messiah had helped him pick out candy, chips, pizza and drinks at the grocery store. Shyhiem wasn't much of a food shopper. He couldn't make his way around a grocery store if he tried. Shania and Sonny had gummy worms, Twinkies, S'mores, popcorn, cheese pizza and grape soda. They were super wired from all the sweets, but Shyhiem knew once they came down from the sugar high, they'd crash.

Everything was going smoothly until Sonny begged to wear one of Shania's nightgowns to bed. Shyhiem wanted to tell him no, but the last thing he wanted to see was his son in tears, after not being around him for weeks. Sonny got enough shit from Keesha at home. Shyhiem didn't like the visual of his only son prancing around like a girl, but he had to find a way to accept that it was who he was.

As Messiah watched the kids shimmy and shake their booties to the energetic song, she couldn't help but notice that Shyhiem had a displeased look on his face. He was staring at Sonny with sadness in his eyes. She knew he struggled with Sonny's sexuality. They'd discussed it in great length, but Shyhiem being the alpha male he was, still didn't like it. Messiah wasn't having it though. He was going to get over it, one way or another. Giddily, she jumped up from the couch and joined the kids. Messiah sang along with them and danced like there was no tomorrow.

Shyhiem arched his brow. Messiah was making a complete fool of herself. She did all kinds of dorky dance moves like the Robot and the Running Man. The kids were cracking up, laughing at her, but mimicked her every move. Shyhiem loved that they liked her a lot. The visual in front of him was all he'd ever wanted. This was the family dynamic he'd always dreamt of. In the bigger scheme of things, it didn't matter if his son liked girls or boys. His sexuality didn't change that he was a good person. Sonny was kind, funny and loving. He was the apple of Shyhiem's eye.

He didn't want his son to live in the shadows. Living in the shadows wasn't a safe place to be. He wanted him to live life freely and abundantly. Shyhiem didn't want to add to his pain. The world would give him enough. Shyhiem wanted to uplift him, when the world let him down. It didn't matter if he liked boys or girls' clothing. He was his son and he'd love him no matter what.

"C'mon, Daddy!" Messiah held out her hand.

Shyhiem drew his head back. There was no way he was getting up and dancing. Thugs didn't dance; they grooved. Shyhiem shook his head no. Messiah wasn't taking no for an answer.

"Come on," she urged, dipping it down low.

Unable to ever tell her no, Shyhiem reluctantly rose to his feet. The twins' faces lit up with joy. Messiah made him take each of their hands. Sonny smiled widely and looked up at his father like a real-life superhero, as he bopped from side to side. Seeing his kids so happy made Shyhiem relax. He didn't have to be hard all the time. It was ok to be softer for his kids. Together, they all danced around in a circle. Laughter filled the room. Shyhiem picked Shania up and swung her around in the air.

"Swing me around too, Pop!" Sonny pleaded.

Shyhiem picked his son up by the stomach and threw him up in the air. When Sonny landed back in his hands, he let out a loud wail. Shyhiem quickly put him down to see what was wrong. Sonny held his side in pain.

"What's wrong, buddy?" Shyhiem questioned, concerned.

"Nothin'," Sonny lied.

Keesha had warned him not to say anything when they left. Shyhiem knew he was lying. He could tell by the look on his face.

"It's ok, buddy. You can tell me," he assured.

"Mama said don't say nothin'." Shania stuck her index finger in-between her teeth.

She was afraid what her daddy might do if he found out the truth.

"Can I see?" Messiah stooped down to Sonny's level.

She could see the hesitation in his eyes.

"I promise, I won't hurt you," she said sincerely.

Sonny allowed her to pull up the hem of the nightgown. On his left side was a purple bruise. Messiah looked over at Shyhiem. He was pissed. A bulging vein strained in his forehead.

"How did you get that?" He asked.

"I fell into the wall," Sonny replied, sheepishly.

"How?" Shyhiem demanded to know.

"Mama pushed me."

Shyhiem had no words. All he could do was rise to his feet and pace back and forth. He wanted to punch a wall. It took everything in him not to grab his keys, find Keesha and kill her.

"We should take him to the emergency room. He might have a broken rib." Messiah whispered, so only he could hear.

"We can't do that." Shyhiem scowled, and continued to pace.

"Why not? He needs medical attention."

"'Cause I said so." Shyhiem stormed past her.

"And what the hell that's supposed to mean?" Messiah followed him to the bedroom.

"It means you heard what the fuck I said!" He turned around and pointed his finger in her face like a gun.

Messiah should've been scared but she wasn't. Arching her brow, she folded her arms across her chest.

"You can yell and scream all you want to. It don't faze me. Sonny needs to go to the emergency room; what I need to know is why you won't take him?"

Shyhiem ran his hand over his head. He wanted to tell her the truth, but the truth would only lead to more problems.

"Just mind your business, ok!" He snapped.

Messiah looked at him like he was crazy. Shyhiem never raised his voice at her.

"I was only tryin' to help." She replied, visibly upset.

"Yeah, well, I don't need your help." Shyhiem went inside the bathroom and slammed the door.

Taking his anger out on Messiah was wrong, but it was the only way he could get her to back off. He wanted to take Sonny to the hospital, but involving the authorities wouldn't be good for either Keesha or him. He didn't want to draw any attention to himself while he was still distro. If DFS got involved, they'd do a thorough investigation on Keesha and him too. He couldn't have that. Messiah deserved to know the truth. It was the right thing to do, but if she found out he was back in the life, the little progress they'd made would be all for nothing. He didn't wanna go two steps back. Keesha would get hers, one way or another.

"I know people backstab you. I feel bad too, but this fuck everybody attitude ain't natural."– Jay Z, "Kill Jay Z"

19

Shyhiem

Shyhiem could feel Messiah's breath, erratic and warm with eagerness. He could feel the rise and fall of her body, desperate to be penetrated by hardened flesh. He could taste her desire in the air. Every nerve ending on her body was standing at attention, begging to be caressed. Shyhiem firmly placed his hands on her hips. His hands squeezed her waist, as the head of his cock gently opened the entry to her wet pussy.

When Messiah straddled his lap, naked, during the middle of the day and the sun shined through the blinds onto her caramel skin was when Shyhiem loved her most. The natural blush tone to her cheeks shined as she smiled. Hunger lit her brown irises. Her wild, black hair surrounded her face, as she rode his dick with reckless abandon. Every time she dropped down on his shaft, he felt ravenous. Messiah popped her booty like a porn star. He loved when she took his long dick like a champ.

Shyhiem gripped her ass cheeks. Messiah's perfect tits bounced in his face, placing him in a trance. Her greedy cunt devoured his cock. Groans of wanton need echoed throughout the room. Her moans, high pitched and desperate, begged for more of his cock.

"You want it?" He asked.

"Yes, I want it."

"I don't believe you. Tell me how much you want it." He licked each of her nipples.

"Oooooooh… baby, I want it!" Messiah threw her head back.

Shyhiem's cock was throbbing so hard inside her she could feel the corded ridges of his veins. She loved riding his dick. It was her favorite position.

"Touch yourself," he demanded.

Loving to please her man, Messiah reached in between her legs and played with her clit.

"Oooooh… yes! Fuck yeah!"

"Don't stop!" Shyhiem bit into his bottom lip and smacked her tit.

Watching her get herself off, while his dick slid in and out of her wet pussy, was the best. Messiah's high-pitched moans let him know she was desperate for more of his long, thick dick. Shyhiem's entire girth was glazed in her slickness.

"Oh my God! I fuckin' love this dick!" Messiah moaned, on the brink of cumming.

"Oh shit!" Shyhiem growled, feeling a nut build in the tip of his dick.

This was his third time cumming. Messiah was the only woman that could make him cum back-to-back. Her pussy was so tight, sticky and wet. He loved when her juices rained down on him. The farther he plunged inside her canal, the more her moans deepened. Inch by desire-filled inch, he pushed deeper inside her trembling walls. Shyhiem was completely buried deep in her hole.

"Ooooooooh… Shyhiem!" Messiah screamed, as he pounded into her pussy harder.

"Fuck! I'm about to cum!" He announced.

Shyhiem's fingers were imprinted on her hips, as his seeds impregnated her honey-coated walls. Messiah's pussy was no longer hers. It was his - forever.

"Shyhiem, baby!" She screamed, as she felt his semen squirt inside her.

Messiah couldn't hold back any longer. It was time for her to cum. Messiah's eyes rolled into the back of her head, as she let out a thunderous moan. Her entire body trembled, as she came all over his dick. She never wanted to get off it. She wanted it in her mouth, pussy and even her ass... but she had to go to work. After coming down from their orgasmic high, they both lay, trying to catch their breath.

Shyhiem wrapped his arm around her neck and inhaled the scent of her hair. They'd been fuckin' for the past two hours. After so much time apart, they had to make up for lost time. Their bodies had to reintroduce themselves to one another. It would take Shyhiem a lifetime to become acquainted with every fold and curve of her shape. He loved tracing her honey-colored skin with his tongue and lips. Although she was very petite and complained about having no booty and no body, she was perfect in his eyes. She had just enough of everything.

Her boobs were more than a mouthful and her booty had just enough bounce to it when he hit it from the back. If he could, he'd stay curled up in the bed with her for the rest of the day. Fucking her brains out was the highlight of his afternoon, but she had to go to work, and he was late for a meeting at the warehouse with Mayhem. It was re-up day - again. Messiah could never know what he was up to. She'd shit a brick if she found out he was back dealing dope. One

157

of the conditions of dating her was that he couldn't sell drugs. She'd let him know that right from the beginning.

When Shyhiem got out of jail, he avoided getting back into the business. His brother had taken over and he was fine with that. With the stress of having Keesha down his throat and losing Messiah, Shyhiem felt as if he had nothing to lose. It was either go big or go home. Doing things the legal way wasn't paying off for him. If anything, it was slowing him down. It would take him years to get to Cali, based off his UPS salary. To make his dream a reality, he had to play in the fast lane.

"I gotta go." He kissed her sweetly on the forehead.

"Noooo... I don't want you to go." She whined, placing what seemed like a thousand kisses on his chest.

"Have you forgot? You gotta go to work," he laughed.

"I'll play hooky," She beamed brightly.

"Nah, you can't do that." Shyhiem sat up, so he could get out of bed.

Messiah poked out her bottom lip and watched as he began to dress. Something was wrong. She felt it in her spirit. Since when did he not want her to take off work? At one point, he used to beg her to stay at home, just so they could have more time together. Hell, he'd asked her to quit, on several occasions, and offered to give her the extra money she needed. Messiah found it quite odd that he was behaving differently now. Red flags were waving in her face but she didn't want to start a war.

They'd only been on good terms a few weeks. She didn't want to rock the boat and put them back on the odds. However, the old, familiar feeling that her man was up to no good resonated in the pit of her stomach. Shyhiem was keeping something from her. They never kept secrets from one another. He'd swore to always tell her the truth. Obviously, that had changed.

"Where you going? You gotta get the kids today?" She fished for answers.

"Uhhhh... yeah." He lied, putting on his jeans.

"Oh." Messiah slouched. "You wouldn't lie to me, now would you?" She blurted out, before she could stop herself.

"Why you ask me that?" Shyhiem eyed her quizzically.

On the outside, he played it cool; but on the inside, his heart was beating rapidly.

"I don't know," Messiah shrugged. "You just seem... different."

"A lot has changed in the last few months."

'I know, but... something is off."

"You buggin'." He made it seem like she was crazy.

"Nah, I trust my instincts. They never steer me wrong," she replied, folding her legs under her.

"Maybe it's you that's off 'cause I'm straight."

"Now I'm the problem," she scoffed. "It's just like you to turn shit around and put it off on me."

"I'm not about to argue wit' you, Messiah," Shyhiem gave her a stern look.

"I'm not tryin' to argue with you, Shyhiem. This is called a conversation."

"Yeah, well, I'm done with this conversation. Change the subject," he ordered, with an attitude.

Messiah licked her bottom lip. A slew of words sat on the tip of her tongue but she held them all in. The fear of pushing him away was far greater than winning an argument. Shyhiem's new, no-nonsense attitude irritated and scared her. He'd began to be curt with her. Whatever he said was the law. She didn't like it at all. Being voiceless in their situationship wasn't cool. Shyhiem's controlling behavior was worse now than before. Until they put a firm stamp on if they were boyfriend and girlfriend again, Messiah wouldn't rock the boat.

"Hey, you busy on the 30th?" She changed the subject, as requested.

"Not that I know of." He finished putting on his clothes.

"My sister's rehearsal dinner is that day. It's at this fancy winery. You wanna come with me? I would love to have you there," she smiled brightly.

"Uhhhh… nah, I'm good." Shyhiem sat on the side of the bed to put his shoes on.

Messiah sat speechless. He didn't even try to be nice about it, when he let her down. He was downright rude. Instead of reacting off emotion, Messiah continued to be submissive and docile, to please him.

"Why?" She crawled over and hugged him from behind.

"From what you told me about your sister, she's a rich, bougie bitch."

"True, but what that got to do with me?" She asked, as he removed her arms.

"I don't wanna be around a bunch of judgmental, rich muthafuckas that's gonna look down on me for a few hours. I gotta put up with that shit every day, all day. Nah, I'm good."

"Do it for me though." She kissed the space in-between his neck and shoulder.

"C'mon, Messiah, we talked about this." He jerked his head away.

"I know we're supposed to take things slow." She sat back, disappointed. "How long is this supposed to last though? I'm sick of being stuck in limbo."

"How many times you gon' ask me that? I told you I don't know. I need more time. A lot has happened between us."

"That sound like an excuse to me," she shot.

"I'm not about to go back and forth with you about this."

"You know you hurt me too, right?" Messiah refused to backdown.

Shyhiem placed on his shoes in silence. This was exactly the reason why he stayed away. Every time he came by to see her, they always ended up arguing. Messiah wasn't the same, cool, go-with-the-flow girl he'd fallen in love with. Now, she was needy, whiny and argumentative. Shyhiem had enough stress in his life already. When he spent time with her, it was supposed to be relaxing.

"You gon' act like you don't hear me, Goodnight?"

"Don't call me that."

"Oh, that got your attention. Why you don't want me to call you Goodnight? That's what your other hoes call you," Messiah spat.

"You are so fuckin' childish," Shyhiem shook his head.

"Now I'm childish? Do you even realize that since we've been back messin' around, the only time we spend together is when you wanna stick your dick in me? Other than that, I don't see you." She rolled her neck.

"That ain't true." Shyhiem denied, even though he knew it was.

He'd been dodging Messiah on purpose. The less time he spent with her, the less he'd have to explain about his day-to-day activities.

"Yes, it is. We haven't even been on a date once. All I see is the ceiling or the sheets, when I'm with you."

"You act like that's a bad thing," he grinned, slyly.

"It's not funny." Messiah threw a pillow at him. "I'm starting to feel like an easy lay. I don't wanna be your fuck buddy. What we have is way bigger than that, and you know it."

Shyhiem hung his head and sighed. This was the part of the game he hated. Living selfishly was only fun for so long, then other people's emotions got involved and forced him to face his transgressions. He didn't wanna be a dick. He never wanted to hurt Messiah or make her cry, but he was so far into his own feelings that he was blind to hers. Having his heart broken by a woman was foreign territory to him. He didn't know how to navigate his way back to a place of forgiveness.

"How many times do I have to say sorry before you forgive me? Don't you want things to go back to the way they used to be?" Messiah died to know.

"You don't get it." Shyhiem chuckled incredulity. "Things will never be how they were. I stood on the sidewalk, begging you to come home with me, and you didn't. I told you I love you time and time again, and you turned your back on me. You knew how big it was for me to open up to you like that, but you still didn't care."

"I did care. I do care. I just needed to love me more in that second. I needed to work on myself so I could be the woman you needed. I'm a better woman now because of the time we spent apart."

"'I see." He picked up one of her ballet slippers and ran his thumb across the smooth material. "You started dancing again?"

"And that's all because of you. You inspired me to follow my dreams and have hope again. I want to do the same for you. If you'll let me."

Shyhiem stared into space. He couldn't focus his attention on her willful, brown eyes. She expected things from him he wasn't ready to give just yet. She hadn't fully earned his trust again, and he honestly wasn't sure she ever would. And yes, he'd done his fair share of dirt that let her down, but his pain was all he cared about. Messiah could never know he was fighting demons bigger than her. Esco's death was eating him alive.

He wasn't the same head-over-heels, in love nigga she met that hot night in August. Resentment now took over the space his heart used to house. This was the side of him he never wanted her to see. Shyhiem hated the side of him that was heartless, selfish and mean. He wanted to snap out of it but couldn't. The fear of the unknown wouldn't allow it.

"I'll see you later, ok?" He palmed the sides of her face with his hands.

Messiah held her head high, despite her organs withering on the inside. Shyhiem wasn't playing fair. He'd completely closed himself off emotionally to her. It would take an ice pick to chip away at the block of ice surrounding his cold heart.

"You walkin' around like you invincible."– Jay Z, "Kill Jay Z"

20

Shyhiem

"Where the fuck is this nigga at?" Mayhem said underneath his breath, as he placed his phone up to his ear.

Shyhiem was supposed to be at the warehouse over two hours ago but he was nowhere to be found. He'd been showing up late a lot lately and Mayhem didn't like it one bit. Whatever was keeping his li'l brother preoccupied had to be removed from the equation immediately. Mayhem just had to find out what that thing was.

"Hello?" Keesha answered on the second ring.

"Aye, you seen Shyhiem today?"

"No."

"Damn, I wonder where this nigga at." He said desperately.

"Why? Y'all got work today?" She spoke in code.

"Something like that." Mayhem watched his words.

"He probably with that li'l mop-head bitch."

"Who; Messiah?" Mayhem screwed up his face.

"Yeah, Shania told me he had her around the last time they were over there."

"He ain't told me shit."

"Mmm… maybe he tryin' to keep it a secret 'cause he ain't said shit to me either. When I confronted him about it, he act like I was crazy. I know Shania ain't lyin'. He

166

fuckin' with that bitch again. Just when I thought I was rid of her ugly-ass." Keesha quipped, rolling her eyes.

Just as Mayhem was about to respond, Shyhiem strolled in.

"Here he come. He walkin' in right now. I'ma ask him and see what he say. Let me hit you back." Mayhem ended the call. "What took you so long? Where the fuck you been?"

"I got caught up with the kids," Shyhiem lied, diverting his attention elsewhere.

Mayhem eyed his brother skeptically. Whenever he didn't look someone in the eye, he was lying, and Mayhem knew for damn sure he wasn't telling the truth after talking to Keesha.

"We're almost done. I need your head on straight."

"I get it. I'm here; ain't I?" Shyhiem frowned.

He despised being reprimanded, especially by Mayhem, of all people.

"I'm just saying, we can't have any fuck ups. I ain't tryin' to go back to jail and neither are you."

"No shit. Let's just get this over with. I gotta go pick Lincoln up in a minute."

"You still hittin' that?"

"You nosy as fuck," Shyhiem chuckled.

"I ain't mad if you are. She bad. She way finer than that Messiah chick."

"Never that," Shyhiem disagreed.

"Let me find out you still hittin' that too." Mayhem said, jokingly, to see his reaction.

"What I do wit' my dick ain't none of yo' business, cuz," Shyhiem laughed.

"Whatever. C'mon, we got people waiting on us."

"You done told on yo' homey. You a pussy."– Meek Mill feat. Yo Gotti & Rick Ross, "Connect The Dots"

21

Messiah

Joe's Diner was a South City staple. Everyone and their mama went there. It had been in the community for over 30 years. Women and men, old and young, frequented the spot for down-home, good eats. The diner stayed open 24 hours a day. Foodies loved coming there for the kind service and 60's, Doo-wop décor. Upon entry, you were transported back in time. There was black and white checkerboard floors, a jukebox, colorful, neon lights, album memorabilia and black, vinyl seats.

Messiah had only been working there a few months. She normally worked afternoons and weekends. Each shift was six to eight hours. The pay was pretty shitty but the tips she got made up for the lack of pay. By the time she got off work each night, her uniform looked like a garbage can had thrown up on her. That day was no different. A kid ran into her while she juggled a tray full of food in her hand. An entire bowl of spaghetti and meatballs fell onto her shirt and apron. It took her a whole minute before she could compose herself long enough to wipe the sauce and noodles off.

It took everything in Messiah not to say fuck it and go home. If her cellphone bill wasn't due, she would've. She was at her wits' end with the overworked and under paid job. The way her body was breaking down from working so hard and doing ballet was making her feel like it all wasn't worth it. If she could dance full-time and get paid for it, she'd be over the moon. But it would take at least a year before her skills were at the level they once were. The only thing that kept her sane was dreaming about the day she'd be able to take a vacation. Unless she hit the lottery, that wouldn't happen anytime soon either.

She shouldn't have listened to Shyhiem and taken the day off and rested in bed. They'd fucked so much, her pussy was swole. Messiah was running herself ragged. The smell of the slow-drying tomato sauce on her chest wasn't making the situation any better. She wanted to vomit but she'd been advised that she had a customer waiting in her section. Messiah reached inside her apron for her notepad, so she could take down the order. She was so in her head about the disgusting way she felt and looked that she didn't pay attention to exactly who was waiting in her station.

"Hi; can I get you anything to drink?" She looked up and made eye contact with the customer.

The smile on her face instantly vanished once she realized who it was. Mayhem sat inside a booth with his fingers intertwined. There was a smug expression on his face. It was funny because he and Shyhiem favored one another. They possessed the same cocoa-colored skin, muscular build and menacing glare. Shyhiem was far better looking though. A long, ugly scar was etched across Mayhem's face. He was buffer than Shyhiem and didn't seem to have a heart.

Messiah had only met him once when he came to pick Shyhiem up from her apartment. That one time had been enough. Mayhem came across very sinister and underhanded. She didn't trust him as far as she could throw him. He'd tried to holla at her with Shyhiem only a few feet away. A nigga like him couldn't be trusted. He made her quite uncomfortable. The last thing she wanted was to serve him.

"Let me find someone else to wait on you." She rolled her eyes.

"I asked for you specifically. Sit down." Mayhem glared at her.

Messiah wanted to tell him to suck a dick but the look on his face told her not to. She didn't know Mayhem that well to know how he'd react to her disrespecting him, so she sat down. She didn't want to cause a scene at her job. If Mayhem acted a fool, she had no one to help her. Mr. Johnson, the owner, was terrified of him and Shyhiem. Besides, getting off her feet for a few seconds wasn't so bad anyway.

"What exactly do you want?" With her tone, Messiah made it clear she did not like him. "You and I don't know each other that well for you to be poppin' up on me at work."

"You back seeing my brother?" Mayhem cut right to the chase.

"That's none of your business. Besides, if you wanna know so bad, ask him. Now, if you'll excuse me." She went to rise.

"Sit… down." Mayhem said, with a violent look in his eye.

"I don't have time for this time. I have to get back to work." Messiah tried to scoot out the booth.

She wanted to get as far away from him as possible. Mayhem was nothing like his brother. She could tell he was a sociopath.

"Don't make me tell you again." He advised, leaning forward.

She didn't know if he was gonna grab her by the throat or slap her. Either way, she wasn't trying to find out. Messiah narrowed her eyes at him and did as she was told.

"I want you to stay away from my brother."

"Excuse me?" Messiah screwed up her face, trying to be tough.

Underneath the table, her legs were shaking. She was terrified of Mayhem.

"I'm tired of you fuckin' wit' his head. You distract him, and right now, we don't need any distractions."

"What is that supposed to mean?"

"It means exactly what the fuck I said. Stay away from Shyhiem."

"Your brother is a grown-ass man who can make decisions for himself. We will stop dealing with each other when, and if, we decide to." She tried to remain strong.

"You funny. You know that," Mayhem chuckled.

"Either order something or leave. If not, I'm callin' Shyhiem. I don't think he would take to kindly to you threatening me."

"You can call him if you want to but he ain't gon' answer." Mayhem sat back, confidently.

"Please, Shyhiem always answers my call." Messiah scoffed, pulling out her phone.

"A'ight. Don't say I didn't warn you."

"You might be all big and ugly but you don't scare me." Messiah rolled her neck.

"Ugly? Bitch, please. Ain't no such thing as an ugly millionaire. I'm cute," Mayhem laughed, appalled.

"Whatever. Shyhiem gon' kick yo' ass when he finds out you came here." She gloated, locating his number.

"Go ahead and embarrass yourself. He ain't gon' pick up." Mayhem toyed with a napkin on the table.

"How you know?" Messiah let the phone ring.

"'Cause he's with Lincoln."

Messiah's heart exploded in her chest. Fragments of it entered her lungs and began to choke her.

"No, he's not. You lyin'." She held the phone to her ear, praying to God Shyhiem would pick up.

After three rings, she was forwarded to voicemail. Messiah ended the call and clenched her jaw.

"He's not answering 'cause he's with his kids," her voice quivered.

"Is that what he told you?" Mayhem chuckled. "That nigga ain't shit."

"Your brother would never cheat on me." She said in disbelief.

"So y'all are together?" Mayhem got the answer he'd been looking for.

"Are we done here?" Messiah asked, staring off into space.

"Yep, I got what I wanted. You be good, Messiah; ya hear?" He gripped her shoulder tightly on the way out.

Messiah wanted to stab him in the neck with a knife but she couldn't move. Her gut had been telling her that something was up. When he'd left earlier that day, she knew deep down something was up with him. There was a time when Shyhiem wanted to spend every second of the day with her. Now, he found every reason in the book to get away from her. Messiah thought it was all in her head. She'd chalked it up to her overreacting because they weren't officially a couple again. Not knowing exactly where they stood was driving her nuts.

Now, it all made sense. He was fuckin' around behind her back, and with Lincoln, no less. As she sat there trembling, Messiah still held out hope that it wasn't true. The only way to know for sure, was if she tried calling him again - so she did. The second time, the phone rang once and went to voicemail. *Oh, hell nah,* she thought, looking down at her phone like it was a bomb. Then, a text message from him came through, causing her to jump. It didn't go unnoticed that he'd texted her back instead of callin'. Red flags were waving frantically in her face. Messiah steadied her breathing and read the message.

Shyhiem: What's up? U good?

Messiah had to play it cool. She didn't wanna come right out and ask if he was cheating.

Messiah: Yeah, you having fun with the kids?

Shyhiem: Yeah we chillin' at the crib.

Messiah: Ok… I'll hit you up when I get off work.

Shyhiem: A'ight

Messiah: I love you

Shyhiem: ☺ ☐

Messiah's nerves had started to die down, until he hit her with the smiley face emoji instead of saying I love you too. Life was repeating itself all over again. This time, she wasn't going to ignore the signs. Tears stung her eyes but she wasn't going to cry. No, it was time to get down to business and find out what the fuck was going on. She had to know if he was with the kids for real or not. Suddenly, it dawned on her how she could find him. She went to the Find Friends app on her iPhone to locate where he was. They'd added each other on it when they first started dating. The app told her he was at Sub Zero in the Central West End.

"That lyin' muthafucka," she hissed.

Messiah raced out of the booth and to the employee room to grab her purse.

"Joe, I gotta leave early! I have a family emergency!" She yelled over her shoulder, not bothering to wait for a reply.

"I seen the innocence leave your eyes."– Jay Z, "4:44"

22

Messiah

Sub Zero Vodka Bar was a prime date spot. Couples all over St. Louis went there for first dates, anniversaries and birthdays. It was dark, sexy and hip. Sub Zero had the largest selection of vodka in the city. They also served some of the best sushi and burgers in the Lou. The food was just as delicious as the drinks. Their bar was made of ice, which added to the place's cool factor. That Friday night, the place was packed. Every table was filled. Messiah walked in and searched the restaurant for Shyhiem. Unbeknownst to her, but the same black crow that had been following her and Shyhiem for weeks, watched from the windowsill. The cab she'd ridden over in waited outside. Messiah didn't plan on staying long. She just came to show her face and let it be known that she'd caught his lying, cheating-ass.

It didn't matter that she looked like a bum off the street. The stares she got from the other patrons didn't deter her from acting like a deranged psycho. She low-key looked like a serial killer, with dried up tomato sauce on her chest that resembled blood. Messiah went from table to table in search of the man who'd betrayed her. It didn't take long to spot him sitting in the back at a candlelit table for two.

Her conscious was telling her to turn around, save herself the embarrassment, but the rage in her wouldn't let her make a logical decision. Shyhiem sat across from Lincoln, looking down at his phone. He wasn't even paying her any attention, as she talked about God knows what. Messiah watched from afar. They were picturesque. The melanin in their skin matched perfectly. Where the chocolate of her skin ended, his began. The two of them were black magic at its finest. They should've been on the cover of Essence magazine.

Lincoln wore a spaghetti-strapped, white, bodycon dress that caressed her bountiful tits and size eight waist. Meanwhile, Messiah stood there helplessly, looking like a gunshot victim. Shyhiem looked just as good - but he was always handsome. His swag, however, that night was on another level. His black snapback had the word BALR written across the face. A black bomber jacket housed his chiseled arms. A white, designer, tank top with holes slashed into it showed off his smooth, cocoa brown chest. A pair of Givenchy, ripped jeans and black and white All-star Adidas completed his edgy look.

Messiah stood watching them, wondering how she'd ended up here again. Was there something about her that caused the men she loved to cheat? There had to be. Maybe she wasn't pretty enough. Maybe her box was trash. Maybe she was too skinny. Maybe she looked too much like a kid. Maybe she was too young. Maybe she expected too much… Whatever it was, she was convinced she was unlovable. God really had it in for her. Just when she thought things in her life was getting on track, he went and threw in another monkey wrench.

Now that she was there, Messiah didn't know how to approach the situation. She could walk up, grab his drink and throw it in his face, or walk over and slap him. Both ideas were great but neither were her. She wasn't the violent type. No, she'd simply make her presence known by saying hello. Taking a much-needed deep breath, she strolled over to their table, as if she didn't have a care in the world. She'd be damned if she let them see how distraught she really was. Messiah grabbed a chair from the neighboring table and sat opposite Shyhiem. He and Lincoln both turned and looked at her. All the color drained out of Shyhiem's face. He'd been caught and there was no way out of it.

"Hey, boo." She took a piece of sushi off his plate, popped it into her mouth and almost choked.

Mortified, she doubled over and coughed profusely into her hand. Afraid that she was choking, Shyhiem smacked her on the back until she began breathing normally again. Still feeling a tickle in her throat, Messiah gulped down his glass of water and then sat up straight, like nothing had happened.

"As I was saying." She placed her folded arms on the table. "Gotcha, bitch!"

"Messiah, what are you doing here?" Shyhiem looked at her exasperated.

"No, the question is: what are you doing here?"

"I thought you had the kids tonight? Where they at, 'cause I don't see 'em anywhere. Sonny! Shania! Where y'all at?" She yelled, causing people to stare.

"What is wrong wit' you? You mad being extra. Calm all that shit down. You embarrassing me," Shyhiem said, instead of, baby, I'm sorry; please let me explain.

"I'm embarrassing you?" She laughed, feeling like he'd punched her in the gut. "Well, hold on to your seat, homeboy, 'cause I'm just gettin' started. Hi, Lincoln. I'm Messiah. You remember me?" She held out her hand.

"Goodnight, what is going on?" Lincoln looked at him, instead of taking her hand.

"You even got her callin' you by your nickname. Let me say it and you get an attitude," Messiah said mockingly.

"Fuck all that. You stalkin' me now? How you even know I was here?" Shyhiem asked, perplexed, as his heart rate accelerated.

"A little birdie told me."

"So, let me guess. You supposed to be mad? It's your fault we're in this situation in the first place. You left me, remember?" He hit her with the hard, cold truth.

"You out with another chick but it's my fault? Ok." Messiah stared at him like he was dumb.

"Will somebody tell me what's going on?" Lincoln questioned, irritated. "What is she doing here? Is there something going on between you two that I need to know?"

"Is there something going on between us, Shyhiem?" Messiah cocked her head to the side.

"Can I talk to you outside for a second?" He scooted his chair back.

"Nah, I'm good. You can say what you gotta say right here. Answer her question." Messiah stared at him. "Who am I to you?"

"You know what it is between me and you."

"Do I?" Messiah's eyes watered.

Shyhiem could see the little innocence she had left fade from her eyes. It was all his fault. He'd done this to her. Because of him, she now knew just how fucked up human beings could be.

"Yeah, you do, but you can't say nothin'; just like I couldn't say nothin' about that nigga stayin' at yo' crib." He hit back.

His pride wouldn't let him admit that he was wrong.

"You still on that shit?" Messiah squinted her eyes, stunned.

"Clearly."

"Are y'all together or nah?" Lincoln jumped in. "'Cause this shit is ridiculous." She threw down her napkin.

"Last time I checked, it was a penny for your thoughts, so why the fuck you puttin' yo' two cents in? Shut the fuck up. Matter-of-fact, you can go." He shooed her away, agitated by her presence.

Lincoln sat horrified. She couldn't believe that he'd spoken to her that way.

"Nah, she ain't gotta leave, I will." Messiah went to stand up.

"Messiah, sit yo' ass the fuck down," Shyhiem warned.

"Uh ah, you can't even tell her who the fuck I am; so obviously, I don't mean shit to you."

"Just like I ain't mean shit to you when you chose that nigga." He shot back.

"I already told you what it was, so if you're going to continue to throw that shit up in my face, then I'm good. You can have him, sweetheart." Messiah rose from the chair.

"Messiah, I swear to God if you don't sit down." Shyhiem said on the verge of losing it.

"Nah, go ahead and finish your li'l date. But let me tell you this, when you're done, don't try and pull up or call me to explain 'cause I don't wanna hear it. It's a wrap between us, homeboy." She shook her head, disgusted by the sight of his gorgeous face.

"Y'all have a good night; ya hear?" She winked her eye and took another piece of sushi off his plate, before leaving.

"Is that anyway for a man to carry on?"– Donny Hathaway, "I Love You More Than You'll Ever Know"

23

Messiah

BAM! BAM! BAM! BAM! BAM!

Messiah sighed heavily and approached her door. Without looking out the peephole, she knew exactly who it was. It didn't take a rocket scientist to figure out it was Shyhiem. She knew he wouldn't heed her warning to stay away. He was hardheaded and fearless that way. It was one of the things she loved about him but now hated. Messiah had meant what she said. She never wanted to see him again. It was over between them. He'd done one of the worst things he could possible do to her. He knew how she felt after Bryson had cheated on her, and then turned around and disrespected her by doing the same, exact thing.

Here she'd been begging his forgiveness like a dummy, trying to win him back. He wasn't the prize she thought he was. Shyhiem's ass wasn't shit. She hated him for what he'd done to them. He'd done one of the worst things a human being could do to another. Because of him, they would never be the same. **BAM! BAM! BAM!** Shyhiem knocked even harder.

"Can you quit knockin' on my door like you the fuckin' police!" She hit her fist against the door, just as hard.

"Messiah, let me in!"

"No. Take yo' ass over Lincoln house!" She folded her arms across her chest.

"Can you at least let me inside so I can apologize?"

185

"What you gon' apologize for? Sticking your dick in another woman?"

"I didn't fuck her. I wouldn't do that to you," he replied, honestly.

"It's sad, 'cause at one point in time, I would've believed you; but now, I don't believe shit that comes out of your mouth. Yo' ass been stringing me along for weeks, making me feel like I was the evil one. When all along, you were the one up to no good. What was the point of saying you wanted to work things out when you knew you were still gon' be fuckin' around?"

"I do wanna be wit' you. I was just hurting and I wanted you to feel the same pain I did," he confessed.

"Oh, so we playin' tit-for-tat now? Wow." Messiah ran her hand down her face and then covered her mouth with it. "You are sick."

Shyhiem leaned his head against the door and closed his eyes. Maybe he was sick. Normal human beings didn't act this way.

"My dad has less than six months to live." He revealed, out of nowhere.

The confession even shocked him. His father's impending death followed him wherever he went. It was something he didn't want to acknowledge because Ricky's mortality made him face his own. Messiah knew it was against her better judgement, but she placed the chain on the door and opened it.

"Look, I know I fucked up. But you gotta understand, I'm going through all this bullshit alone. I'm having these nightmares. I can't see my kids like I want to, I lost you, my dad dyin'. I barely even fuckin' know him and now I'll never get the chance to. How the fuck am I suppose to process that shit? It's like I'm bleeding out and there's nobody there to save me."

"I'm sorry you're going through all of that, Shyhiem. I really am but—"

"C'mon, Messiah, now ain't the time to shut me out. I need you. Like, for real. I need you bad."

Messiah bit the inside of her lip. *I am not gonna let him see me cry.*

"I can't... I can't be there for you this time. I think it's best we go our separate ways. You focus on you and I'll focus on me." She closed the door in his face, before he could utter another word.

"Messiah, wait! I get it! I fucked up but I can't lose you!" He twisted the knob repeatedly.

Tears rapidly ran down Messiah's cheeks, as she tuned him out and went back to her room. Giving Shyhiem another chance wasn't in the cards. The love she had for him didn't matter anymore. She had to love herself more.

The next morning, Messiah grabbed her coat and purse to head to work. Puffy bags were under her eyes from crying herself to sleep. She didn't even know how she'd gotten dressed, she was so distraught. But she'd managed to piece together a decent enough outfit for her job at Charter that day. She wore a high-neck, crème, Chantilly lace, long sleeve top, skin-tight, light denim jeans and camel-colored, over-the-knee-boots she'd gotten from a second-hand store. Her hair was pulled up into a high ponytail. Her bountiful curls cascaded like a waterfall on top of her head.

For weeks, she'd tasted dishonesty on Shyhiem's breath and ignored it. *Silly girl,* she thought. But Messiah couldn't dwell on the pain that resided in her veins. She had to push forward. She'd sat in sadness for far too long. She refused to let the evils of the world keep her down. She refused to fix things with Shyhiem. Messiah had to make a grown woman decision and move on. Sometimes, love wasn't enough to keep two people together. Shyhiem had ruined them for good. There was nothing he could do to make things right. He'd violated the trust she had for him. She'd never be able to look at him the same. The days ahead of her would be dark, lonely and filled with tears, but she'd made it through worse things than this.

Shyhiem would have a harder time adjusting to their separation than she would. Her conscious was clean. His would eat him alive. He'd made their good love go to waste. He'd done her wrong and the memory of that would terrorize him forever.

Messiah placed on her $5 shades. She didn't want Bird to know she'd been crying all night. The last thing she needed was to be hit with a bunch of questions. She wasn't in the mood to rehash what had happened. As she opened the door to walk out, she almost fell over. To her shock and dismay, Shyhiem lay curled up in a ball outside her door, asleep. She was pissed and touched, at the same time, that he was there. Her heart melted for 1.2 seconds, then anger took over.

"Get up!" She kicked him in the back.

Shyhiem jumped out of his sleep, startled.

"Move." She pushed him out of the way, so she could lock up.

"Messiah, wait." He scrambled to stand up.

Shyhiem wasn't going to let the day start without seeing her face.

"Shyhiem, go home. You gon' be late for work." Messiah stomped past him.

Shyhiem looked down at this watch. It was 8:30am. His shift started at 7:00.

"Fuck," he whispered.

He'd forgotten all about his job. There was a pretty good chance he'd be fired but he'd risk it all for Messiah.

"Will you just stop and talk to me for a second?" He stood behind her, as she pressed the button for the elevator.

"I ain't got nothin' to say to you."

"It's a whole bunch I wanna say to you. I know I should've handled things different but I'm new to this love shit. Everything is new to me."

"Boo hoo. Poor you." Messiah rolled her eyes, as the elevator doors opened.

Shyhiem quickly followed behind her. Messiah inhaled deeply. He was getting on her nerves. This was not how she envisioned her day starting off. She didn't need Shyhiem getting in her head. Her defenses weren't strong enough to ward him off. Tuning him out, she pressed the 1st floor button. Seeing he was getting nowhere with her, Shyhiem hit the emergency stop button.

"What are you doing? Bird is downstairs waiting for me."

"I'll take you to work."

"I don't want you to do shit for me, besides leave me the hell alone."

Shyhiem wasn't willing to accept that. He'd be damned if he ever left her alone. That wasn't what either of them wanted and she knew it. Before she could restart the elevator, he palmed both sides of her face.

"Please, don't do this to me." He pleaded, on the edge of insanity.

"This isn't about you. It's about me. You hurt me! You lied to me!" Messiah hit him continually, as tears spilled from her eyes.

"I know, baby. I know." He tried to calm her down, while taking every hit. "Shhhhhhh... Shhh." He kissed her lips, lovingly, as his tears mixed with hers.

With each tear that fell, it felt like his life was slipping away.

"Don't leave me. I need more time."

"Shyhiem, just leave me alone, please." She squeezed her eyes tightly.

She couldn't bear to look at his face. Unwilling to let her go, he wrapped his arms around her and squeezed tightly. Messiah stood frozen. He felt the stiffness in her limbs and became sick to his stomach. The love she once had for him wasn't there. Shyhiem panicked.

"Messiah, please don't leave me. I love you."

"You gon' make me late for work, Shyhiem. I can't lose my job," she ignored his plea.

Shyhiem didn't move an inch. He didn't want to release her from his grasp. He knew once he did, he wouldn't be able to get her back. The selfish part of him wanted to kidnap her and make her go with him to his crib, but he couldn't keep her captive. It wasn't fair to her. She'd been through enough. Shyhiem wiped his eyes and stepped back. Messiah wiped her face and unstopped the elevator. An uncomfortable silence filled the tiny space, as they went down.

So many hidden emotions swarmed them. The doors couldn't open fast enough for Messiah. Once they did, she made a mad dash to Bird's car. Shyhiem was hot on her heels, but the twins were standing in the hallway with their book bags on, ready for school. Keesha was locking up to take them to the bus stop.

"Daddy!" Shania shrilled happily.

Shyhiem gazed at her, and then over at Messiah's back as she raced out the door. He wanted to continue to plead his case but he'd never pass up the opportunity to spend time with his kids. Keesha could tell some major shit had gone down between he and Messiah. Mayhem's little visit to her job must've done the trick. Pleased with the outcome, a sly smile graced the corners of her lips. Shyhiem's life was falling apart and she couldn't be happier.

"Rich nigga, poor nigga, house nigga, FIELD nigga; still nigga."– Jay Z, "The Story Of O.J"

24

Shyhiem

By the time Shyhiem showed up to work, it was almost 10:00am. He was beyond late. Shyhiem dragged his feet, walking in. He was in deep shit. There was no excuse for being this damn late. He could say he was physically ill - because he was. He'd fucked up a good thing with the love of his life. Messiah was heaven-sent from God. He'd let his foolish pride and ego get in the way of loving her without resentment. Instead of just leaving her alone until he was fully healed, he played with her heart. The sad part was he secretly enjoyed seeing her in limbo.

He'd been stuck in the same place for months. He thought he would feel better once he returned the favor. Messiah was the first woman, and probably the last, he'd ever love. His heart had been open from day one. He laid everything on the line for her and asked only for her love in return. He wined and dined her, took care of her emotional needs, held her when she cried, kissed her scars - both the physical and invisible ones. He'd done it all, only for his heart to be stomped on in the end.

He'd thought losing his mother had been tough to handle, but Messiah leaving him made him feel weak and insecure. It didn't make sense to him that the woman he'd lay down his life for could so easily walk away. Shyhiem was never the type to doubt himself. He was always confident in who he was as a man, but losing Messiah made him feel unworthy. From the start, he didn't think he was worthy enough of her. He was a black-ass nigga from the slums who'd grown up dirt poor. He'd barely graduated from high school. He didn't go to college or pick up a trade. All he knew how to do was survive to live another day. Messiah was beautiful, worldly, smart and classy. She wasn't like the hood bitches he was used to. To him, she was a real-life Disney princess.

Shyhiem was unlovable. Everyone he ever loved left him. Hell, his own father didn't love him enough to stick around. At first, he thought he was dumb to think a girl like Messiah would love him unconditionally, but she did. And being the spiteful nigga he was, he fucked it up. He was no longer the superhero he'd built himself up to be in her eyes. He'd toyed with her emotions 'cause he was emotionless.

Now, here he was, numb to the world. Keesha's words were stuck on repeat. She'd warned him that Messiah would see him for the spiteful, monster he was. He'd kept that side of him hidden until she broke his heart. After that, he never wanted to feel again. It was better to live life being emotionally unavailable. It was the only way to survive in a world that didn't love you back.

"What's up, Shyhiem?" A few of his coworkers spoke, as he headed to clock in.

Shyhiem gave them a quick head nod. He didn't want to draw too much attention to himself, in case Tom was somewhere snooping around. Shyhiem was just about to make it outside to his truck when Tom stopped him. Shyhiem stopped dead in his tracks and exhaled slowly. *Fuck,* he thought, turning around to face him.

"My office - now!" Tom ordered.

Shyhiem groaned and followed him back inside.

If Tom was about to lecture him, he could save it. He'd been told off enough in the last 24 hours. Shyhiem walked inside his junky office and closed the door behind him. It was a pigsty in there. Papers, empty soda cans and food containers were thrown everywhere. If that wasn't bad enough, it smelled like wet dog in there. Shyhiem breathed through his mouth, instead of his nose.

"Have a seat." Tom sat behind his desk.

"I'm good. I'll stand." Shyhiem refused to give him eye contact.

The sight of Tom disgusted him. He was a fat fuck with bad body odor.

"You know you're on your third strike, right?" Tom smirked, taking a bite out of a jelly donut.

The jelly inside squirted into his mouth and squished out into the corners of his lips. Tom didn't even bother wiping his mouth. Shyhiem was revolted.

"My bad for being late. It won't happen again." He tried to sound as sincere as possible.

"This is like what, your fourth or fifth time sayin' that?"

"I'm being honest. Today was the last time."

"Why should I believe you this time? Tell me why I shouldn't fire your sorry-ass."

It took everything in Shyhiem not to go off. Groveling wasn't his strong suit. Tom was trying his manhood by talking to him crazy, but he couldn't pop off. He had to keep his composure to keep his job.

"Like I said, I'm sorry for being late. I'm having some issues at home that's been getting the best of me. I know that probably don't mean shit," Shyhiem stopped himself. "I mean, much to you, but I really need this job.

I'm a good worker. I work my ass off around here and you know it. I'll do whatever you need me to. I'll work overtime. I'll stay late. I'll pick up extra shifts; just please, give me another chance. I need it. I can't lose this job."

Tom swiveled in his chair from left to right.

"I hear you. I feel you, homey." He mocked Shyhiem by talking black. "But I don't think this is a good fit for you. I know your kind likes being on color people time, but that don't work around here; ya feel me?"

Shyhiem furrowed his brows.

"You're fired."

"But what am I gonna tell my P.O.?"

"Tell her the truth. That you're another, entitled nigger that thinks the world owes you something 'cause you're black and grew up in the ghetto. Well, let me tell you something, boy. Ain't no reparations. You ain't getting no 40 acres or a mule. All you're getting is a one-way ticket to the welfare line. Now, turn in your badge and get the fuck out of my office."

Shyhiem's nostrils flared. All he saw was red, as he stormed over to Tom's desk and grabbed him by the collar of his shirt. With his fist balled, he reared his hand back, ready to punch him in the nose.

"Do it, monkey. I dare you." Tom egged him on.

He wanted Shyhiem to hit him so he could call the police. Shyhiem would end up right back in jail, where his black ass belonged. Coming to his senses, Shyhiem released Tom from his grasp and stepped back. His parole was ending in just a few weeks. He couldn't fuck up now.

Instead of spazzing out, he snatched the clip-on badge off, threw it onto his desk and stormed out.

"Better day than yesterday. I just take it day by day."– SZA, "Broken Clocks"

25

Messiah

It was Christmas day and Messiah was spending it alone. She lay on her couch, curled up in one of her mother's old, quilted blankets, watching A Christmas Story for what had to be the 50th time. The classic movie was her favorite Christmas movie of all-time. It reminded her of the close-knit bond she and her family had - once upon a time. She missed waking up on Christmas morning to her mother's homemade cinnamon buns and the sound of The Temptations' *Merry Christmas* playing throughout the house.

Since her father was Jewish, they celebrated Hanukkah as well. Her mother, nor her father, forced their religious beliefs upon her and Lake. They wanted them to choose which religion they wanted to practice. Messiah connected to both in different ways, but didn't devote herself to either religion. She missed going to church with her mom and listening to the all-black choir sing their hearts out. She also missed Shabbat dinner: the three-night, Jewish tradition where they ate challah bread and sipped wine, was a staple in their household.

She had the best of both worlds. Now, she had nothing. Her holiday tradition now consisted of eating a microwavable dinner and sleeping the day away. She and Lake usually texted each other *Merry Christmas*, but that was about it. Lake had her fiancé, so she had his family to spend the day with. Messiah thought she would've been spending the day with Shyhiem and the kids.

She planned on cooking a big breakfast, after opening presents. It sucked that she and Shyhiem weren't together because she missed him and the kids terribly. They filled the void of not having her own children to spoil. Bird had invited her over to her parents' house, but Messiah was too down in the dumps to go. She didn't want to be a party pooper and bring the festive mood down.

Messiah gazed over at the window. It had started to snow. Giddily, she ran over to see the snow flurries fall from the sky. She loved the snow. As a kid, she'd race outside in her snowsuit and make snow angels. Sometimes, Lake would join her. They'd laugh and throw snow balls at each other until their fingers were numb. She missed those sisterly bonding moments they once shared. She wished like hell, sometimes, they could get them back.

Quite some time passed by before Messiah left the window. She hadn't even noticed the black crow perched on top of the tree, watching her every move. Messiah reclaimed her spot on the couch and pulled the quilt over her legs. She was about to lay down and go back to sleep when a text message came through her phone. Messiah snatched up her phone, quickly. Not having any communication with the outside world on Christmas was a lonely feeling. Messiah looked down at her screen. Tears welled in her eyes, when she saw Shyhiem's name appear.

Since she refused to see him, he made it his business to send her postcards in the mail every day, like she'd done for him. Messiah stuffed them inside a kitchen drawer and acted like his words of love didn't matter, but they meant more to her than he would ever know. Shyhiem wasn't expressive with his feelings, so for him to send her postcards was a huge deal. Some of them read:

The first time I saw you, my heart whispered, "That's the one."

When I tell you I love you, I don't say it out of habit or to make conversation. I say it to remind you that you are the best thing that ever happened to me.

I want to wake up at 2am, rollover, see your face, and know that I'm right where I'm supposed to be.

The fact that he was texting her must've meant he'd opened the gift she'd left for him under the tree. She'd gotten them both one-way tickets to California that could be used in January, on the last day of his parole. It was her way of letting him know she was all-in. After learning he'd cheated on her, moving away with him was nowhere on her radar. That didn't stop her from reading his text.

Shyhiem: I pray we'll get to use these.

Messiah thought about responding back but her pride wouldn't let her. She wasn't ready to forgive him. It wasn't possible that she could. He'd misused her trust. It was over for she and Shyhiem. No amount of beautifully, handwritten postcards would change that, but her fingers still hovered over the keyboard anyway. Just as she was about to type back, there was a knock at the door. Messiah's heart skipped a beat. She would surely shit a brick if it was Shyhiem on the other side. She wasn't prepared for an unexpected visit from him. Messiah fretfully removed the blanket and walked over to the door.

"Who is it?" She asked, biting her bottom lip.

"Merry Christmas, beautiful." Bryson said cheerfully.

Messiah's face instantly dropped. Bryson was the last person she expected to visit her.

"Go away," she groaned.

"It's Christmas, Messiah. For God sake, stop being mean and open the door."

Messiah rolled her eyes and removed the chain.

"Why are you here?" She asked, with an attitude.

"I brought you breakfast." He held up a bag of bagels and cream cheese. "I also got your favorite coffee. Cream and two sugars, just how you like it." He smiled.

Messiah's stomach started to growl. The smell of the warm bagels made her mouth water.

"Come in but don't get too comfortable. Yo' ass ain't stayin' long."

"Merry Christmas to you too," he grinned.

"Whatever, just give me the food. I'm starving." She snatched the bag from his hand.

Bryson watched as her ass jiggled when she walked.

"You can stop lookin' at my ass, pervert." She hissed, making her way to the kitchen island.

"Hey, I wouldn't be a man if I didn't." He took off his coat and hung it on the back of the chair.

Messiah rolled her eyes and opened the bag. On top of the bagels was another brown bag. Perplexed, she took it out and opened it up as well. Two stacks of one hundred-dollar bills were inside.

"What is this?" She pulled out the stack of cash, which added up to be two grand.

"It's your Christmas present from me. I know it's not as much as what I owe, but it's a start at paying my debt off to you."

Messiah was at a loss for words.

"Thank you, Bryson." She held the money up to her chest. "You have no idea how much this means to me. This is gonna help me out tremendously."

"No, thank you."

Not wanting to become emotional, Messiah sat the money down and dug into the bag for a bagel.

"Why aren't you at your parents' house?" She asked.

"You mean, why ain't I at my ugly-ass mama house," he laughed.

"Yeah, that too," Messiah giggled.

"Dinner don't start until two."

"Yo' mama still make that watered-down macaroni and cheese?"

"You always said you liked my mama macaroni and cheese." He noted, making himself comfortable at the kitchen island.

"Yeah, well, I lied. That shit is nasty as hell."
"I ain't gon' lie, it ain't that good."

"See, even you know yo' mama can't cook for shit." Messiah smeared honey-flavored cream cheese on a cinnamon-crusted bagel.

"I ain't gon' say all that. She gets some things right."

"That's a lie; but umm… thanks for the yummy bagels. You can leave now." She shooed him away with her hand.

"Damn, you gon' do me like that?" Bryson grinned.

"Absolutely; we ain't cool."

"You know, I took a chance on coming by here today. I just knew you were gonna be gone."

"You thought I would be with Shyhiem?"

"Yeah, that's yo' boo thang, right?" He teased.

"Nope." Messiah rolled up the paper bag.

"I thought y'all were back together."

"We were. Now we ain't." She sat back down on the couch.

"Sorry to hear that." Bryson tried to seem empathetic.

Secretly, he was overjoyed that Shyhiem was out of the picture. It gave him a chance to move in.

"No, you're not."

"You know me so well," Bryson chuckled. "What happened? I mean, if you don't mind me asking."

"I do, but if you must know, it turns out he's no different than you. He cheated on me too."

"Whoa… can't say I didn't see that coming. The nigga is trash. He's a street thug. You can do better."

"You don't know anything about him, so hush." Messiah rolled her eyes.

"My bad. I apologize." He surrendered, holding up his hands.

"It just blows 'cause now I have to go to my sister's rehearsal dinner alone. I don't wanna be around her Ivy League, Rich Kids of Beverly Hills friends."

"You'll be a'ight." Bryson assured.

"No, I won't. You know them heffas don't like me."

"I'll go with you… if you want."

Messiah contemplated his offer. Having Bryson attend the dinner with her was like signing a deal with the devil. Nothing good ever came from being around him. Yet, the thought of sticking out like a sour thumb without having any allies around Lake and her crew wasn't a risk she was willing to take.

"Ok… you can go."

"That don't check the box of what I thought. That don't check the box of somebody who wasn't shit."– Jay Z, "Footnotes of 'Adnis'"

26

Shyhiem

The twins held onto their father's hands tightly. They were amazed by the big house and glamourous cars in the driveway. Shyhiem told them they were going to meet someone special, before heading to his house to open presents. Keesha only allowed him to have them for a few hours. He'd asked that they spend Christmas night with him, since she had them Christmas Eve, but the evil bitch said no. Keesha was pushing him to the edge. Keeping him away from his kids was the harshest form of punishment anyone could receive.

Keesha knew just how to get under his skin. He hated her for keeping him and the twins apart. The distance was not only affecting him but them as well. Shania had started to wet the bed again, and Sonny had become damn near mute. Shyhiem hated seeing his kids that way. They needed him now, more than ever, and there was nothing he could do about it. Being an unemployed, ex-convict wouldn't help his case in court, if he tried for full custody. That's why he needed his father's help.

Once again, he found himself at Ricky's doorstep. He didn't want to spend the little time he had with the kids begging his father for help, but he had no choice. He had to find steady employment before his next parole visit. Plus, the twins needed to meet their grandfather before he passed away. Shyhiem might've had his issue with him, but that had nothing to do with Shania and Sonny creating memories with their grandfather.

"Shyhiem, come on in." Gloria ushered him inside with a huge smile.

Shyhiem looked at Gloria, awkwardly. The last time he was there, she treated him like yesterday's trash and threatened to spray him with mace. At least this time she knew his name.

"Can I take your coat, sir?"

"Uh, yeah, sure." Shyhiem hesitantly handed it to her.

"Daddy, where are we?" Shania looked around wide-eyed, as Gloria took their coats too.

"We're at Uncle Mayhem's dad's house." He explained, as Mayhem turned the corner, stuffing his face.

He had a full plate of greens, dressing, sweet potatoes, ham and cornbread on his plate. The food looked delicious but Shyhiem wasn't there to eat. Mayhem paused eating and stared at Shyhiem. He had no idea he would be stopping by. Shyhiem had never come to Christmas dinner before. Mayhem wondered if he was there to confront him about running up on Messiah.

"Merry Christmas, li'l bro." He approached him, watchfully.

Shyhiem was known to punch first and ask questions later.

"I'm surprised to see you here."

Shyhiem held out his hand for a shake. Mayhem gave him a pound and let out a sigh of relief. It was apparent Messiah hadn't ratted him out like she said she would.

"Where yo' mama at?"

"In the dining room with the rest of the fam. You wanna go say hi?"

"Nah, I'm good." Shyhiem shook his head.

"Y'all hungry?" Mayhem looked down at the kids.

"Yeah." Shania spoke up, before Shyhiem could say no.

Mayhem laughed.

"You hungry too, li'l man?" He asked.

Sonny shook his head no and clung to his father's leg.

"We ain't staying long. I just stopped by to see Ricky."

"He's in his room. C'mon." Mayhem led them upstairs.

Ricky lay in his bed under the cover with the television on. He was far worse off than he was the last time Shyhiem saw him. He was hooked up to a breathing machine and an IV. He'd lost more weight. The skin on his face was sunken in. This wasn't how Shyhiem wanted the twins to see him, but it was too late. Shyhiem felt bad that he had to spend Christmas on his deathbed.

"Pop, you awake?" Mayhem asked.

"Yeah, son." Ricky spoke hoarsely.

He was losing his voice, just like he was losing his life. Even though his days were numbered, Ricky's eyes lit up when he saw Shyhiem.

"Uncle Mayhem, this yo' daddy?" Shania looked up at her uncle.

"Yeah."

"He's my daddy too." Shyhiem brought the kids closer to Ricky's bed.

"I though you said we ain't have no granddaddy?"

"Daddy made a mistake." Shyhiem admitted, afraid to get too close to Ricky.

Hesitation was written all over his face. Ricky couldn't ignore it.

"I didn't take you for the scared type." He tried to make light of the situation.

"Never that, old man." Shyhiem smiled, slightly, as he came closer to the bed.

"Who are these little people?"

"Shania and Sonny, I want you to meet your grandpa, Ricky."

"Hi." They both waved, timidly.

"So, God really does answer prayers." Ricky winked his eye at Shyheim. "I've been praying a long time that I'd get to meet you two." He looked at the twins, adoringly.

"You did good, son."

Normally, Shyhiem would take offense to Ricky calling him that, but with the circumstances at hand, it didn't matter. He was his son, whether he liked it or not.

"Thank you."

"Daddy, I'm hungry." Shania tugged on his shirt sleeve.

"I got you, baby girl." Mayhem took her by the hand.

Being that close to his daughter and she not know he was her father was a hard pill to swallow. There were many occasions where Mayhem wanted to come clean, but he kept his mouth shut out of his own, selfish need. He loved Sonny and Shania. They were his flesh and blood; but being a full-time parent didn't work with his lifestyle. He didn't want to interrupt his life. Shyhiem was the only father they knew. It would fuck up their little world if the truth came out. With all the enemies he'd acquired over the years, he didn't want to put their lives in jeopardy. The twins were better off under Shyhiem's care, as they had been. Keesha was a bad enough parent. Add him to the equation and all hell would break loose.

"Pop, I wanna stay with you." Sonny said to his father, softly.

"Go downstairs with your uncle for me. I need to talk to your grandpa."

"Ok." Sonny responded sadly.

Lately, whenever he was around Shyhiem, he clung to him for dear life.

"I'll be down in a minute," Shyhiem guaranteed. "Get you some food but don't eat it all up. Save Daddy some, ok?"

"Alright." Sonny replied weakly.

The sadness in Sonny's eyes killed Shyhiem. He'd do anything to take all the gloom that consumed him away. When they were alone, Shyhiem pulled a chair up to the side of his father's bed.

211

"What you need?" Ricky asked.

He wasn't fool enough to think Shyhiem only came by to wish him a Merry Christmas.

"Is it that obvious? You must think I ain't shit, huh? Only time I come around is when I need something."

"I can't blame you. It's a lot of stuff you don't know. If you did, things between you and I would be much different."

"And what exactly is that?" Shyhiem leaned his elbows on his knees.

"I know this is gonna be hard for you to believe, but I always wanted to be in your life." Ricky cut right to the chase.

"You had a shitty way of showing it."

"You're not gonna like what I'm about to say, but the reason I was never around is because your mother made it that way."

"I understand you're sick and everything... I feel bad for you, I do, but you not gon' lie on my mother. You're not gonna tarnish her name."

"Shyhiem, your mother was a good woman, but she wasn't perfect."

"This wasn't a good idea. I should go. I can figure this shit out on my own." He rose to his feet.

"Shyhiem, please listen. I don't have much time," Ricky begged.

Shyhiem sat back down with an attitude.

"Say what you got to say, man."

"When your mother and I met, we were young. Carol and I had already been together since high school. She was my high school sweetheart; but like all couples, we had our fair share of problems. Whenever we would get into it, I'd get mad and go to your mother."

"So, you're tryin' to tell me my mama was your side chick?"

"I hate to say it, but yes."

"Your mother loved me and I had love for her too, but Carol was always the girl for me. I played with your mother's heart, I did. I used her when it benefited me. But when she became pregnant with you, I was all in. I made it clear to her that I wanted to be a part of your life. Carol wasn't happy with it because she was pregnant with your brother too, but I swore that I would always be there for my kids. I made a lot of mistakes growing up, but you weren't one of them."

"If you wanted to be there, then why weren't you?"

"Your mother wouldn't let me. She wanted us to be a family, and when I chose to stay with Carol, she didn't like it. She got mad and kept you away from me. Since I didn't want her, she took away the one thing she knew would hurt me, which was you."

"Bullshit, I don't believe that. We could barely keep the lights on. If you wanted to be there, then why didn't you at least help out financially?" Shyhiem argued.

"I did."

"When? 'Cause I clearly remember having to heat water up on the stove 'cause the gas was off, or eating Ramen noodles for breakfast, lunch and dinner 'cause it was cheap. Muthafuckas made fun of me every day 'cause I

213

ain't have shit. I wore the same raggedy-ass clothes and shoes for years. Why you think I hit the block at 13? I got tired of fuckin' struggling. I got tired of seeing my mother cry all the time."

"Shyhiem, I gave your mother money every month for you," Ricky stated, calmly.

"Now I know you lyin'."

"I deposited $1500 every month in a bank account I had set up for you. You didn't know that?"

"No, 'cause it doesn't exist."

"Open that drawer and get that black folder out for me," Ricky pointed.

Shyhiem did as he was told and pulled out a black folder with his name on it. Inside, was a stack of deposit records. Sure enough, every month, for the last 27 years, his father had deposited $1500 into a savings account for him. The total added up to be $486,000.

"I thought your mother told you about it. I figured you just didn't want it. Shyhiem, it killed me not being able to see you. I hated that your mother kept me away from you because she and I had problems. I never wanted you to feel like I didn't love you 'cause I did. I do. You're my son. You're an extension of me. I would go to the end of the earth for you."

Shyhiem was blown away. Everything he knew to be true was now a lie. His whole world had been turned upside down. His mother had chosen poverty because her ego was shattered. He couldn't believe it. They never had to struggle. His life could've been so different if he'd known the truth. He'd spent his entire life hating his father for no reason, and it was all his mother's fault. She'd made him look at Ricky like a monster. The hate he had for him was a catalyst for the majority of the decisions he made - bad or good.

"I don't know what to say." Shyhiem sat back, bewildered.

"Just say you'll give me a chance. I don't have much time left, but the little time I do have, I want to spend with you."

"I'd like that," Shyhiem admitted. "There's so much about you I don't know."

"Where do you wanna start?" Ricky smiled.

This was the happiest he'd been in months.

"Ummm…what's your favorite color?"

"Green," Ricky laughed.

"That figures," Shyhiem laughed. "LeBron or Curry?"

Ricky's answer would make or break their relationship.

"Neither; MJ."

"Aww… you trippin'," Shyhiem waved him off.

For hours, he and his father sat and talked. Shyhiem even joined the rest of the family for dinner. It wasn't how he envisioned his day going, but it turned out to be one of the best days of his life. Shyhiem couldn't get over the fact that his mother had lied to him for years. He'd always thought of his mom as an angel. In his eyes, she could do no wrong. Now, he realized that she was just as flawed as everyone else. He wanted to hate her for what she'd done but she was dead and gone. Living with hatred would only affect him. Shyhiem had enough shit to be sad about. Instead of being mad, he decided to devote his time to getting to know his father. He was grateful to God that he'd learned the truth before it was too late.

"You can't make me love you if I don't."– H.E.R., "I Won't"

27

Messiah

Lake's rehearsal dinner was so extravagant, Messiah didn't know what to expect for the reception. She'd spent a fortune on it. Austin allowed her to spare no expense. The event was being held at a winery inside the wine barrel room. A long, rectangular-shaped table, which seated 40 people, sat in the center of the space. A white table cloth, Hermès tableware, red rose petals and a single candelabra decorated the table. The lights were dimmed low. On each wine barrel was a tea-light. Light from the individually-placed tea-lights on each wine barrel gave the room a soft, amber glow.

All of Lake and Austin's closest friends and family were there. Messiah and Bryson made their way over to Lake to say hi. She was in her element. Lake stood in the center of a small crowd, captivating them with her timeless good looks. Like always, she was dressed to impress. Messiah didn't admire much about her sister, but the bitch knew how to put a look together flawlessly.

Lake had the finest taste in everything she did. The white, Elie Saab, spring 2017, couture dress she wore was completely sheer and showcased her delectable, honey-colored skin. A rainfall of crystals began a little past her shoulders and cascaded over her breasts and trickled down to the hem of the dress. A pair of flesh tone panties covered her lady bits, but everything else was on full display to see, except her nipples. The dress was classy with a hint of sex appeal. It reminded Messiah of something Grace Kelly would've worn, if she was at the height of her success in 2016.

The dress was perfect. Lake was the bell of the ball and she wouldn't have it any other way. She was glowing. Messiah loved seeing her sister so happy. It was a rarity to witness. Lake kept her feelings close to her chest 'cause she was always playing a game of chess with everyone around her. That night, her usually high guard was anchored low. She smiled brightly. Messiah figured she was on cloud nine because she was hours away from being the wife to a multi-millionaire. Lake's dream of landing and bagging a baller was coming true. It was all she'd ever wanted. At one point, Messiah was jealous of her sister's good fortune. She'd gotten engaged before her and Lake still beat her to the alter. Messiah quickly learned there was no competing with Lake. She would always lose.

Lake spotted her baby sister out of the corner of her eye and prayed to God she didn't show up lookin' like Janis Joplin. Messiah had a strange sense of fashion that she did not understand. Lake was a classic beauty with a sophisticated edge. Messiah was a wild child and her sense of style represented that. Lake didn't know what to expect from her, but for the first time in ages, she wasn't embarrassed by her appearance.

She didn't look like an old negro spiritual, but she did look like Rainbow Brite. She wore her hair down in an abundance of loose, wavy curls. A soft, natural beat adorned her face. Her after-five attire consisted of a purple, green, and mustard yellow, satin, bomber jacket and a spaghetti-strapped, pink and gold-striped gown that pleated at the skirt. The outfit wasn't something she would've worn, personally, but Messiah looked beautiful. For once, Lake wouldn't be embarrassed to call her *sister*. Now, what she did have a problem with was her plus-one.

"Well, look what the cat drug in." She greeted Messiah with an air-kiss to the cheek. "You're late."

"Traffic was backed up. Wasn't it, Bryson?" Messiah looked to him for confirmation.

"Yeah, it was. How you doing, Lake? Congratulations." He spoke politely.

Lake ignored him and focused her attention on Messiah.

"Why did you bring this parasite with you? You know damn well I don't like him." She asked, with a plastered on, fake smile.

"I didn't wanna come by myself and Bird would rather slit her wrist than be around you."

"Ditto. Well, since you're both here, let's make the best of it." Lake snarled at Bryson. "Let me introduce you to everyone."

"Lake, who is this beautiful young lady?" Tyler, Austin's best man asked.

"I'm so glad you asked." She escorted Messiah over to him.

"Tyler, this is my baby sister, Messiah. Isn't she gorgeous? I mean, besides the fact that she's dressed like Willy Wonka; she's pretty, right?"

"She is." Tyler liked what he saw.

"She's a ballerina, which means she's very flexible. If you know what I mean." Lake winked her eye twice.

Messiah's face turned beet red; she was so mortified. Bryson was infuriated. He couldn't believe that Lake had the audacity to try and hook Messiah up with another man in front of his face.

"It's a pleasure to meet you, Messiah." Tyler kissed the outside of her hand.

Messiah gave him the once-over. He had skin the color of a brown paper bag, was 6'1 in height and had an athletic build. He was an attractive man but he wasn't her type. There was only one man that made her salivate at the tongue.

"Messiah, Tyler is an accountant. He's single, with no kids and has several homes."

"Keep it up and you're gonna make a black man blush," Tyler grinned.

"No blushing necessary. She's here with me." Bryson jumped in.

Lake dropped her head back, exasperated.

"Oh God. Just die, Satan, die!" She rolled her eyes.

"I have to say, my sister is absolutely glowing. Marriage looks good on her. I've never seen her smile this much." Messiah quickly changed the subject.

"Austin makes me smile every day," Lake gushed, linking her arm with his.

"You hate smiling." Messiah pointed out.

"I mean, I still don't smile at strangers. I can't use all the collagen I have left in my face." Lake flipped her hair.

"I've been thinking, you guys," Lake's best friend, Kat, spoke up. "We need to start planning our summer trip."

"Ooooooh... we should," Lake agreed.

"I just got back from yachting in the South of France and Italy for like three weeks. It was cute." Her bridesmaid, Cristin, said.

"That might be an option." Austin nodded his head.

"Or we could like, go to Greece or Ibiza," Kat replied cheerfully.

"I'm going to Greece, Wednesday." Tyler announced.

"You didn't tell me that." Lake said surprised.

"It was a last-minute trip," Tyler clarified. "Since my homeboy here is leaving town for y'all honeymoon, I decided to take me a trip too."

"Cute." Lake took a sip of champagne.

"I've always heard Cabo is fun," Bryson interjected, trying to fit in.

"Eww… who are you?" Kat pretended to gag.

"We do not do Cabo, darling. That is so pedestrian," Lake laughed.

"I say we just charter a yacht somewhere." Cristin downed the rest of her drink.

"Can't do it." Lake shook her head. "One of my spiritual advisors told me that I was a passenger on the Titanic. Unfortunately, I didn't survive the voyage. There will be no yachts or boats for me."

"Messiah, where do you vacation?" Tyler died to know.

"Ummm," she said, feeling suffocated.

She'd stayed out of the conversation on purpose. She didn't want them to know that she didn't have a pot to piss in or a nickel to rub together.

"My sister is a workaholic." Lake jumped in and saved her. "She doesn't do much for fun."

"That's no way to live. A pretty girl like you should always have her feet up. You should let me take you out sometime." Tyler smiled confidently.

"Didn't I tell you she was with me?" Bryson shot, feeling disrespected.

"Bryson, how is Kenya?" Lake quizzed, cocking her head to the side.

"How has she been? I haven't seen her in a while." Kat asked.

"You guys remember my line sister, Kenya, don't you?" Lake asked everyone.

They all nodded.

"Tragic thing happened. She had a miscarriage recently. Poor thing. Bryson was the father. She's torn up about it, as any woman would be; but, Bryson, you seem to be doing quite well."

Bryson boiled over with anger. Lake always made it her business to embarrass him.

"I think we're gonna go get a drink." Messiah pulled him away from the crowd, before things escalated.

"If I wasn't a fuckin' man. I would—"

"But you are, so chill," Messiah handed him a glass of champagne.

"Where the fuck does she get off embarrassing me like that?" Bryson fumed.

"I mean, to keep it 100, what are you doing when it comes to ole girl? Have you even checked on her?"

"Of course I have. I just told her that I needed a minute to sort through some things."

"I hope not anything involving me. I've told you before, that door is closed."

"But it doesn't have to be. We can work through the pain. Hell, Jay Z and Beyoncé did."

"Jay Z didn't get another girl pregnant; and, nigga, don't ever compare yourself to Jay Z. You ain't got Jay Z money." Messiah checked him.

"I'm just sayin', Messiah, give me another chance to prove to you that I've changed. I wouldn't be here right now, if you didn't have some kind of feelings for me."

Messiah saw the eagerness in his eyes. He wanted her to agree with him so badly, it was almost pathetic.

"Baby, I love you. I've loved you since I was 16. I know I hurt you, but I swear I will never do it again." He hugged her close.

Messiah couldn't even release herself from his grasp before she was yanked by the arm. Caught off guard by the forceful pull, she almost lost her balance, until she fell into Shyhiem's strong arms.

"C'mon." He ordered, not taking no for an answer.

Surprised that he was there, Messiah tried to collect her thoughts. Shyhiem looked like an angel sent down from heaven. He never looked so good in his life. His deep brown skin was poppin'. His hair and beard were freshly cut and trimmed. A pair of aviator shades shielded his eyes. He donned a camel-colored, cashmere, trench coat, crisp, white button-up, light denim, fitted jeans and gray, YSL Chelsea boots. The man looked like he jumped out of a GQ magazine. He took her breath away; but that didn't mean he could come uninvited and boss her around.

"I'm not going anywhere with you." She pulled her arm away.

"You heard the lady. Let her go." Bryson stepped up.

"You betta tell yo' friend to fall back," Shyhiem warned, taking off his shades.

Messiah knew he wasn't playing. She didn't want to cause a scene at her sister's rehearsal dinner. Lake would have her head on a spike.

"Bryson, I got this," she said, before pulling Shyhiem to the side.

People were starting to stare.

"What are you doing here? You're embarrassing me." She asked in a hushed tone.

"I came to take you home with me - where you belong. I'm done with all this back and forth bullshit. I'm sorry for what I did; and if I could take it back, I would, but I can't. So please," He got down on one knee. "Do me the honor of being my wife, so I can spend the rest of my life making it up to you?" He pulled out the engagement ring she'd so desperately wanted to see.

Messiah's chest heaved up and down, as the ring sparkled under the candlelight. This wasn't how she ever imagined the moment would be, but because it was Shyhiem, she wouldn't have it any other way. She tried to hate him. He'd done things to her she would never forget. Shyhiem was as imperfect as a man could get. His flaws were more than a handful. The fact that he'd cheated would never be forgotten. With all those things against him, she should say no. It was the most logical thing to do.

But when it came to Shyhiem, logic went out the window. She'd searched her whole life for him. With him, there was no consequence or doubt. The road ahead of them may be rocky. He could break her heart again, but Messiah wouldn't know unless they took the first step together.

"Yes." She held out her shaky hand.

Shyhiem placed the ring on her ring finger and then stood up. Messiah lovingly wrapped her arms around his neck and kissed him, passionately, on the lips.

"Umm... I don't know what kind of Love & Hip Hop shit y'all got going on over here, but y'all gotta chill," Lake informed.

"I'm sorry, Lake, but look," Messiah gushed, showing off her ring.

"Congratulations; but who is this? And why did he just pop the question to you at *my* wedding rehearsal dinner? Have all y'all lost y'all damn minds? That is so fuckin' tacky."

"This is Shyhiem, the guy I was tellin' you about." Messiah smiled with glee.

She was the happiest woman on earth.

"You mean, the UPS driver?" Lake curled her upper lip.

"Former UPS driver. I'm now in the real estate business. You may have heard of my father, Ricky Simmons," Shyhiem bragged.

He had to let Lake know that he was on the same playing field as her.

"I have." Lake arched her brow. "Impressive. You might not be so dumb after all, baby sis."

"Did you really just say yes to this clown?" Bryson stormed over.

"You need to calm down." Messiah urged.

"Nah, fuck that! This nigga is a clown! He doesn't deserve you!"

"And let me guess, you do?" She quizzed.

"Look, this is cute; and believe me, any other day, I would sit back and watch with a bowl of popcorn, but I'ma need you to take this ratchet shit elsewhere," Lake demanded. "Y'all are starting to scare my white in-laws."

"You let this fake-ass jailbird propose to you after he cheated on you? What the fuck are you thinkin'? I'm starting to think you might be as dumb as Lake said you are!" Bryson exclaimed.

Before Bryson could get in another word edgewise, Shyhiem reared his fist back and punched him in the mouth. He hit him so hard, he knocked his front tooth out. Bryson tried to fight back but it was futile. He was no match for Shyhiem. He'd hit Bryson several times, and all Bryson had got in was one jab to the jaw. Messiah and Lake screamed for them to stop, but neither man was willing to backdown. Austin tried to step in to break it up, but as he pulled Shyhiem off Bryson, Shyhiem clocked him in the nose too. Blood instantly spewed down his face.

"MY NOSE!" He yelled, holding his face.

"OH, HELL NO! Y'all muthafuckas got to go!" Lake's ghetto side came out in full effect. "Baby, are you ok?" She examined Austin's bloody nose.

"I think I'm gonna need surgery. Am I hemorrhaging?" Austin cried, as he looked down at all the blood. "Holy shit." He closed his eyes and fainted.

"Oh my God! Somebody call 911!" Lake screamed. "Baby, it's gonna be alright! Don't go towards the light!"

Austin's eyes flickered open.

"Oh, thank God," Lake exhaled.

"Shyhiem, stop, please!" Messiah pleaded.

Hearing her cries brought Shyhiem back to reality. Huffing and puffing, he let Bryson go and fixed his clothes. He'd fucked up again, but he couldn't let Bryson's punk-ass get away with talking to her that way. Their engagement was probably over before it had even begun.

"Messiah, I'm sorry," He instantly apologized.

"It's ok. I'm not mad."

"You should be! Look at his face!" Lake shrilled, pointing back at her fiancé.

"It's just a bloody nose, Lake. Calm down," Messiah urged.

"Calm down? Calm down?" Lake said, appalled by her choice of words. "Bitch, tomorrow is my wedding day!

Look at my fiancé's fuckin' face! None of this would've happened if you wouldn't have invited Booker T and 'Stone Cold' Steve Austin! This is all your fault!"

"My fault?" Messiah placed her hand on her chest.

"Did I stutter? Hell, yeah, it's your fault. You done brought the whole East Side to my fuckin' wedding rehearsal!"

"You're right, I'm sorry," Messiah sincerely apologized.

She was completely in the wrong. There was no if, ands or buts about it.

"C'mon, Shyhiem, let's go."

"C'mon, Shyhiem? You really about to leave with this nigga? Look at what the fuck he did to my face! My fuckin' tooth is missing!" Bryson followed them outside.

"Messiah!!! I know you hear me! He's a fuckin' criminal!"

"You ain't had enough yet?" Shyhiem went to charge at him again.

"Shyhiem, stop. Just give me a second," Messiah held him back.

"You got two minutes." He said, done with the bullshit.

"What the hell is your problem?" Messiah pushed Bryson in the chest.

For the first time since the brawl was over, she got a good look at all the damage Shyhiem had done. There were three knots on Bryson's forehead and his right eye was slowly starting to close.

"You're makin' a big mistake, Messiah. I'm tellin' you." He shot, holding his eye.

"And if I am, it's my mistake to make! You don't get to tell me what I should and shouldn't do with my life!"

"How could you say yes to him? You were just crying over this muthafucka a week ago."

"First of all, I wasn't cryin'." Messiah rolled her neck.

"It doesn't matter. He doesn't deserve you! He doesn't even treat you right!"

"And you do? Bitch, do you have amnesia? Shyhiem might not have a college degree, and we might fight all the time, but time stands still when I'm with him. I love that man and I would follow him to the ends of the earth, if need be."

"Messiah, please don't—"

"Listen." She cut him off. "He may not be right, but he's just right for me. I'm not about to keep going back and forth with you on who I choose to spend the rest of my life with. It's none of your fuckin' business. You and I are over. Go back to Philly and leave me the fuck alone."

"That's really how you feel?"

"Yes!"

"Ok," Bryson shrugged. "It's your funeral, but tell your fiancé this ain't over," he threatened.

"Whatever," Messiah waved him off and went back over to Shyhiem. "Baby, are you ok?" She examined him closely.

"That fuckboy can't even fight. He was doing the windmill. Ain't no scratch on me." He grabbed a handful of her ass and kissed her roughly. "You read to go, wifey?"

"Yes." She smiled, loving the sound of her soon-to-be name.

"A'ight, let's go."

"Shit, I left my coat inside. I'll be right back." She raced back in the building.

Messiah looked around for the coat girl but she wasn't at her station. With no time to waste, she unlatched the door and walked inside. As she rummaged through the racks of coats, she couldn't help but overhear muffled voices close by. Curious to who it was, she quietly tiptoed towards the sound. What Messiah saw next, shocked her to the point that she almost let out a squeal. Pressed against the racks of coats was Austin and Tyler. Tyler wiped Austin's bloody nose and then placed a tender kiss on his lips.

"Why didn't you help me?" Austin whined.

"I ain't want my face t get messed up too," Tyler admitted. "Tomorrow is gonna be hard enough. What's the point of adding a black eye on top of that too?"

"Yeah, you ain't tell me you were going out of town either."

"I don't wanna be here all alone while you honeymoon in Monaco with her," Tyler rolled his eyes.

Messiah left her coat behind and ran out of the room. She knew Lake was mad at her, but she had to tell her what she'd seen.

"Lake! Come here, I need to talk to you." She yelled across the room.

"I thought I told you to leave." Lake furiously walked over to her. "Haven't you embarrassed me enough?"

"I'm gonna go. There's something I have to tell you first."

"Whatever it is, it can wait." Lake tried to walk away.

"No, Lake, you gotta hear me out." Messiah stopped her from leaving and pulled her over to the side.

"What is it, Messiah?" Lake slapped her hand against her thigh, infuriated.

Messiah held her by each of her arms.

"You can't go through with this wedding." She said out of breath.

"Bitch, whet?" Lake drew her head back.

"Oh my God." Messiah said, becoming dizzy. "Ummm... I don't even know how to tell you this." Her hands shook.

"Fuckin' spit it out already, Messiah! I ain't got all damn day. My white in-laws probably think I'm one of y'all."

"I just saw Tyler kissing—"

"I don't give a fuck about Tyler kissing no damn body! Is that really what you dragged me over here for?"

"He was kissing Austin."

Lake paused and looked at her.

"Really, Messiah?" She looked at her like she was insane. "You really expect for me to believe that?"

"Yes."

"Let me get this straight; not only do you ruin my wedding rehearsal, but now you gon' sit up here and lie in my face? That accident must've fucked you up more than I thought."

"I swear to God I'm telling you the truth. I would never lie to you about something like that."

"You are fuckin' crazy. You're delusional. You are so fuckin' jealous of me it's not even funny. Haven't you ruined my life enough? You took Mama and Daddy away from me, now you're tryin' to ruin the one piece of happiness I got." Hot tears filled Lake's eyes.

"Is that really how you feel?" Messiah swallowed back the tears in her throat.

"Yes, it is," Lake lied.

She was hurt and was lashing out, as always.

"I don't know why Mama and Daddy even had you. You were a fuckin' mistake. All you do is ruin everything around you. You would've been better off swallowed," Lake spat.

Messiah inhaled deeply. That was it. That was the last straw. She and Lake had verbally sparred more than once; but this time, she'd taken it too far.

"Fuck you, Lake." She said after a pause. "I swear to God you bet not call me, when this shit blows up in your face." Messiah mushed her in the forehead before walking off.

"Yeah, that's right! You betta leave!" Lake tried to save face. "And I told you not to come smelling like mothballs but you did anyway!"

"Couldn't we be happily ever After?"–
Case, "Happily Ever After"

28
Lake

The Romona Keveža, blush & French violet, printed, silk organza, ball gown with a draped, one-shoulder bodice fit Lake's body like a glove. A vibrant mix of pink, garden roses, ivory mums and dramatic, wine-colored dahlias rested in her French-manicured hands. A cathedral veil hung from the back of her head. Lake examined herself in the mirror. It was almost time for her to walk down the aisle. Nervous butterflies danced in the pit of her stomach, making her sick.

Since she was a little girl, she'd fantasized about wearing a wedding dress. She and Messiah would play dress-up. She'd be the bride and Messiah would be the flower girl. Now, she didn't have to pretend anymore. The day was finally here. She'd made Messiah believe that she was only marrying Austin for money, but secretly, a small part of her loved him. Was she head-over-heels in love; no, but love was there.

Every woman on the planet wanted him, but she'd been the one to claim him as her own. Their faces would be plastered all over every major blog by the end of the week. People magazine had bought the exclusive rights to their wedding photos for a million dollars. They'd lied and told the journalist that the proceeds would go to their favorite charity, but really, Lake was keeping every, red cent for herself. It was a part of her prenuptial agreement. She'd get the money after a full year of marriage. If Austin ever cheated, she'd get that, as well as another three million for pain and suffering.

She prayed to God that day would never happen. She'd been hurt before. It was one of the reasons she never showed her true colors. Lake had given Austin just enough of her to get this far. It would be years before she fully gave herself to him. In the meantime, she asked God to bless her with a marriage as great as her parents'. They'd literally loved each other – literally - till the day they died. She wanted that kind of unbreakable love for herself and was hopeful she'd have it.

"You ready?" Kat asked, admiring her through the full-length mirror.

"No. Not yet. Not until my sister gets here." Lake tried to calm her nerves.

"After what happened last night... she might not come."

"She'll be here." Lake tried to convince herself.

"But, sweetie, we have to go," Kat insisted. "We've waited long enough."

Lake looked over at her sister's bouquet. It was the only one left. Her heart broke that she wasn't there. Getting married without her there by her side wasn't in her vision. She and Messiah weren't particularly close, but she loved her sister. They were all each other had. Maybe she shouldn't have been so hard on her the night before. She knew the venom she spewed would cut her deeply, but she couldn't stop herself. Messiah was accusing the man she was about to marry of being gay.

If Austin was gay, Lake would know it. Her *gaydar* was always on high alert. She would've picked up on the signals, at some point. Even if there was a sprinkle of truth to her lies, it was too late to turn back now. The crème de la crème of St. Louis was waiting for her to make her grand debut. She'd be the laughingstock of the town, if she backed out now. Despite all of that, she loved Austin and was ready to commit her life to him. Messiah not being there wouldn't stop her day. The wedge between them would just grow wider.

"Here." She picked up the bouquet, which was different from the rest of the bridesmaids' and handed it to Kat. "You're my maid of honor now."

"Yes!" Kat balled up her fist and pulled back.

Lake stood on the side of the door, so the crowd wouldn't see her, as the bridesmaids made their way down the aisle in their lavender dresses. It was finally her moment to shine. The doors closed briefly, giving her enough time to situate herself. Lake stood all by herself. A feeling of sadness washed over her, as she steadied her breathing. More than ever, she wished her dad was there to walk her down the aisle. But he wasn't. He was dead and gone. She had no one but Messiah and she'd pushed her away - probably for good.

With no time to dwell over her family issues, Lake held her head high, as the doors opened and Felix Mendelssohn's *Wedding March* began to play. All the guests rose to their feet, as if she were royalty. Lake smiled and looked at them all like they were her royal peasants. This was her moment and nothing or no one would put a damper on it. Everything was perfect. Her man stood at the end of the isle in a custom-made Valentino tuxedo. He was the Ken to her Barbie. They were a match made in heaven. His dashing good looks and her effortless beauty were unparalleled.

The only problem was, the closer she got to the alter, the sight of Tyler crying as if someone had died caught her attention. Austin had shed a tear or two when the doors opened, but this nigga was doing some next level shit. Homeboy was full on weeping with snot coming out of his nose. The shit was weird and made Lake's antennas go up. What the fuck was he so distraught about? Then it dawned on Lake that maybe Messiah's confession was true. *Nah, it couldn't be,* she thought, as she took Austin's hand. *It couldn't be.*

"You take Wednesday/Thursday; then just send him my way."– SZA, "The Weekend"

29

Lake

Lake and Austin's honeymoon in Monaco had been nothing short of a fairytale. They made love daily, shopped till they dropped, ate at the finest restaurants, gambled and got couples' massages on the beach. By the time they landed back in St. Louis, off their chartered plane, Lake was tan and relaxed. During their honeymoon, she'd revealed to Austin about missing her parents and regretting not having Messiah at the wedding. Lake wasn't the type to talk about her feelings. She had to trust you with her life to do so.

Austin seemed to understand her pain. She cried on his shoulder for hours. Not having her parents around to share in the important moment left her devastated. Since their deaths, she'd blamed Messiah. She despised her for it. That's why she kept her at arm's-length. Seeing her sister reminded her too much of the tragic loss. Messiah was the perfect blend of their father and mother. Looking at her face was like starring into her parents' eyes. She couldn't handle it.

Adding her to the wedding party was a huge deal for Lake. It was her way of trying to build somewhat of a relationship with her. But once again, Messiah went and ruined everything. It was like a black cloud followed her wherever she went. Lake couldn't have that kind of negativity around in her life. She'd worked too hard to get where she was at. She wasn't going to let Messiah bring her down. From the looks of it, they would never have a sisterly relationship with one another. It, evidently, wasn't written in the stars and Lake had to be ok with that. Austin was her family now. She'd cried all the tears she could over the family she once knew before the accident. It was now time to move forward.

"You ready, Mrs. Rhodes?" Austin asked, as they stood outside their mansion door.

"Yes." Lake beamed.

Austin scooped her up in his arms and carried her across the threshold. Her new life was finally about to begin. Inside their foyer, Austin kissed her softly and whispered, "I got something I need to tell you."

Lake lovingly gazed into his crystal clear blue eyes. Whatever he had to say, they'd deal with it as a couple. Nothing could ruin this moment.

"Baby, you're home!" Tyler traipsed down the staircase in a pink, silk robe and furry kitten heels.

Lake looked over her shoulder at him. He was nice and tan from his trip to Greece.

"What in the gay hell?" She said, struggling to get out of Austin's arms.

"Baby, calm down."

"No! Why is this nigga in my shit? That is brand new La Perla lingerie!" Lake fumed, ready to fight.

"Oh, it is?" Tyler looked at the tag. "Well, it's mine now, girl. You'll get used to sharing things with me in this nice, Caucasian house." He winked his eye.

"Messiah wasn't lyin'. Y'all are fuckin'." Lake looked back and forth between the two men, mortified.

"I thought you were gonna tell her before you got back." Tyler placed his hand on his invisible hip.

"There wasn't a right time."

"There wasn't a right time to tell me what?" Lake screamed. "That you like dick?!"

"And vagina. You forgot about that," Tyler corrected her.

"You shut up!" Lake pointed her finger at him.

"You gon' let her talk to me like that?" Tyler bopped down the steps, switching his hips.

"Baby, calm down," Austin pleaded.

"No, you better check her," Tyler ordered.

"Check me? I'm his wife!" Lake yelled.

"You might wear his ring, but I'm the main bitch," Tyler exclaimed.

"Is this a joke? Like, am I in the Twilight Zone?" Lake looked around.

"Listen, baby, I love you, but I like men and women. The world can't know that though. My career would be over," Austin explained.

"So, basically I'm your fuckin' beard?"

"I wouldn't say that."

"I would! Don't sugarcoat shit for her. Tell her the truth," Tyler commanded.

Austin stood quietly. The anger and hurt on Lake's face rendered him speechless. He expected her to be mad, but she was livid.

"If you won't do it, I will." Tyler wrapped his arms around Austin's neck. "Tell her, baby. Tell her for me."

"To the public, you and I will be this loving couple; but behind closed doors, I'll be with Tyler."

"What the fuck do you mean you'll be with Tyler?"

"I'll be living here, honey," Tyler smirked.

"Oh, no the fuck you won't!"

"It's already done. Your things have been moved to the guest room. Tyler will be in the master suite with me," Austin announced.

"Bloop!" Tyler mushed her in the forehead.

Lake tried to slap the shit out of him but Austin stood in her way.

"I can't believe you're doing this to me."

"Doing what to you?" Austin drew his head back. "I know you only married me for my money. Now, you get the best of both worlds. You get to spend my money and fuck whoever you want to."

"I really loved you. Do you know how hard that is for me to admit? I don't love nobody," Lake said honestly. "I trusted you!"

"Giiiiiiiiiiiiiiiiiirl, shut up! That is enough. He is my man. It's done! Shit! Let it go! I'm tellin' you now, Austin, I ain't gon' be able to put up with all this damn whining!" Tyler said, fed up.

"You fuckin' faggot!"

"Uh ah, bitch! We don't do that up in here! Don't be droppin' the F bomb in my house!"

"Your house?" Lake exclaimed, taken aback.

"I never meant to hurt you, but we both know this marriage isn't real. I know you don't love me," Austin clarified.

But I do, Lake thought, on the verge of tears.

"Alright, babe. Are we done here? Let's go have lunch by the pool, as she cries." Tyler sashayed away with her robe flying in the wind behind him.

Distraught, Lake went to the only person she knew would have her back - no matter what. Messiah opened her apartment door and stared at her sister. Tears were streaming down her face, at lightning speed, but she didn't care. She felt nothing for her. Nine times out of 10, whatever caused her to cry, she had it coming.

"Are you gonna let me in or no?" Lake asked.

"No, what do you want?" Messiah held the door steady.

"Messiah, please, let me in. I need you right now."

"Tough titty." Messiah shrugged.

"Messiah, please!" Lake begged.

Messiah rolled her eyes and stepped to the side. Lake walked in and sat in Messiah's furry chair.

"Let me guess, you found out I was tellin' the truth," Messiah gloated.

"You were right, ok!" Lake sobbed. "My whole marriage is a sham. He only married me so no one would know his secret."

"Hmmm...God don't like ugly." Messiah plopped down on the couch.

She couldn't contain her joy. Lake was finally getting what she deserved. She'd been nothing but an evil, vindictive bitch her whole life. She'd treated Messiah like an ugly stepsister, when all she'd did was try to love her. It was of no surprise to her that Lake came running to her when the walls started closing in.

"I'm fucked." Lake buried her face in the palm of her hands.

"You sure are," Messiah laughed.

"I'm happy you're getting so much pleasure from my misery."

"I sure am. This nut that should've been swallowed has always had your back but you continuously turned your back on me. Now, look at you. Just pathetic. Maybe if you would've got an UPS driver like me, you wouldn't be in this position."

Lake held her head back and cried.

"You are a nasty, vile, gutter snake, Lake. All you do is take-take-take. You never give. You have cussed me out, like a dog, and gave me the cold shoulder on several occasions. After Mama and Daddy died, you acted like I didn't even exist. You never called and checked on me. You stayed in L.A. and left me here to fend for myself. What have I ever done to you to make you treat me so bad? Why don't you like me?" Messiah died to know.

"I was mad because I felt like you took Mama and Daddy away from me. I never got the chance to say goodbye. One minute Mama and Daddy were alive, and the next, they were gone," Lake confessed.

"And you're right. I've been nothing but a bitch to you. I've just been so hurt." Tears slid from the corners of her eyes.

Messiah let out a loud sigh. She'd never took that into consideration. Lake had been away at college and hadn't seen their parents for months before they passed away.

I'm sorry, but you can't continue to punish me for something I had no control over."

"I know," Lake nodded. "I was wrong for making you feel like the accident was your fault. I shouldn't have done that. I should've told you I loved you, instead of pushing you away. You needed me. I was your big sister. I should've been there for you. And it may sound corny and sappy, but will you forgive me?"

Messiah didn't know what to say. Lake wasn't the apologetic type. Finding out Austin was gay must've really done a number on her.

"Mmm," she placed her finger up to her chin. "Let me think about it."

Lake bugged up laughing.

"Of course, I forgive you. You're my sister. Family comes first."

"Thank you. You're a far better person than me," Lake wiped her nose on the back of her sleeve.

"Ah... duh."

"What am I gonna do, Messiah? I can't stay married to him now."

"Didn't you say you had a cheating clause in your prenup?"

"Yeah."

"Use that bitch."

You're right." Lake perked up. "All I have to do is get proof of his infidelity, which will be easy to prove since Tyler lives with us."

"You say what now? He lives with y'all?"

"Yeah, girl, that's a whole 'nother story." Lake flicked her wrist.

"Jesus, be a fence."

"Mama and Daddy probably in heaven lookin' at us like we crazy," Lake wiped her face.

"Hey, we were branded from birth. I'm a coward and you're the brave one. Daddy always said that," Messiah retorted.

"No, Daddy said you're the brave one and I'm the pretty one," Lake corrected her.

"No, I'm the smart one," Messiah giggled.

"Oh, whatever," Lake giggled.

It felt good to have a genuine conversation with her sister, where there was no animosity or hate. They might not ever be the best of friends, but this was a start towards redemption.

"Niggas ain't thorough like I always thought."– Meek Mill, "Heavy Heart"

30
Shyhiem

"Ugh, I don't wanna go to work today." Messiah groaned, on her way to the diner.

"Just hang in there, babe." Shyhiem kissed her hand, while focusing on the road. "With the money my pops left me, we'll be straight for a while."

Shyhiem wanted to be honest and tell her about the drug money he had stashed away too. The money from his father, and the bank he'd made off being Mayhem's distro, added up to be a cool 2.5 million dollars. It wasn't a lot, but it would hold them for a while. At least until his film career popped off. He didn't want to go into their marriage sitting on a bed of lies, but he didn't want to rock the boat either. Messiah was finally at a place of peace. He wasn't going to be the one to steal her joy.

"I can't wait to get out of here. It's so much fuckin' drama in St. Louis. I can't stand it. I'm just happy you and I are finally on the same page." Messiah looked at him lovingly, as the black crow soared above them in the sky.

"Me too, baby. The day I marry you will be the happiest day of my life."

"I think about it every day." Messiah blushed.

"You wanna have a big wedding or a small wedding?"

"Something simple. Hell, we can go to the courthouse, for all I care," she laughed.

"You serious?" Shyhiem took his eyes off the road and stared at her.

"Yeah, I don't care where it is. We can get married in a box under a bridge. What matters most, is that we'll be committing our lives to one another. I say we go to the courthouse the day before we leave and just do it. Why wait?"

"I'm down, shit. Whatever you want, baby," he caressed her hand. "Who you wanna invite?"

"The only people I have to invite are Bird, Twan and my sister."

"I ain't got that many people to invite either. My old dude is sick, so he can't come; so that just leaves the kids and Mayhem.

"I know that's your brother and all, but he can't come." Messiah said, not willing to budge.

"Why not? That's my brother." Shyhiem screwed up his face.

"He's the one who told me you were with Lincoln that night."

"What?" Shyhiem slammed on the brakes.

Messiah jerked forward and held onto the dashboard.

"Shyhiem, calm down," she spoke, soothingly.

"Nah, tell me what the fuck happened." He replied, furiously.

"He came to my job and threatened me to stop seeing you."

"What? When?"

"The same night I pulled up on you at the restaurant."

"That happened weeks ago. Why are you just now tellin' me this?" Shyhiem gripped the steering wheel and resumed driving.

"We broke up, then you proposed and everything went down with my sister. I haven't had the time to tell you. Plus, I didn't want you to do anything stupid. You know how you get when you mad." Messiah eyed the vein thumping in his neck.

"Nah, you know how I get when somebody fuck wit' you." Shyhiem parked the car in front of the diner and looked at her. "But it's all good. I'm straight. I just wish you would've told me sooner."

"You sure you're ok?" She asked, concerned.

"Yeah, I swear," he lied.

"Pinky swear." Messiah held up her pinky finger.

"Man, get the fuck outta here with that shit," Shyhiem laughed, pushing her hand away.

"You wack. I'll see you when I get off work." Messiah caressed the side of his face and placed her lips on his. "I love you."

"I love you too."

Shyhiem watched until Messiah's back disappeared inside the building. Once she was out of sight, he picked up the phone and called Mayhem.

"What up?" He panted out of breath, answering on the fourth ring.

"Where you at?"

"At the gym. What's good?"

"I need to holla at you for a second?"

"A'ight, I'll hit you when I get to the crib."

"Bet." Shyhiem placed the car in drive and ended the call.

He knew his brother could be foul, but he never thought he'd betray him by snitching to Messiah. What did he have to gain by it? She was of no threat to him. Whatever Mayhem's reasoning was, it didn't matter. The trust had been broken and now Shyhiem would never look at his brother the same. They were a week from finishing off the supply, but he was done. There was no way in hell he was going to put his life on the line for someone who didn't have his back.

While he waited on Mayhem, Shyhiem decided to head over to Keesha's house to see the kids. He normally called and asked if he could come by in advance, but he was tired of being at her beck and call. If he wanted to see his kids, he should be able to, if she was at home. In a minute, he'd be gone and would only get to see them on holidays or summer vacation. He was determined to spend as much time with his kids as possible, before he boarded the plane. Shyhiem pulled in front of the apartment building and got out. Using his fist, he knocked lightly on the door.

"Who is it?" Sonny asked.

"It's your dad, buddy." Shyhiem smiled at the sound of his li'l man's voice.

"Shania, Daddy at the door!"

"Yay!" She jumped up and down.

Sonny grabbed a kitchen chair and scooted it over to the door to open it.

Shyhiem walked in and looked around. The kids never answered the door on their own. Something was off. The TV was up so high, he could barely think straight. Shyhiem surveyed his surroundings. As usual, the apartment was a wreck. Shyhiem got the heebie-jeebies, on sight. The twins were in the living room alone. Covers, for them to lay on, were on the floor. *Why are they sleeping in the living room,* he wondered. Their toys were everywhere. Dirty plates and cups were all over the place. What really caught Shyhiem's eye was a leftover blunt in an ashtray. The inner guts from a cigar were all over the coffee table. When Shyhiem walked over to clean up the mess, he noticed two, white lines of coke.

"What the fuck?" He said underneath his breath, pissed.

Just the thought of the twins getting their hands on it sent him over the edge.

"Where is your mother?" He wiped the coke off the table with his sleeve.

"She in her room," Sonny responded.

"She got company?" Shyhiem questioned.

Her door was closed.

"Uncle Mayhem back there," Sonny admitted.

"Ooooh… you gon' get in trouble." Shania teased.

"The fuck?" Shyhiem stormed towards the bedroom and barged through the door.

What he saw took his breath away. The tart smell of sex permeated the room. Keesha was on all fours, moaning loudly, while Mayhem fucked her, hard, from the back. Sweat poured from his brows, as he pounded into her.

"You wanna run yo' mouth about me but you fuckin' my baby mama?" Shyhiem barked, catching their attention.

Mayhem immediately stopped fuckin' Keesha mid-stroke and hopped off her.

"What are you doing in my house?" Keesha covered herself up with the sheet.

"Fuck all that! How long y'all been fuckin'?"

"None of yo' damn business. Get the fuck out my house!" Keesha shouted, wrapping the sheet around her.

"If you wanted to fuck her, you ain't have to do it behind my back, dawg. That pussy for everybody. I wouldn't have gave a fuck." Shyhiem said to his brother.

"I wanted to tell you—"

"You ain't gotta explain shit to him!" Keesha cut Mayhem off. "I'm a grown-ass woman! I can fuck whoever I want!"

"Look, Shy, it ain't what you think," Mayhem tried to explain.

"It ain't what I think? I walk in here and you fuckin' my baby mama raw, doggy-style, while my kids in

255

the living room, unattended, with weed and shit everywhere! It's fuckin' coke on the table! Who shit is that?"

"Mine, nigga! Miiiiine! Now get the fuck out!" Keesha spat.

"You doing coke around my kids?" Shyhiem said, in disbelief. "And you let her do the shit in front of my kids? What the fuck is wrong wit' you?"

"You know I wouldn't put the kids in harm's way. Just so you know, I don't give a fuck about her," Mayhem declared.

"You don't give a fuck about me?" Keesha quipped. "After all the shit I have done for you?"

"That's not the point! My brother come before you any day," Mayhem clarified.

"Yo, y'all can have this shit!" Shyhiem waved them off. "Sonny! Shania! Put your shoes on! We outta here!"

He would be damned if his kids spent one more night in that fucked-up-ass environment.

"You ain't taking them nowhere!" Keesha ran and blocked his path.

"Bitch, move!" He pushed her out the way, forcefully.

"You really gon' let him put his hands on me?" Keesha turned to Mayhem for protection.

"That's y'all business. I ain't gettin' involved in that." He placed on his pants.

"Oh, word?" She shot him a death glare. "That's how you feel? Fuck it then!" Keesha said, ready to fight dirty. "You ain't takin' my kids 'cause they ain't yours to take!" She followed Shyhiem down the hallway.

Knowing exactly what she was about to say, Mayhem quickly tried to stop her.

"Keesha, chill!" He tried to cover her mouth.

"No! Remember, I don't mean shit to you; right? I'm tired of hiding this shit!" She pushed his hand away.
"I'm warning you! Shut the fuck up!" Mayhem shouted.

"Sonny and Shania ain't yours!" Keesha called his bluff and focused her attention on Shyhiem.

"I ain't got time for this dumb shit. Kids, put yo' shit on!" Shyhiem ignored her revelation.

"You heard what I said! You ain't they daddy! Mayhem is!" Keesha folded her arms across her chest.

Shyhiem looked at his brother's reaction to prove she was lying, but the panicked expression on his face revealed that she wasn't.

"It can't be." Shyhiem tried to keep his balance.

No one said anything.

"Nah, it can't be." He said, feeling sick to his stomach.

"I'm sorry, man," Mayhem shook his head. "I wanted to tell you."

Shyhiem didn't even think twice. Right there, in the hallway, he pushed past Keesha and charged at his brother.

Mayhem stood firm, accepting his fate. He wasn't going to fight his brother. He couldn't beat him anyway. Mayhem knew this day would come, eventually. He deserved every punch he was about to receive. Shyhiem grabbed Mayhem by the throat and tackled him to the bedroom floor.

"Get off of him!" Keesha screamed in the background, to no avail.

Her screams were like white noise to Shyhiem's ears. Nothing anyone could say would get him to stop. His fist slammed into Mayhem's face, repeatedly, causing blood to gush from his nose and mouth. His face started to swell, immediately. Shyhiem was beyond livid. A rage soared in him that he'd never felt before. What pissed him off more, was that he didn't even try to fight back.

"You still a fuckin' pussy!" Shyhiem growled, squeezing his neck.

He wanted to kill him. He was going to do it. Mayhem needed to die. He'd betrayed him in the worst way. He'd hate him forever, after this. He and Keesha had taken the best part of him away. Bits of his soul disappeared with every jab he landed. Spotting Mayhem's gun on the nightstand, he got up and grabbed it. Neither Mayhem or Keesha was going to walk out of that room alive. Shyhiem cocked the gun back and pointed it at Mayhem's head. He lay on the floor with a busted lip and two, swollen, black eyes. The skin above his brow had split open. Blood was everywhere but Shyhiem didn't care. They'd taken his heart away, so he was going to take their life away.

"Shyhiem, the kids! Stop!" Keesha wailed.

Shyhiem turned and aimed the gun at her. She was seconds away from dying too. Keesha fell back against the wall, afraid.

"Bitch, fuck you!" He pressed his finger on the trigger. "Do you realize what you just did?"

"Leave or I'ma call the police!" Keesha warned, trying to sound tough.

Shyhiem gazed over at the kids, who were crying hysterically. He couldn't kill their mother and Mayhem in front of them. It would scar them for life. They'd seen enough. Plus, he was only weeks away from being off parole. He and Messiah were on the cusp of starting their new life together. He wasn't going to throw everything he'd accomplished down the drain for these two losers. Keesha and Mayhem would get theirs, one way or another.

"You gon' pay for this shit, bitch!" He hacked up as much spit as he could and spat in Keesha's face.

Violated, Keesha wiped the glob of spit away with the sheet but didn't say a word. Shyhiem was on a warpath. There was no telling what he might do.

"Fuckin' pussy!" He kicked Mayhem in the stomach, one last time, and left with the gun in his hand.

When Messiah walked into her apartment that night, she had no idea she'd find Shyhiem sitting on her couch. He sat in the dark with a glass of Hennessy in hand. Messiah went to turn on the light.

"Leave them off," he said.

"Baby, are you ok?" She asked, worried.

Shyhiem was acting very strange. She didn't know what had gotten into him. Concerned, she sat next to him on the couch. That's when she saw the gun resting on his thigh. Cuts and scrapes were all over his hands.

"Baby, what happened to you?" She questioned. "Did you and Mayhem get into a fight over what I told you?" She examined his face.

"They've been lyin' to me all this time."

"Who, baby?" She said, on the verge of tears.

"Keesha and my brother."

Everything around Messiah went silent. He'd finally learned the truth.

"You found out they were fuckin' around behind your back?"

Shyhiem faced her.

"You knew?" He screwed up his face.

"I put two and two together a long time ago."

"And you ain't tell me?" He snapped. "I can't trust nobody around this muthafucka!" He threw the glass of Hennessy across the room.

Messiah flinched. Once her heartbeat steadied, she resumed speaking.

"That's not true. You know you can trust me. Now, calm down and stop throwing shit and talk to me."

"Why didn't you tell me?"

"I was going to tell you, but so much shit went down between us that honestly I forgot. I'm sorry. I really am."

Shyhiem wanted to be mad at her but it wasn't her fault his piece-of-shit-ass brother and cokehead-ass baby mom wasn't shit.

"Well, that ain't all. I hope you don't know this part; but Sonny and Shania ain't mine."

"Fuck nah, I ain't know that. Who kids are they?" She asked, shocked.

"Mayhem's."

"Whaaaat? Get the fuck outta here. You lyin'." Messiah shrieked. "Baby, I can't believe it. I'm so sorry." She took him into her arms.

"How could they do this to me?" Shyhiem broke down and cried.

"Shhhhhh, baby. I know; I know." Messiah began to cry too, as Shyhiem rested his head on her lap.

"My whole life, people been making decisions for me. They ain't give a fuck how it would affect me. I knew Keesha wasn't shit, but I never thought my mama and Mayhem would fuck me over too."

"I know, baby." Messiah rubbed his head.

"I love those kids to death. I can't just go on with life like they ain't mine."

Messiah sat silent. So much shit had happened, neither of them could absorb it. She, nor Shyhiem, didn't know who they could trust now. They were truly all each other had. Seeing her future husband cry tears of sorrow cut

Messiah deep. She was furious that they'd done this to him. From the looks of it, Shyhiem would never recover. She couldn't have that. He couldn't be the only one suffering. Keesha and Mayhem had to pay too.

"How can you feel no love?"– Alex Isley, "Feel NO Love"

31

Keesha

At 26 years of age, Keesha Perry had gotten away with doing some of the grimiest shit known to man. She'd lied about the paternity of her children, helped rob niggas, stolen money from the state, wrote bad checks, did credit card fraud, jumped bitches, fucked her homegirl's boyfriends, and even fought her mother. She'd done it all with no remorse. For her, life came with no consequences. But the old saying, you reap what you sow, was true. Karma was a son of a bitch and hit you when you least expected it...

It was a typical day for Keesha. Long, 32-inch, blonde weave hung down her back. Her eyebrows were freshly threaded and a new set of gel nails decorated her pretty, little fingers. She sat on the couch in a wife-beater, booty shorts and flips flops, smoking a cocaine-laced blunt. Wendy Williams was on. It was the Hot Topic segment, which Keesha loved. She always wanted to know the latest celebrity gossip. The kids were in their room playing, despite the fact that it was a school day. Keesha was too tired to get up and take them to the bus stop that morning. It was the third day they'd missed that month but she didn't care.

They were only in the first grade. First grade, in Keesha's mind, didn't matter. The shit they learned at school, they could learn at home by watching Doc McStuffins. Keesha needed her beauty rest. That night, she was planning on going out with her girls. She had to look her best. Mad niggas would be at HQ nightclub. Mayhem would probably even be there. He hadn't spoken to her since she'd spilled the beans to Shyhiem about the paternity of the kids. She should've felt bad but she didn't.

In her fucked up mind, Shyhiem deserved to have his world rocked. If he'd never left her, this would've never happened. He'd brought this misery on himself. He could be mad all he wanted. Being mad wouldn't change the fact that his name was on the birth certificate, so until a paternity test proved he wasn't the twins' father, he'd still have to pay child support. She wasn't sure if he was going to request a DNA test or not. Whether he did or not, Keesha still came out winning. Mayhem would have to step in and take over financial responsibility of her and the kids. Keesha still wouldn't have to work. She could spend her time focusing on being cute and running niggas' pockets. Life was great. People around St. Louis didn't call her a bad bitch for nothin'.

A knock on the door took her focus off Wendy, pissing Keesha off. She wasn't expecting any company. Placing the blunt in the ashtray, she got up and opened the door, without seeing who it was. Keesha rolled her eyes, as soon as she opened it. An older, black woman with a small fro, dressed in brown, dowdy clothes and ugly, square-toe, 2-inch heels was there. Keesha just knew she was a Jehovah's Witness.

"I'm an atheist." She went to close the door in the woman's face.

"Excuse me, but are you Miss Perry?" The woman stopped her from closing the door.

"Who are you?" Keesha looked her up and down.

"My name is Rhonda Collins. I'm from the Department of Social Services. There was an anonymous referral with regards to abuse or neglect for Shania and Sonny Simmons. May I come in and speak to you?"

"Who in the hell called you? I'm a good mother to my kids!"

"Unfortunately, ma'am, I'm not at liberty to discuss who referred you, but I have to ensure the safety of your children. Are they home?"

"Yeah, they in their room," Keesha pursed her lips.

"Can I come in?" Rhonda asked, politely.

"Yeah, but hurry this shit up. I got shit I need to do."

The social worker walked in and eyed the apartment with disdain. The place was revolting. The apartment was damn near inhabitable. She was shocked to see a lit blunt, an ounce of weed and coke on the coffee table. Before Keesha could hide it, Rhonda quickly snapped a photo of the illegal substances, when Keesha's head was turned.

"You can't give me a hint who called you?" Keesha wanted to know so badly, she was oblivious to her afternoon ritual out in plain sight. "I bet it was that old bitch across the hall," Keesha snarled.

"Once again, I can't disclose that information, ma'am. Are there drugs in the house?" Rhonda arched her brow.

Keesha looked over at the coffee table. Chill bumps developed on her skin. She'd completely forgotten about her afternoon delight.

"No." She moved, hoping she blocked the social worker's view of the table before she could notice. "Didn't you want to talk to my kids?"

"Yes, may I go back to their room?"

"Mmm hmm… it's the second door on the right," Keesha smiled.

When the social worker disappeared down the hall, she hurriedly grabbed the weed and coke and placed it under the couch cushion. The blunt she'd been smoking was put down the garbage disposal. Once it was all gone, she went and stood by the kids' door. It was cracked open, so she could hear everything.

"Hi, my name is Rhonda." She sat down in one of the tiny chairs. "What's your name?" Ms. Collins directed her attention to the beautiful, little girl with friendly eyes.

"Shania." She spoke, playing with her dolls.

"And yours?" Rhonda focused her attention on Sonny; he was equally cute, but his eyes were cautious.

He sat on his bed, holding a stuffed teddy bear to his chest. Fear now resonated in his small, brown eyes.

"He don't talk much no more, but his name is Sonny," Shania responded.

"And why is that?"

"I'll get in trouble if I tell you."

"It's ok. My job is to make sure kids are safe. Do you know what safe means?"

"That's like when you're not supposed to cross the street by yourself. If you do, that's not being safe, right?"

"Yes," Rhonda laughed, impressed with the child's answer. "I need to ask you guys a couple of questions, and I need you to be honest with me, ok?"

"Uh huh." Shania stopped playing and gave Rhonda her full attention.

"Has your mother ever hit you?"

"That's enough!" Keesha barged into the room. "You gotta go!"

"Ma'am, I'm not finished with my investigation. If you have any questions or concerns, we can speak after I'm done talking to the kids," Rhonda said bluntly.

Keesha licked her bottom lip.

"Can you please step out of the room?"

Heated, Keesha stepped back into the hallway. Nervous, it dawned on her that this meeting wasn't going to go well. She had to figure out a way to get herself out of this.

"Shania and Sonny, has your mom ever hit you?" Rhonda resumed her line of questioning.

"Yeah," Sonny spoke up.

He didn't know who the woman was, but his mother feared her, which meant something.

"She does?" Rhonda said, surprised by the sound of his voice. "How often, sweetie?

"Everyday."

"Uh ah! She don't whoop me every day! She whoop you every day!" Shania argued.

"Why?" Rhonda asked.

"'Cause she say I act like a girl," Sonny said, softly.

"And how does she spank you?"

"With her hand, a belt, an extension cord, a switch or her shoe."

Writing their answers down in her notebook, she continued, "Do you guys know what drugs are?"

"Oooooh... I do!" Shania raised her hand. "They the green leaves Mama be smoking."

"And that white candy she put up her nose, but she say we ain't supposed to do it too," Sonny chimed in.

"Is that so?" Rhonda took all the information down.

"Thank you for being honest with me." Having heard enough, she gathered her things to leave the room.

"You done, 'cause I'm ready for you to leave?" Keesha spat with an attitude.

"No, ma'am, I'm not. Why are the children at home today?"

"They sick, didn't you hear them coughing in there?" Keesha shot, sarcastically.

"Miss Perry, I'm going to need you to take a drug test. Are you willing to go for a urine screen?" Rhonda asked.

"For what?" She spat furiously.

"It was reported that you may use drugs, so I need to test you for confirmation."

"Girl, please, I think not. You need to get your shit and get the fuck out of my house." Keesha pointed towards the door.

"I think not," Rhonda spat right back, with just as much attitude. "I'm letting you know now, if you don't go for the urine screen, I'm going to assume you're hiding something, and it's grounds for removal of your children," Rhonda warned.

"Do what you gotta do then, 'cause I ain't takin' no damn drug test."

"Are you sure?" Rhonda asked again.

"You heard what I said." Keesha rolled her neck.

"Ok," Having seen and heard enough, Rhonda pulled out her phone and stepped outside the apartment to call the police.

Ten minutes later, the police arrived. Rhonda showed them the picture of the substances on Keesha's coffee table that she'd taken without being seen, and told them what she smelled and what the children reported. Rhonda stayed outside while the officers entered Keesha's apartment. Twenty minutes later, one of the officers brought the children to her, reporting that they found bricks of coke under Keesha's kitchen sink, as well as ounces of weed. The other officer brought Keesha outside in handcuffs. All the neighbors were outside watching, as she was escorted to the police car.

"Excuse me," Rhonda stopped the officers. "Before you take her in, let me ask her if there's anyone that can take the children."

"Call my mother." Keesha tried to hide her face with her hair.

After obtaining her information from Keesha, Rhonda ran a check on her mother, but it came back that she had an extensive criminal history herself.

"I'm sorry, ma'am, but your mother won't be able to take them. She has numerous offenses on her record. Is there anyone else I can call before these kids go into placement?"

Keesha inhaled deeply. The last person she wanted to call was Shyhiem, but she had no choice. If she didn't, the kids would end up in foster care until she got out.

"Fuck," she yelled and placed her weight from one foot to another. "You can call their father, Shyhiem Simmons."

After being detained for five hours, Keesha finally got to make her one phone call. The first person she dialed was Mayhem. It was because of him that she was in this mess. It was his drugs that were stashed in her house. He had no choice but to help her. She was the mother of his kids.

"Didn't I tell you not to call me no more?" He barked into the phone.

"Shut up! Mayhem, listen; I'm in jail. I need your help." She looked around before she continued speaking. "Somebody called DFS on me; the police were called and they took the kids. They found everything. I need you to get me out."

"Yo, I don't know who you tryin' to reach, but you got the wrong number." He hung up in her ear.

"Mayhem!" She called out his name. "Mayhem!"

When she realized he'd hung up, Keesha slammed the phone down. She realized that she was royally fucked; but if she was going down, so was he.

"Who wants that hero love that saves the day?"– Jay Z feat. Beyoncé, "Part II (On The Run)"

32

Shyhiem

When Shyhiem got the call that Keesha had been taken into custody, he couldn't believe his ears. He'd been fucked up since he learned the kids weren't his. He didn't know what his place in their life would be or how he would proceed. With Keesha being locked up until only God knew when, he had no choice but to be the loving, doting father he'd always been. It had been an all-day process to assure the social worker he was fit to take care of the twins; doubt had started to creep in. She had to assess his house, run a background check and more. It was a strenuous process, but in the end, the kids were with him, where they belonged and not in foster care.

Shyhiem couldn't have been happier. His prayers had finally come true. He no longer would have to worry about their safety and well-being. With him, they wouldn't have to worry about anything. They'd get the best education, love and care. Between he and Messiah, Sonny and Shania would receive so much love, their little hearts wouldn't be able to take it.

Messiah gazed at the twins adoringly, as Shyhiem held her hand. They'd just put the kids to bed. They were knocked out in their room. Shyhiem had been having such a rough time, to see him finally score a win overjoyed Messiah. Their family was finally complete. Good would always prevail over evil. Shyhiem led her to their bedroom and started to peel her clothes off. The only thing that would make the night better, was making love to his soon-to-be wife. Their tongues did the forbidden dance of love, as he laid her down onto the bed.

"You called DFS, didn't you?" Shyhiem asked, in-between kisses.

"I don't know what you're talkin' about," Messiah tried her best to say, with a straight face.

"What would I do without you?"

"Thankfully, you'll never have to know."

"Preparing this new life we were gon' have together and he had passed the next month."– Jay Z, "Footnotes of 'Adnis'"

33

Shyhiem

On January 21st, Ricky Simmons lost his battle with cancer. His entire family, including Shyhiem, had been by his side when he took his last breath. Despite the obvious tension between Mayhem and Shyhiem, his father went on in peace. His last, dying wish, was that his two sons set aside their beef and make up. What Mayhem had done was deplorable, but blood was thicker than water. He demanded that they protect each other at all costs. Shyhiem was pleased that he'd gotten the closure he'd so frantically wanted from his father. He'd learned a lot about him in the last few weeks of his life.

Turns out, they had a lot more in common than he thought. All animosity that he had for him over the years had vanished. Neither of his parents were perfect, but he loved them both, despite their flaws. He wished he could set aside his differences with Mayhem. He wanted to fulfill his father's dying wish, but he'd never be able to look at his brother the same. Mayhem was dead to him. As far as Shyhiem was concerned, he could've been buried six feet under ground as well.

Being at the wake had been awkward. Carol still gave him the cold shoulder and acted like he wasn't welcome in her house, but Shyhiem didn't give a fuck. Now that his father was dead, he'd have no reason to come back there. He only got through it because of Messiah. She never left his side once. She was a godsend. When the black suit he wore became too constricting and he wanted to run outside for air, she eased his spirit. Asking her to be his wife had been the best decision he'd ever made.

The kids clung to her just as much as he did. She'd become the mother figure they'd never had. She did arts and crafts with them, taught them ballet, let them help her in the kitchen and read them bedtime stories every night when they went to bed. The twins' lives were now stable because of her. All their lives were better because of the unconditional love she showered them with.

All day long, Mayhem hovered around his brother. He kept just enough distance not to crowd him, but was close enough to feel his pain. It physically ailed him to overhear Shyhiem tell their aunt that he and Messiah were getting married in a few days at the court house. He always thought he'd be by his brother's side when he said I do. Now, things were all messed up and he had no one to blame but himself. He'd felt like shit since the fight. Many nights went by where he wanted to pick up the phone and call to say sorry. Words of regret and sorrow wouldn't be good enough. He'd ruined his brother's life, all so he could run the streets freely, with no obligations. I'm sorry would never be enough.

"Nothin' is promised to me and you."–
Jagged Edge "Promise"

34

Messiah/Shyhiem

Messiah never envisioned herself being a typical bride. She never wanted to go the traditional route. Getting married at the courthouse to the man she loved might've been cheap and ghetto to some, but for her it was perfect. She never wanted to spend thousands of dollars on one day, just to prove to people how much they loved each other. What mattered most to her was the commitment they were going to make.

Lake respected her sister's wishes but demanded that she allow her to spend a coin or two on her wedding dress. She refused to let her baby sister walk down the aisle in an inexpensive, cotton, shift dress from Target. Messiah and Shyhiem might've been getting married at the courthouse, but she didn't have to look like it. Lake went all out. She hired a hair stylist, a makeup artist and a photographer. It was the least she could do, after all the hell she'd taken Messiah through.

As Lake watched her walk down the short, sterile aisle, a bright smile shined from her face. Messiah was a vision in white. She wore her hair to the back in a heap of ethereal curls. A few tendrils of hair hung past her delicate shoulders. The makeup artist gave her a warm, smoky eye and a gorgeous, nude lip. The gown they picked out was a perfect reflection of Messiah. It had a hippie vibe to it but was sexy and classic at the same time. The sheer, nude-lined gown hung off her shoulders, showing off her glowing, golden skin. Strategically-placed lace and crystal embroidered leaves cascaded over her arms, breasts and hips. What really set the dress off, was the split in the center of the leg area that stopped midway up the middle of her thigh. A pair of gold, Giuseppe, ankle strap heels finished the bridal look off.

Shyhiem couldn't believe his eyes when Messiah walked down the aisle. He'd always thought she was beautiful, but that day she surpassed beautiful. Messiah was a goddess. He was so happy that she was going to be his wife and the mother of his kids. Messiah made her way to the man she adored and placed her hand in his. He was just as handsome as the first day they met. Shyhiem wore a navy blue suit with a white shirt and pink tie. A navy blue and white handkerchief peeked out of his breast pocket. The suit fit him like a glove.

Twan and the twins sat in the pews while Lake and Bird stood beside Messiah and Shyhiem, as they dedicated their lives to one another. Bird stood as Shyhiem's witness, since he and Mayhem were on the outs. Once the ceremony was over, the two love birds kissed for what seemed like hours. Messiah couldn't stop smiling. She was over the moon. For the first time in her life, everything was how it should be. It was damn near perfect. She'd never had a moment in life like this. Everything was going her way. Their future was so bright, it was almost blinding their sight.

Neither she or Shyhiem had a care or worry in the world. The following day, they, along with the twins, would be on the first flight to California. Messiah was so overjoyed, she never wanted the moment to end. If she could, she would bottle up the feelings she felt for a rainy day.

After saying their vows, the bride and groom walked hand in hand out of the courthouse. Their very small bridal party followed behind them. It was a chilly January day. The sun hid behind the gray clouds. The smell of rain was in the air. They all were about to head to brunch to celebrate Messiah and Shyhiem's nuptials, when Shyhiem spotted his brother leaning against his truck. Shyhiem furrowed his brow. He didn't know why he was there. Messiah could see how upset he was. She hated that Mayhem's presence was ruining their cherished day.

"Uncle Mayhem!" The twins ran towards him with open arms.

The sight of his kids hugging the man they knew and loved as uncle, but who was really their father, sickened him. He'd never get over Mayhem's betrayal.

"Just stay calm, ok? Don't let him rattle you," Messiah whispered in his ear.

"What the fuck you doing here?" Shyhiem barked, instead of taking his wife's advice.

Messiah could only shake her head and laugh. Shyhiem would never be chill. He'd always go from 0 to a 100 - real quick.

"I overheard that you were getting married at the wake and wanted to come and say congratulations."

Shyhiem held his wife's hand and stared at his brother with disdain. He wanted to punch him in the face, all over again, but the twins were holding onto to his leg like he was the second coming of Jesus.

"So this is the brother?" Lake asked her sister.

"Yeah," Messiah scowled.

"Mmm," Lake looked Mayhem up and down with lust. "If I still dated black men, he'd be my next victim."

"Eww," Messiah almost gagged. "Simmer that puss down, ma'am."

"Friend!" Bird called out.

"Huh?" Messiah replied.

"We about to head to the restaurant. We'll see you there." Bird said, as she and Twan got into the car to leave.

"Ok." Messiah waved goodbye. "Baby, it's cold. We need to get going." She rubbed Shyhiem's arm.

"I ain't tryin' to hold y'all up. I just wanted to tell you, I'm sorry... for everything," Mayhem apologized.

He wanted to say more but nothing he said would ever mend their relationship. He could tell by the look in Shyhiem's eyes that they would never speak again after that day. That fact would sting him for the rest of his life. Even though he had a fucked up way of showing it, deep down, he really loved his brother. Shyhiem glared at his brother. For half of his life, he'd placed Mayhem's wants and needs ahead of his own. He'd protected him at all cost. Although he'd found himself jealous of Mayhem's good fortune at times, his love for him knew no end. Now, he felt nothing.

He wasn't angry and he didn't hate him. An emptiness filled the space his love for him once resided. It didn't matter that the twins weren't biologically his. He was the only father they knew and it would remain that way. Shyhiem's life hadn't been easy, but now, it was on the right path. He had the woman of his dreams by his side and two, little angels that brought him constant joy. Nothing or no one, including Mayhem, was going to take that away from him.

"C'mon, kids." He took the twins by the hand.

Without saying another word, Shyhiem and his family walked away towards their new life together. The problems they once had were all in the past. The crow that had been following them for months had other plans.

"Ay yo, Shyhiem!" A male voice shouted.

Knowing it wasn't his brother calling his name, Shyhiem turned around, cautiously. An eerie feeling swept over him. Shyhiem made eye contact with the stranger. His heart instantly froze. The dude came across the street in a black ski mask, aiming a gun at his head. Shyhiem's whole life flashed before his eyes. This wasn't how the happiest day of his life was supposed to go. His past transgressions weren't supposed to rear their ugly head now. He'd feared that murdering Esco would come back to haunt him. Seeing the hatred in the killer's eyes told Shyhiem that it was one of his men. Shyhiem's number was up. He didn't want to leave Messiah like this, but if it was his time to go, then his main concern was the safety of his wife and kids.

Messiah turned and looked over her shoulder, as she heard someone call Shyhiem's name. Goosebumps developed on her skin, as she spotted a masked man rush towards them with a gun. Like in a nightmare, everything around her, including her limbs moved slowly. A million things ran through her head, as the monster neared. The first thought was that the person behind the mask was Bryson. He'd said to tell Shyhiem to watch his back. She didn't relay the message because she assumed he was just talking shit. Now, as the masked man approached with venom in his eyes, she wondered had she misjudged his threat. Maybe she shouldn't have taken it so lightly. There was no time to contemplate words spoken in the heat of the moment. She had to protect her family at all cost. She would be damned if they got hurt in her presence.

Without hesitation, Messiah pushed the twins out of the way and turned to face her husband. Trying to protect her, Shyhiem quickly grabbed Messiah to block her from the shooter's range. His back faced the masked man, as a gun shot rang through the air. An excruciating spark of fire blew through Shyhiem's right shoulder and landed inside Messiah's chest, as they both fell to the ground. Messiah gasped for air, as the bullet paralyzed her lungs. Visions of her parents and baby flooded her mind, on the way down to the ground. Shyhiem clutched Messiah tightly, as the masked man let off three more rounds into his back. Each shot felt like he'd been stabbed with hot coals a million times each.

The masked man smiled with delight, as Shyhiem lay in a pool of his own blood. He hadn't meant to shoot Messiah but all was fair in love and war. What the killer hadn't anticipated was that while he was targeting his prey, he'd become the prey as well. Mayhem cocked his gun, aimed it at the back of the masked man's head and pulled the trigger. His brother's killer fell to the ground, face first. Lake let out a blood-curdling scream, as she looked at the three, lifeless bodies on the sidewalk.

"Somebody call 911!" Mayhem demanded, placing his gun in the back of his pants.

On bended knee, he peeled back the mask on the guy's face. He had to know who'd set out to kill his brother on his wedding day. At first, he couldn't recognize the man's face. The guy was young-looking. He had light skin with a thick beard and a tear drop tattoo under his eye. It quickly dawned on him who the guy was. It was the li'l nigga they'd stomped out months before at Blank Space. Shocked, he pulled the mask back down and stood up. He didn't wanna leave his brother, but he had to get out of there. Police and ambulance sirens were nearby.

Shyhiem wanted to prevent his death but there was no such thing as immortality. He'd heard that loving the wrong person could get you killed but pride would be the death of him. His pride and ego led him to this place. He'd faked being strong when deep down he was insecure. His insecurities caused him to lash out and beat a man when he should've walked away. Now the decision he made that fateful night was catching up to him. Those untamed emotions now brought him to his death bed.

Shyhiem lay on top of Messiah as a tear slipped from her eye. He could feel her breathing slow. His beautiful bride was dying. He wanted to tell her everything would be okay, but he too was beginning to fade. Tears welled in his eyes but he couldn't feel a thing. All he could hear was the sound of his kids crying and Lake's screams. His blood mixed with Messiah's. Her white gown was now red. They were now officially one. This was it. This was the end. Their love on earth was no more. They both were on their way home.

"I refuse to think I'm gonna walk this earth alone, no. I wanna be with you."– Dawn Richard feat. PJ Morton, "Vines (Interlude)"

35

Shyhiem

For years, Shyhiem saw himself as nothing but a criminal. He'd screamed fuck the law since the age of 13. That was until his wife, of only a few minutes, died laying underneath him. The police and paramedics couldn't come fast enough. Fuck saving himself. He needed Messiah to survive but she didn't. She was pronounced dead on sight. Shyhiem didn't know how he was going to go on. If it wasn't for the twins, he would've taken his life, after surviving getting shot four times. It wasn't fair that the sweetest, kindest girl in the world had to die. She'd wanted to join her son and parents in heaven for years, but she'd just begun to love life on earth. When Messiah took her last breath, she wasn't ready to go. She'd told Shyhiem on more than one occasion that she looked forward to growing gray and old with him under the California sun.

Now, he stood looking out the kitchen window of his L.A. home, wishing she was there. Life wasn't worth living without her. He'd never love a woman like he loved her. She brought out the best of him. The twins asked when she was coming back every day. Shyhiem wanted to tell them soon. He was still in denial of her death. Every day was like Ground Hog's Day. His whole life revolved around the kids. He was a real-life Mister Mom. That day was no different. Shania and Sonny sat at the kitchen table doing their homework while he cooked dinner.

He was trying to make spaghetti and garlic bread. Shyhiem didn't know what he was doing. Months had passed by and he still didn't know his way around a kitchen. He needed Messiah. She could cook anything. She never needed a recipe book like he did. The kitchen was a mess. Tomato sauce was splattered all over the stove. Shyhiem had wasted numerous seasonings on the counter. He'd dropped pieces of cooked ground beef on the floor. The kids laughed, as he tried to maneuver his way around the kitchen. It was useless. Shyhiem looked like a chicken with its head cut off.

He was a disheveled mess. Sweat poured from his forehead. Sauce was all over his shirt. If the twins weren't watching his every move, he would've broken down and cried. He needed his fuckin' wife back. She would've helped calm his nerves. Messiah always knew how to talk him off the ledge of insanity. Wiping the sweat from his brow, he picked up the pot of tomato sauce without a glove. The heat from the handle burned his hand, causing him to drop the pot of piping hot sauce on the floor. Thick, red tomato sauce was everywhere.

"Fuck!" He screamed, jumping out of the way.

Once the initial shock of ruining dinner wore off, Shyhiem stopped dead in his tracks and placed his face in his hands. He couldn't take it anymore. He was tired of feeling low. All he wanted to do was cry. The walls were closing in on him but there was nowhere to hide. There was nowhere to go but down from here.

"Messiah, I need you." He whispered, distraught. "Come back home to me. Please, I need more time."

"It's ok, Daddy." Shania hugged her daddy around the neck.

Shyhiem wept silently. He wanted to believe his daughter but it would never ok. Without Messiah, he didn't want to go on.

"Daddy you hear me? Daddy!" Shania called out his name, tugging on his arm.

Shyhiem stirred in his sleep.

"Daddy, wake up!" She rocked his arm back and forth.

Groggily, Shyhiem's eyes popped open. His heart was beating at a rapid pace. Disoriented, he studied his surroundings to see where he was at. The warm sun, pristine sand and ocean view reminded him that he was in Malibu.

"Look what me and Sonny made." Shania pointed to the makeshift sand castle.

"Good job, baby." Shyhiem kissed her on the forehead.

Shania ran back over to where she'd been sitting. Her little, pink and white, polka dot swimsuit and ponytail made her look even more adorable than she already was. Her brother ran along the shore, blowing bubbles, as happy as he could be. Shyhiem sat up. His long feet sunk into the soothing white sand. The gunshot wounds in his back still hurt. It had only been five months since the shooting. He still couldn't get over the fact that he survived, what would normally be a fatal shooting. All he could do was thank God.

After the incident, Shyhiem didn't take anything for granted. Every breath he inhaled and exhaled, every step he took, he cherished more than ever. God had sparred his life. He would be eternally grateful. His brother didn't fare so well afterwards. After taking a plea deal that gave her only three years in jail, Keesha snitched on Mayhem. He ended up being taken into custody and landing 10 years in jail.

Shyhiem wanted to feel bad for his brother but karma was a bitch. He and Keesha deserved everything they got.

Shyhiem placed his hand over his mouth and yawned. He didn't even remember falling asleep. The beach was such a calming place. Every time he came, he was refreshed and renewed. It truly was the most peaceful place on earth.

Relocating to California had been the best decision he'd ever made, outside of marrying Messiah. Shyhiem looked down at the gold band on his ring finger. Loving her had brought him here. Because of her, he was as free as a bird catching the wind. She'd loved all the negativity out of him. She was his best friend. The sound of her voice sent chills down his spine. He'd follow her around the world.

Straight through his heart, she shot an arrow with her name all over it. Shyhiem never thought he'd feel the way he did for her towards anyone. Shyhiem never knew intimacy could exist so deeply without penetration. He loved everything about her, especially her mouth and how it felt on his. When they were together, sparks flew everywhere. He could never lose with her by his side. He'd want her always.

Picking up his camera, he pressed record. The sun was beginning to set over the horizon. A mystical pink hue graced the afternoon sky. Messiah's back was to him. She'd been looking out at the ocean. Waves of water crashed onto her pretty, little toes then flowed back into the ocean. She wore a white, African inspired, fringed, two-piece bikini that fit her perfectly. One of her legs was crossed over the other, as she stood. Shyhiem recorded her, without saying a word. He loved looking at her when she didn't know he was watching. Messiah didn't have to do much to capture his attention. She'd always be his muse.

"Baby!" He called her name.

Messiah turned slowly and gazed at him. The wind caused her honey-blonde and brown hair to blow in her face, as her round stomach came into view. Messiah pulled her hair back and waved. Shyhiem smiled back at her. They'd learned two months prior that they were having a baby girl. Messiah becoming pregnant was a shocking miracle. Since the age of 16, she'd been told she'd never be able to conceive again. God had other plans. As she lay on the hospital bed, fighting for her life after being shot right above the heart, the doctor's informed Lake she was pregnant.

When Messiah came to after being unconscious for 72 hours, she told her sister and Bird that she overheard the doctor's news while under. Hearing that she was pregnant gave her the will to fight. She had a lot to live for. She had her husband and kids to get back to. She hadn't fought her way through hell for it to be over. Messiah was no longer afraid to live. For so long she resided in darkness. But as she stood with her feet in the sand, she thanked god for not allowing her to sink into oblivion.

She was so happy Shyhiem had brought her here. Their pride and ego had been set aside. There were no more games to be played. It would take more than a few bullets to pull her away from him. She and Shyhiem's love story was one for the history books. It couldn't be explained or contained. He had her heart forever. No one would ever take his place. The baby growing in her stomach proved they were meant to be. Time was on their side. She was his and he was hers. Their love couldn't be stopped. There was no end in sight. Shyhiem and Messiah's love story wasn't over. It had just begun.

Afterword

After ten years, I finally decided to give you, the readers, what you wanted and bring Shyhiem and Messiah the full story that they deserved. Bringing their love story to life and breathing air into their lungs was an experience I'll never forget. Writing Messiah's character was a challenge for me because she is so unlike me, but I fell in love with her innocence and perseverance. If you loved this story as much as I loved writing it, please leave a short review. I love hearing you guys feedback!!!

XOXO,

Keisha

P.S.

Keep reading for a teaser of War IV Love. The 5th installment in the Chyna Black series.

War IV Love

"Wish I was comfortable just with myself but I need you." – SZA, "Supermodel"

#1

I fuckin' hate weddings. Muthafucka's all happy and shit. Little do they know, love don't last forever, Chyna thought, rolling her eyes while taking a sip of champagne. It was her sixth glass but she didn't care. She needed to get fucked up in order to sit through this romantic-ass bullshit. Chyna sat with her short hair slicked back in a one-arm, black, skin-tight gown that wrapped around her neck and showcased her bare left arm and toned back. A sultry, dark, smoky eye, pink blush and nude lip gloss emphasized the features on her oval-shaped face.

Chyna Danea Black was a rare beauty. She had big, brown eyes, long, thick lashes, a button nose, sumptuous, full lips and dimples as deep as the Atlantic Ocean. She only reached 5 feet 3 in height but her take-no-prisoners attitude and cocky demeanor made her seem 10 feet tall. She had soft, caramel, 38DD breasts that were more than a mouthful. Since she was a child, her breasts were a focal point of her looks. She used to hate them but now she showed them off as much as possible.

She was drop-dead gorgeous. If she were taller, she could've been a supermodel, but as she sat alone nursing the chilled glass of champagne, her devastating good looks couldn't stop the loneliness she so desperately wanted to escape. Chyna was in a room full of people but she never felt more alone in her life. Everyone at Mo and Boss' wedding slow danced to Beyoncé's *All Night Long*. Chyna wanted to stab herself in the neck with a fork. Love was in the air and she wanted to vomit. *I don't even know why the hell I'm here,* she sighed.

She didn't know anyone there except her friend, Delicious. The only reason she came was because Delicious didn't want to come alone; but as soon as some light skin nigga that looked like Drake eye-fucked him from across the room, Chyna quickly became a distant memory. Chyna was ready to go but she'd rode to the wedding with Delicious. She couldn't leave until his funky-ass was ready to go.

She looked over to the dance floor and groaned. By the way he was slow dragging on Champagnepapi, Jr., there was no telling when they would be out of there. *This is some straight bullshit,* she inhaled deeply and sighed. Everybody at the reception had someone but her. Even the little kids had found love on the dance floor. It had been months since Chyna felt the touch of a man. Chyna used to be a dick magnet, but lately, no one was trying to get at her. If she did get hollered at, it was by some old-ass man or a thirsty-ass African, professing his love in her DM's.

Homegirl needed some dick and fast and she didn't want just any old dick. She wanted a big, fat, juicy, python dick with veins pulsating under the rigid, hard skin. The old Chyna would've hit up a club and threw her pussy at the first fine man she laid eyes on - but those days were over. She wanted something real. She was over having one-night stands and giving her heart to men that didn't deserve her affection.

At the age of 35, she'd only been in love three times. Each time ended in excruciating heartbreak. Chyna didn't want to go through that ever again. Her last heartbreak almost ended her life. She still hadn't gotten over the man that will not be named. He was the love of her life; but He Who Will Not Be Named, wanted nothing to do with her. Chyna figured after a year of unanswered calls, emails and texts, that if she refused to say or hear his name, she'd get over him.

A year had gone by and she still thought of him every day. She missed everything about him; from the way he smelled to the way his caramel skin tasted on the buds of her tongue. Chyna thought about getting back out there and dating but only he held the keys to her heart. She had to get over him. It was evident that they were through. He despised her and she couldn't blame him. She'd fucked up royally and made another dumb decision that cost her everything.

Her biggest fear was coming true. Chyna was destined to die alone. Since her 20's, she feared she'd be old and single - just like her mother. All she wanted was someone to love her unconditionally. Every man she gave her heart to promised to love her forever, but in the end, they all left.

Maybe she was unlovable. She wasn't the easiest person to get along with or get close to. Chyna had been through hell and back, which had made her cold as ice. To say she was tough was an understatement. She didn't take shit from anyone and would cut you deeply if you crossed her. She had a foul mouth and a short temper. Outside of her readers and YouTube audience, Chyna didn't have very many friends. Her circle was super small. Her two best friends, since the age of 10, Brooke and Asia, put up with her 'cause they knew deep down inside she was a softy. The only reason she and Delicious became friends is because they fucked the same man and loved each other's fashion sense.

Brooke, Asia and Delicious were her only friends. Chyna didn't mind not having many friends. She was a loner at heart. If she wasn't with one of them, she was with

. 17-year-old daughter, India. Soon, India would be ᴊrning 18. She was a junior in high school. The dread of knowing she would be graduating soon softly killed Chyna. When India went off to college, she'd be all alone. Loneliness would swallow her whole. She wouldn't be able to survive it.

Chyna didn't do well when she had too much idle time on her hands. She often ended up acting out and doing some shit she had no business doing. Since He Who Will Not Be Named broke up with her, she buried herself in her work. Chyna was a best-selling author, writer for the hit TV show, *The Girlfriend Experience,* and a YouTube star. Instead of stressing over her ex and letting random guys bang her back out, she wrote several, best-selling novels; two, which were based on her life, called Heartless and Radio Silence.

Radio Silence was a love letter to the last man to ever share her bed and capture her heart. She hoped that he would read it and see just how much she loved him. She needed him to see that she'd never betray his trust. He was her lifeline. No other man came before or after him. Her heart belonged to him and only him. She would give her last dollar, limb, breath and heartbeat to have him back. Days, weeks and months passed by, but it never got easier to be without him. He was perfect, in her eyes. Chyna wished she could be comfortable being by herself but her life wouldn't be complete until she had He Who Wil Not Be Named back in her arms.

Inhaling deeply, she sat up and stretched. Her back was killing her and the Spanx she wore was cutting off her circulation. She couldn't wait to get home and pull the death trap off. Chyna wanted nothing more than to curl up in bed with a pint of ice cream and watch her favorite movie: Clueless, for the 100th time. She'd worn the bad-ass

Valentino gown for nothing. Nobody was checking for her, which irked the fucked out of her. Everyone was boo'd up and in love. Over 100 people were at the reception and there wasn't an eligible bachelor in attendance.

Chyna didn't think the night could get any worse until the DJ began to spin Jon B's classic hit song, *They Don't Know*. The song used to be her and her ex, Tyreik's song. *Uh ah, it's time for me to go,* Chyna shook her head. She didn't want to be reminded of another, unrequited love she'd lost. She didn't care if she had to hitch hike home; she would. There was no way in hell she was gonna sit through the torture of hearing Jon B's smooth, velvety voice sing his heart out to the woman he loved. The song did nothing but remind Chyna just how miserable she was.

Grabbing her gold clutch purse, she rose to her feet. As she stood and smoothed down the front of her dress, she couldn't help but feel a set of eyes bore into her. The hair on her arms stood up. A cold chill swept over her entire body. Chyna looked around to see who was watching her, and then her heart dropped down to her pedicured-toes.

For a second, she thought she was dreaming. Chyna's mind was obviously playing tricks on her. There was no way he was there. Before she knew it, her feet started moving. The bottom of her gown flapped, as she quickly walked across the room to him. She had to make sure he was real. Chyna stopped and stood inches away from him. Her chest heaved up and down, as her body quaked. *This can't be real,* she thought. If it was, she didn't know what she'd do.

She'd dreamt of this moment for months, but as time went on, she never thought it would come true. Slowly, she raised her hand to caress his face. As soon as her palm ran across the prickly hair on his cheek, Chyna's

, watered with tears. This was real. He wasn't a figment her imagination.

She didn't know how long he'd been there. It didn't matter. All that mattered was that he was there. The air in her lungs felt lighter and clearer than it ever had before. She'd promised him that she'd wait a lifetime for him. As he stood before her, she realized she'd wait for him even beyond the grave. Tears slipped from her eyes and landed on his crisp, white, button-up shirt. He wore a five-thousand-dollar, custom-made Tom Ford tuxedo. The tuxedo was molded to his body. His muscular biceps shown through the expensive fabric.

He was just as beautiful as she'd remembered. His low-cut hair was freshly cut and lined. His bushy brows, piercing, almond-shaped, mocha eyes, scruffy beard and tantalizing lips caused her pussy to cream with desire. He towered over her at 5'11 and weighed 185 pounds. His lean, athletic physique and tattoos that graced his face, neck, chest, back, arms and hands, added to his bad boy demeanor. Chyna wanted to place a thousand kisses all over his honey-colored skin.

Instead, she ran her small hands down his neck, broad shoulders and long arms. She didn't stop till she grasped his hand and brought it up to her lips. Lovingly, she kissed the outside of his tattooed-hand. Closing her eyes, she ran his hand across her cheek. The smell of his cologne engulfed her senses, as she became lost in his touch. Unable to contain herself, Chyna wrapped her arms around his neck and held him as tight as she could. She could feel his breath hitch, as she touched him, but Chyna didn't care. She never wanted to let him go. Her breasts pressed up against his hard chest, as she cried what felt like a million tears. It wasn't until that moment that she realized just how much she missed his presence in her life.

L.A. stood there as stiff as a board, as she held onto him for dear life. He hated the feel of her arms wrapped around his neck. Everything she touched, she tainted. If he would've known Chyna was gonna be there, he wouldn't have come to the wedding. He'd done his best to avoid her for a year. He'd done a damn good job - until now. He knew if he ever laid eyes on her, he'd cave. He couldn't get sucked into her deceitful web of lies again. She'd done damage that was irreparable. Every inch of him still loved her but he would never forgive her.

As far as he was concerned, Chyna Danea Black was the devil. She'd warned him not to fall in love with her. She told him she'd only end up breaking his heart in the end; but like a fool, he didn't listen. It wasn't until he saw pics of her on Instagram, naked, at her ex-boyfriend and his former friend, Carlos' house, that he learned his lesson. She'd embarrassed him and tarnished the love he had for her. He'd done nothing but show her how real love looked and felt like and she'd returned the favor by shitting on him.

He missed her and her daughter, India, terribly but once he was done, there was no turning back. He could never trust her again. Her word was nothing to him. He wanted nothing else to do with her. L.A. wanted to push her away. The feel of her arms wrapped around his neck made him feel like he was suffocating but he couldn't move his limbs. Unbeknownst to him, the need to feel her up against him surpassed his want to rid himself of her.

Chyna was his heart. He loved her ever since the first time he laid on her eyes. He needed her just as much as she needed him. She was the first woman he'd ever loved. He'd tried turning off his feelings for her but it was impossible. She was just as pretty as he remembered. L.A. could stare into her warm, chocolate eyes for the rest of his days and never tire. She was low-key his favorite person on the planet. He'd follow her to the depths of the earth and back.

Unable to resist her any longer, he hesitantly wrapped his arms around her small waist. Chyna let out a long sigh of relief. This was what her body needed. L.A. buried his nose in her hair and inhaled her mesmerizing scent. This woman was etched in his veins. He could never rid himself of her. Having her back in his embrace was the best feeling in the world. He'd been miserable without her.

About The Author

Keisha Ervin is the critically acclaimed, best-selling author of numerous novels, including: The Untold Stories by Chyna Black, Cashmere Mafia, Material Girl 3: Secrets & Betrayals, Paper Heart, Pure Heroine, Emotionally Unavailable, Heartless, Radio Silence, Smells Like Teen Spirit Vol 1: Heiress, Mina's Joint 2: The Perfect Illusion and Cranes in the Sky.

For news on Keisha's upcoming work, keep in touch by following her on any of the social media accounts listed:

INSTAGRAM >> @keishaervin

SNAPCHAT >> kyrese99

TWITTER >> www.twitter.com/keishaervin

FACEBOOK >> www.facebook.com/keisha.ervin

Please, subscribe to my YouTube channel to watch all of my hilarious reviews on your favorite reality shows and drama series!!!

YOUTUBE >> www.youtube.com/ColorMePynk